Madame's Daughter

C.K. Crigger

WOLFPACK
PUBLISHING
— EST 2013 —

Published by Wolfpack Publishing
5130 S. Fort Apache Road, 215-380
Las Vegas, NV 89148

Paperback IBSN 978-1-64734-551-8
eBook ISBN 978-1-64734-569-3

Madame's Daughter

Chapter 1

July 31, 1909

The soot-smeared train window did nothing to dim the sun's intensity as it blazed into Jacoba DeGroot's face. Perspiration beaded under her fashionably tall, wide-brimmed hat, gathered on her scalp and along her hairline, itching almost unbearably before sliding down her cheek in a soft drizzle.

It seemed to Jacoba that the train, a Spokane and Inland Empire special headed west out of Coeur d'Alene, lingered interminably on the siding at Gibbs station, waiting for the oncoming regular to pass on its way east. The car windows were locked up tight, without a breath of fresh air to stir the sweltering heat. The special broiled under the direct rays of the afternoon sun, and Jacoba boiled within it. For some reason, she hadn't expected northern Idaho to be so hot.

Self-conscious at being seen to sweat, she patted a recurring dribble with her lace-edged handkerchief. The hanky, she noticed with a grimace of distaste, was soggy and streaked with gray. She couldn't help wondering if corresponding streaks of white patterned her face.

Could be, judging by the way the dark-skinned man standing in the crowded aisle two seat rows away fixed his gaze on her. Unless—a chill that did nothing to cool ran up her erect spine— unless he had been sent by her mother to take her home and he was only biding his time.

She discarded this thought almost as soon as it occurred. No. Madame wouldn't have *tried* to drag her back. She either would have, or not bothered in the first place. More than likely, Madame Ludke had disowned her errant daughter as soon as she discovered Jacoba's empty bed that Sunday morning. Anyway, Charlie had planned their elopement well, even had Madame wished to stop them. But why, in that case, was the dark man watching her?

Her elbow nudged her husband of seventeen days in the ribs, startling him from a heat-induced doze.

"Charlie," she said, leaning toward him and speaking directly into his ear, "a man is staring at us. Do you suppose Mother . . ."

There was no use trying to talk. The noise level in the railroad car escalated as heat-fired tempers, already fraught with nervous expectation—and Jacoba suspected a little liquor— boiled over and soared louder. They were only a mile and a half out of Coeur d'Alene which made this halt wear at every passenger's nerves. Everyone on the train was anxious to get back to Spokane after registering for the reservation land lottery, and she and Charlie were every bit as fretful as the rest. Although not, she hoped, as argumentative and loud as some.

Folks just wanted off the train and Jacoba sympathized whole-heartedly with the desire. People took up every available inch of space inside the car, filling the aisle, crowding three into two seats—though not in her row, for which she was grateful—and outside, too, on the coach platforms, the car roofs, even on the cowcatcher and running gear. Those whose luck decreed they stand for the entire trip into Spokane were hot, tired and touchy as gunpowder. They were giving the conductor what-for in no uncertain terms at the delay, as though it were his fault.

Impossible, therefore, to hear her or anyone else over the racket, although Charlie smiled.

"Thirsty, Jake?" His more powerful lungs propelled his words over the noise. "Your face is awfully flushed. I can go forward and see if there's a dipper of water left, if you like."

He looked as if he could use a swallow of water, himself. His sweat-darkened brown hair clung to his skull like that of a little boy who had played himself out. His shirt collar, exquisitely starched and stiff when they boarded the train this morning, was even more limp and grayer, if possible, than Jacoba's handkerchief.

"No, Charlie." She shook her head and spoke louder. "Don't trouble yourself. Someone might take your seat. Anyway, it's too hard to get through all these people. I'm all right. I just wish we'd hurry up and get there." To tell the truth, she would have appreciated the water, but not at the cost of him losing his seat. Or of being left on her own surrounded by all these men.

Nothing could stop Charlie when his mind was set. He braced himself on the back of the seat in front of him and stood up. "It's no trouble, honey. Don't want you fainting."

In this heat, she'd deliberately left her corset strings slack. She was in no danger of swooning.

"I won't faint," she said, her words lost to him. So was her quick grab at his arm. "Don't leave me alone, Charlie."

He patted her hand. "I'll be right back."

He was already shuffling away, pushing through the throng. She saw the dark man look at him and open his mouth as if to speak. Charlie never noticed. "Sorry," he was saying as he trod on booted toes. "Pardon me. Excuse me."

One man, sweating so badly his acrid stench spread before him like a fog, tried to take Charlie's empty seat. Jacoba forestalled him mid-sit by placing her handbag in his way and, drawing a nine-inch hatpin from her high-crowned hat, displaying that, pointed up, on top. Her arched brow and the tilt of her chin stopped an imprecation before it fully formed. He turned from her, angry and red-faced.

Perhaps, she mused, more than a little astonished by the idea and not altogether happy with it, there was more of her mother in her than she liked to admit. Madame Ludke could stop a…a train…with one blink of her steely eyes, let alone one stinky little man. Madame enjoyed the power, which a great deal of practice had perfected. Jacoba, having been on the receiving end of *the eye* more than once, wasn't sure she wanted the knack for herself. She dabbed at a drop of perspiration trickling beneath her ear.

A sudden jerk, then a couple more accompanied by a squeal of released brakes signified they were at last getting ready to move. Wishing Charlie would hurry and get back, she leaned forward, cupping her eyes with her hands to see through the grimy window. The passengers cheered, more noisy and raucous than ever. Someone sang out a "Hip, hip, hooray!" that everyone in the car echoed.

Jacoba, although not quite in as boisterous manner, cheered along with the rest. She couldn't wait to arrive in Spokane and escape this hot, overcrowded train. Stretch her legs and cool down. Their hotel had high ceiling fans ventilating both the public areas and their room. How she longed for a bath using Madame's special bath salts, followed by a soothing lotion, the one using aloe sap, on her face. She needed food, as well. Her empty stomach gave a rumble.

Her musings were interrupted as the train shuddered once, then lurched forward with a force that threw people off balance. In the center aisle, a boy cried out as he fell and was immediately hidden from view behind a dozen sets of legs. Those seated were slung about, Jacoba among them. A sun-darkened hand reached for her, stopping her just before she landed on the floor on her knees. A second hand saved her handbag, although the hatpin rolled beneath the seats, irretrievably lost.

"Oh!" she said, a frisson of uneasiness inching through her. It was him. The man who'd been staring at her.

"Caught you," he said.

"Caught me?" she repeated, wary and worried. *Had* Madame

sent him?

"You about got tossed. Could've hurt yourself."

His voice was soft, light, and almost undetectable in the racket. Jacoba snatched her arm from him and sank onto the seat again, glancing up through a veil of eyelashes. He was quite young, she saw, although older than she or Charlie, and while not above medium height, sturdily built. Not fat. Just sturdy, as though every bit of nourishment he'd ever partaken had turned into solid muscle.

He made no claim on her. In fact, he wasn't paying her any mind at all now. Jacoba realized the reason he'd been able to prevent her from landing in a heap was because he'd leaned past her in an attempt to see out the dirty window. His eyes narrowed as he stared ahead, appearing almost black even with the sun shining on them. He looked, she decided, not only concerned, but tense.

"Is something the matter?" Alarmed, Jacoba turned her head to follow the direction of his gaze. She wished her new husband back at her side, with or without the water.

The train had pulled out of the siding onto the main track, inching onto the right of way.

The man swore, the words harsh and angry for all they were barely louder than a whisper.

Jacoba had heard worse, although his vehemence startled her a little. For instance, Madame never hesitated to make her displeasure known by such methods. But in this case, Jacoba was not the one in the line of fire. In truth, the stranger didn't appear aware of her at all as he pushed past her, his face right up against the window in an effort to see ahead.

"What is it? Is something wrong?" she demanded again, apprehension prickling along her nerves. If he had ever stared at her, which she'd begun to doubt, he was certainly ignoring her now. She wished she could wrench him out of the way so she could see for herself what held his attention. He seemed anxious. Disturbed. She settled for clutching at his arm, braced on the seat beside her, and shaking it. "Mister?"

He straightened and for a brief instant, his dark eyes met hers. "I didn't see the regular go by. Did you?"

The apprehension Jacoba had felt only a second ago shifted and turned into something else. Fear. What was he telling her?

"The regular? No," she said. "Do you mean it's— Did they cancel it?" Stupid question. He wouldn't be looking for it if they had. Anyway, how would he know?

Face sober, he answered as if her questions had merit. "Dunno. But I doubt they'd cancel a regular."

A part of her noticed that he had an odd way of speaking. Almost an accent, yet not. Certainly different from hers. But although his voice was still quiet, the words slow, there was something tightly drawn that told her that he was infected with the same tension frazzling her nerves.

He leaned past her again as the train picked up speed. The car swayed as they started into a curve and Jacoba braced herself against touching him again. She sensed Charlie wouldn't be pleased if he came back and found a stranger this close to her.

She flinched as though she'd been struck when the man jerked erect.

"*Merde*!" he said.

She saw the corners of his wide mouth tighten and go ash white. With hardly a blink, he fastened onto her arm and pulled her with him as he backed into the aisle. His elbows and stiff arms made room for both himself and her. For a moment, she was too shocked to do anything other than let him carry her along.

Without waiting until she was steady on her feet, he said, "Come on. We've gotta get out of here."

Go with him? Jacoba wrenched her arm away. "What do you mean? Let go of me!" Where was Charlie? Panic rose in her, starting in her gut and driving straight on into her head. Blood rushed through her veins, the surge making her dizzy.

As though unaware of her resistance, the stranger grabbed her again and without another word began hauling her along in his wake. There seemed nothing she could do but go with him as he headed toward the back of the train.

"Charlie!" she yelled, voice soaring. "Charlie."

But Charlie was nowhere in sight. Jacoba tried to hang onto the back of one of the seats, only to have its occupant glare and brush her hand aside. Her captor plowed through the crowded aisle like Moses parting the Red Sea, dragging her with him. At every point her opposition was blocked, not only by the overcrowded conditions, but by the rattling and rocking of the train.

"Help me," she cried once, catching the eye of a man dressed in farmer overalls. But there was no help there. He flushed and looked away. Jacoba's hand went numb below her wrist where her captor held it in a too-tight grasp.

"Let me go," she said, a little breathless now, after her struggles.

He spared her one glance. "If you want to live, shut up and run."

Run? Did he really expect her to aid in her own kidnapping? Yet as quickly as this question flashed through her mind, a disclaimer followed it. He didn't act like an abductor. There was nothing furtive about the urgent way he hurried her along.

He stopped, thrust his wide shoulders through the throng at the door, then yanked her out onto the platform where wind rushed around her ears and tugged at her hat. She put up her spare hand to save it, which is when she finally discovered the cause of his urgency. A scream rose in her throat. Instead of struggling against the man, she harried him, pushing against his back when the crowd in the next car forced him to slow.

Charlie! Oh, God! Where was Charlie? Pray, pray he'd seen what this man had seen. Pray, pray he would catch up.

Battling a way through the aisles, they reached the open platform of the second car. The stranger flicked a glance backward, over the top of Jacoba's head. His mouth grew tauter, more tightly stretched than before. There were many people out here, and she saw they, too, had finally realized what was happening. Terror stricken, they scattered like sage hens, most of them trying to push a way through into the next car in line. That she was too small to see over the top of them may have been a blessing. The yelling and screaming that broke out in the cars both behind and in front of them was bad enough. Word had spread.

Her self-appointed savior didn't follow the crowd, but let himself be shunted to the side to where a waist-high railing caged the platform. Beneath her feet, the train wheels vibrated. The screech of metal on metal raised the hair on her head as someone finally applied the air brakes. Sparks flew, smoking as they settled in the grass beside the track.

He pulled her closer, until she was level with him. "We're going to jump," he said in her ear, never letting go of her arm.

"Jump?" Sheer panic cranked her voice high and strained. "No. No, I can't."

But she could. Almost paralyzing terror, along with the long, tight skirt hobbling her, made no difference because when the man flung himself out the gate, he took her with him. He launched himself and her, jumping as high and wide as a man hampered by a hundred pounds of dead weight can.

They landed in grass and gravel only a few feet beyond the train. In the moment of contact, Jacoba felt nothing, heard nothing. The world became a smear of brown and green, her eyes closing against the tremendous jolt. Then pain exploded in her right knee and the palms of her hands shredded to bloody rags as she slid along the ground.

Before they stopped tumbling, bones bruised and without a whiff of air left in her lungs, the Spokane and Inland Empire Special and the missing regular train came together. Sound and fury erupted with the clash of metal shrieking as it ripped apart, a tormented noise straight from the door to Hades.

The platform, from which seconds earlier they had launched from the train, crumpled and collapsed as the next car in line rammed into it. People still on the platform were not as lucky as she and the man she now deemed "savior" in her mind. Bodies sailed through the air like fleas from a dog, some landing in safety beyond the car as it rose in a parody of a rearing horse, and some falling beneath the wheels as it came down again. Cries of agony, of panic, of hysteria, rose over the clamor of tortured steel.

A few lengths to the front, the lead car of the special train fought head on with the lead car of the regular. And lost.

Horrified, Jacoba watched the car virtually disintegrate, telescoping into a splintered mass of wood and steel. *Charlie!* Where was Charlie? Had he been caught in there? A moan rose in her throat on an acid tide of sickness.

The train was still moving, only instead of driving forward, the regular pushed it backward down the tracks. The car from which they had jumped went past, then the first car and finally the engine. There were people beneath the wheels, people running, people lying still — too still. Some cried out. Two men lay sprawled, one on his back, one face down, not a dozen feet from her. She knew they were dead.

"You hurt?"

Her savior's calm question penetrated her brain. Dimly aware of having heard him ask before, the capacity to reply eluded her. Besides, she didn't know the answer yet.

She tried to think. "I don't know. Are you?" In turn, she finally forced her own question.

He favored an arm as he crouched, then lurched to his feet and stood, swaying. Pallor lay beneath his brown skin. "Guess I'll live," he said. "It ain't safe here, missus. Gotta move you back. Can you get up?"

She nodded, but then she couldn't rise, not until he reached down and helped her. One of her knees protested, pain shooting all the way to her hip, as she turned toward the wreck. Blood dripped from a cut above her eyebrow and she had a vague idea it had come from a bit of debris flung from the wreckage, more of which still shot from the tracks and split the seams of the railroad cars. The cars themselves had finally quit moving. Overheated

metal and burning oil boosted a stench into the air. Underlying it
was the smell of blood.

Oh, dear God. Was Charlie trapped in that? "Come on," her
savior said. "Get under those trees over there. They will help
protect you."

"No." Jacoba dodged away from him. "I've got to find Charlie—
my husband."

But he caught her before she'd gone a step and, ignoring her
protests, half carried, half dragged her a few feet in the direction
he wanted her to go. "You'll get in the men's way, missus. You
can't help. Go sit over under that tree and stay put. Believe me,
your man will find you."

She started to argue, drawing breath to counter this piece of
nonsense, but whatever she been about to say was masked by a
woman's sharp, piercing scream for help. Savior's head whipped
around, toward the cry.

"You head on over there," he told Jacoba, pointing to the stand
of hemlock a few yards away. "You will be all right. If I see that
feller you were with, I'll tell him where you are."

"Yes," she said. "I'll be fine. Go. Someone else needs your help."

Without another glance in her direction, Savior hurried toward
the woman who had screamed. He reached her, bent to look where
she was pointing, then plunged off behind a pile of wreckage.
Soon, pieces of metal and smoking wood were being flung over
the top of the rubble.

Jacoba moved then. Straight toward the place where the car had
been reduced to a pile of twisted metal and broken wood. To where
she had last seen Charlie.

Chapter 2

Jacoba dodged around a bush that, dry with the heat of summer, burned with fierce explosive pops. Set alight by embers from the train, it blazed like an oil-soaked torch, as it emitted more sparks of its own. Several spot fires smoldered here and there, some of them in danger of jumping the graveled ditch alongside the track and spreading to nearby trees. A few men had already rallied, beating at the flames with their coats and kicking dirt over the coals.

Although she searched the firefighters' smoke-blackened faces, she didn't find Charlie's among them. Sobs catching in her throat, she hobbled on, closer to the derailed passenger car.

The crushed lead car, like a behemoth of the sea stranded out of water, seemed to pant and gasp and groan. Hot metal ticked as it cooled. The machine loomed high above Jacoba, making those eerie sounds as though it were alive and in pain. She distrusted its present immobility. She had the feeling of an entity waiting to roll over on top of her, and that she would not be able to escape. Her chest tightened in fear as she walked along beside it.

Someone had organized a rescue team in the shadow of the first coach and the wreckage of the second and third cars following it. The men were hurrying, carting the injured off to the side where there was less danger from fire or explosion, in case something, the boiler, she guessed, ruptured and blew up. Periodically, they freed another person from the wreckage and placed him, or her, in one of two rows. The row where folks cried out, occasionally moaned and just as often cursed, contained the lucky ones. The second group, thankfully fewer, was made up of the dead. Charlie couldn't be with them. She was certain of that. She would know if he—

She refused to let the conclusion of that thought go all the way to the end.

"Charlie," she called out, a pitiful effort, then. "Charles De Groot?" Her voice was somewhat stronger on the second try, although it did no good. Charlie didn't answer.

Marching—if her swollen knee could be said to march—up to an assemblage of three men frantically shifting hot timbers, Jacoba tugged on the back of one man's shirt. He kept working, muttering low, almost to himself.

"Sir," she said, plucking at him again, "Please, sir, can you help me? I'm looking for my husband." Despite herself, her voice shook.

"I can't find him," he said without glancing around at her. "I don't know where he is."

He didn't, she realized, mean Charlie.

Another of the men, his face scraped to the bloody bone on one side, paused in holding a board clear while the man crawled on his knees to peer under it. "He can't hear you, miss—something must have happened to his ears. He's looking for his son."

The deaf man was young, Jacoba noted. His son could hardly be out of leading strings. "I'm sorry. Tell him I'm sorry. But my husband . . . have you seen—"

Too late. He had dropped the board and the three of them hurried to move on to the next likely pile of debris. Tears ran down the father's cheeks, making pale runnels in the grime.

Heart pounding, Jacoba swiped at her own blurred eyes and

blundered on, her feet crunching in the gravel alongside the track
where embers glowed. How had the father and son become separated? She couldn't imagine allowing a child to run about in that
crowd by himself. Nor of being sent on an errand. An errand, perhaps, like the one Charlie had posed for himself.

Within her core, something shivered. Guilt? Charlie was always
rescuing her. Now it was her turn to rescue him.

Think. Where would he have gone to find a drink of water? That
is where she must search for him. Earlier, there had been a container
of water in their coach, but if it had been a simple matter, Charlie
would have returned to his seat long before the accident. Therefore,
or so Jacoba's flustered brain told her, her husband had not found
what he sought there. He had gone on, into the same car that had
taken the worst punishment. She must focus her quest there.

Then why did her resolve lag, giving her pause before she lifted
her skirt to her knees and climbed through the narrow gap remaining between the cars? Perhaps she'd find Charlie just there, over
on the other side.

But the chaos she found when she had ducked beneath a bent
steel rail was just as bad here as where she'd come from. Maybe
worse, because it didn't look as though anyone had stepped forward
to organize the turmoil as yet, or put together teams of rescuers and
set up orderly rows of survivors. Or of the dead.

Jacoba swayed where she stood, dread coursing through her.
She didn't want to look on more pain. More death. She wanted to
find Charlie. No. She wanted Charlie to find her, and together, they
would walk away and she would be safe and protected, and she
wouldn't have to see and smell and hear and feel.

But life didn't work that way. She had always known it didn't.
Taking a deep, smoke-laden breath, she plunged over to where she
saw a cluster of bodies stirring.

"Charlie," she called. "Charles De Groot. Where are you?"

With all the speed she could muster, she approached the huddle
of dazed survivors. A family, she saw, with a middle-aged father, his

pale and shocked wife, and three sons in stair steps ranging from perhaps ten years of age to sixteen. Miraculously, they all appeared unharmed beyond cuts and bruises.

Jacoba herself was more damaged than they, what with her injured knee and the cut over her eye. Unconscious of the action, one performed without thinking several times previously, she swept blood from her lashes and cheek, and wiped her hand on the skirt of her dress.

"Sir, please," she said, "can you help me? I'm looking for my husband. He's…"

A swift chopping motion silenced her. The man wouldn't meet her eyes, but stared over the top of her head. "Find someone else," he said in thin, sharp voice. "Can't you see we're in trouble ourselves? I can't help you."

The middle of the three boys shuffled restlessly.

"Walter," the father said, stern and with warning.

"Are you looking for someone, too?" Jacoba asked. "Maybe I can help."

He made that silencing gesture again. "Go away. You're frightening my wife. Don't you know you're covered in blood? Hideous!" He took his wife's shoulder and firmly turned her so she would not have to look at Jacoba. However, his voice came clearly enough even with his back to her.

"I'm going to sue the Spokane and Inland Empire," he said. "Carrying a bunch of damn riffraff that'll accost anybody."

"But, John," his wife replied. "Her traveling costume is very fine. She can't help being injured. I'm sure she's…"

"Boys!" her husband barked, overriding her smattering of generosity. "Come."

He got his family moving, picking a way through bodies and the injured, and the field of debris without a second look. They left an incredulous and shocked Jacoba standing like a petrified stump, wiping once again at her blood-smeared face. Only the middle boy spared a backward glance, leading her to believe he, at least, might have helped if only his father had let him.

Unfortunately, a boy's regrets wouldn't help her find Charlie, Jacoba reminded herself. And time spent curbing the anger and hurt that blazed through her could be better spent in her search.

Head pounding with pain, she trudged on, every step harder than the one that came before. Impressions flooded her senses. The smell of hot oil. The stain of fresh-spilled blood. The sound of mourning, of shattered hopes, of squelched dreams. Of fear and of pain. Jacoba wanted to scream and scream and scream. She didn't.

"Charlie," she called. "Charles De Groot."

There was a woman, her hands outstretched beseechingly. Death had overcome her as she tried to stop herself from being skewered by the ragged piece of steel penetrating her chest. The steel rod held her upright and she stood in a puddle of her own blood, still red and wet.

Jacoba, trembling hard enough to rattle her teeth and with her heart pounding within her rib cage, edged around the dead woman. She didn't know whether she was frightened by the specter of death, or if she was afraid the woman would suddenly come alive again, regardless of the stake through her heart. It was enough to almost— *almost*—discourage Jacoba from searching further, and yet she gritted her teeth and went on.

Perhaps she should do as *Savior* had told her. Perhaps she should find a place under a tree to sit and let Charlie find her. Except, what if Charlie lay in one of those rows of wounded or dead? What if he was trapped beneath some of the shattered pieces of railroad car and couldn't come for her? *What if he had a stake through his heart?*

No. No! He was only out of her sight for a little while, and surely she'd find Charlie helping others.

She ignored the niggling voice in her head insisting that if Charlie were able, his wife would be the first one he helped.

Jacoba searched on. Spots danced in front of her eyes, her head felt ready to float off her shoulders, and she was aware of staggering around like Madame's Irish coachman after his Saturday afternoon visit to the tavern.

"Charlie," she cried for perhaps the fiftieth time, the words quaking. "Charles De Groot?"

A voice answered. "J...Jacoba?"

Charlie!

At first Jacoba thought she might be hearing things, a product of her own wishful thinking, as the sound barely touched her ears. But then it came again. "Jacoba," accompanied by a hoarse groan.

"Charlie?" She couldn't see him anywhere, although she circled all the way around twice. "Charlie, where are you?"

The answer was long in coming.

"Here." He sounded as though speaking took every ounce of strength he possessed. Off to her left, a pile of broken lumber and the outside panel of a railroad car rustled before settling down again. She heard another groan and a faint whistling sound.

Fear dogged her footsteps as, hardly feeling her own pain, she followed his voice to the source. Dear Lord, but he, her Charlie, sounded so weak. How could that be her strong young husband?

"I'm here, Charlie." She halted with her toes touching the metal panel. "Tell me what to do."

What seemed an age passed before she heard him again.

"I'm buried...under...a pile of..." He paused, voice failing, then went on. "I'm hurt, Jake...can't get loose." He gasped. "Get help."

"Get help?" she cried. She turned another full loop, seeking someone—anyone.

Desperation seized her. "There isn't anybody, Charlie. Only me."

Nobody alive, she meant, everyone else in sight being either hurt or dead. She kept that to herself.

And Charlie hurt, too. Her heart swelled right up into her throat. What would they do if he were crippled? *No.* She couldn't let herself think of that now. *Not ever.* First she had to free him. Maybe he wasn't as bad off as he feared, or as bad as he sounded. Maybe he was just scared. Like her.

The pile of debris shifted a little as he moved, and he groaned again with the effort.

"Hurry," he said, his whisper fading.

Opening her mouth, Jacoba let out a yell that under different circumstances could have been heard in Coeur d'Alene. Here, mixed
with the other cries already ululating heavenward in the aftermath
of disaster, it got lost. As she had known it would be. She, Jacoba
Ludke De Groot, was the only one Charlie had to depend on for
help. A weak vessel, as anyone—especially Madame—could have
told him. Dread lay heavy on her.

Dropping to her good knee, she started digging. Little animal
noises issued from her mouth. A fingernail tore down to the quick.
Blood welled up smearing a board which, grunting under its weight,
she tossed to the side. More blood from the cut on her forehead
dripped onto the ground in front of her. Seeing the splash of red,
for the first time she became aware of how much it hurt.

What would she do if Charlie's head had been mangled like
that of the fellow over on the other side of the wreck? She'd
seen all the way to the skull, the bone glistening white and red
and raw. What if—

Some ridged metal that looked like part of the coach steps lay
across a network of timbers. Jacoba tugged and pulled, not making
much progress although sweat poured off her, stinging like fire in
the cut, but diluting the blood to pink.

She leaned forward, bracing on one hand in order to gain better
purchase, then froze as Charlie cried out.

"Sorry," she cried, retreating. She felt where he lay buried
now, his body resilient beneath her. "I'm so sorry, Charlie. I didn't
mean to hurt you."

He knew that. Of course he did.

"Get someone…to help." he said, his wheezy panting loud
enough to be heard over her own. "You can't…do this…by
yourself."

Jacoba spared another glance around while drawing more air
into her lungs. Thank the Lord that, because of the heat, she hadn't

laced her corset as tightly as usual this morning, so at least she hadn't become dizzy. Yet.

Charlie's plea to the contrary, no one had come forward to help. A dozen yards away a man wandered about making a search of his own, while farther still, two ladies had collapsed on the ground beside a body and were wailing their sorrow. More people, men in railroad uniforms, were coming this way, but they appeared headed towards the two women. The noise, Jacoba supposed, attracted them like flies.

She stood up and called, "Help. Please come help me. There's a man under this rubble."

But it was as if they all had been struck deaf and dumb.

"It'll be all right, Charlie." Kneeling down again, she peered beneath the sheet of metal. Her hand smarted as she touched the hot steel. "Hang on."

"Yes," he breathed. "That's what…I'm doing."

Jacoba didn't like the way he sounded. She dug a bit more, then set her eye to an opening, able to see a little of Charlie from this angle. What she saw made her heart skip a beat. Her husband lay still as the dead.

"Charlie?" Her voice quavered. His face, barely visible in the poor light, shone as ashen as though someone had powdered him with flour. But, to her immeasurable relief, it appeared unmarked in any dire way aside from a swollen lump along his jaw line. His eyes were closed.

"Charlie, speak to me. Where are you hurt?" He should be talking to her. A memory from her school days surfaced; a reminder of reading a rule that stated a person with a head injury must not be allowed to go to sleep.

At her question, his lids fluttered and his face turned a half-inch towards her.

"Jacoba… can't feel …my legs."

"Oh, Charlie," she said, trying to think what to say. "It's all right, my love. There's something laying on top of them, is all. You'll be fine as soon as you're freed." If only she really believed that.

His eyes had closed again. She didn't think he heard.

Wiping blood from her eyes yet again, Jacoba renewed her task, the need unearthing a frantic strength from somewhere. She found a length of broken timber to use as a pry and worked at levering the metal piece up and off of Charlie's legs. Unfortunately, it tilted almost to the point of crushing his face. She had to quit, then, on the realization she might kill him herself if she kept on.

A sob rose, choking her. She couldn't do this herself. She couldn't!

With the back of her wrist, Jacoba wiped the sweat-diluted sheen of blood from over her eye and cast around. Relief made her legs shake as she saw at long last, an organized group of men making their way around the damaged engine and who seemed bound in her general direction. One of the men she recognized, the dark man from the train who had saved her once already.

"Help!" she cried. "Sir, please come help me. Hurry. Please hurry."

She saw him touch the arms of two of the men with him, an indication to come along with him as he jogged over to where she stood.

"Find your husband?" he asked.

"I found him," she replied, gesturing to the mound of debris in front of her. "He's trapped under here. He quit talking to me. I'm afraid..." She started over. "I'm afraid he's badly hurt."

Tears clogged her throat. *I'm afraid he is dead.*

Her savior lost no time in getting his crew busy digging. He proved remarkably efficient for a man using only one arm.

"Sit down over there," he told Jacoba, indicating a grassy spot a few yards away. "Give us room to work."

Mutely, she nodded, glad to stand back and let him take over.

"I saw you didn't stay put before," he said, taking a breather while the other two lifted the sheet of metal, now stabilized so it wouldn't fall back on Charlie. They heaved it aside.

"No," Jacoba said. "And it's a good thing I didn't."

The other two men hovered at the cleared space where Charlie lay and stared down at him. One knelt and felt for a heartbeat.

"Gagne," she heard one of them say on a note of warning. "Better..."

Warned—and alarmed—by something in his voice, she hurried over to join them before the dark man had a chance to catch at her arm and stop her. Her breath hissed painfully past the clog in her throat.

Charlie appeared as fragile as a porcelain doll, sprawled at the bottom of the heap of debris. One leg crooked at an unnatural angle, but that, she saw, was the least of it. A thin metal spike protruded from his chest, driven there God knows how. A small amount of blood seeped into his shirt around it.

A vision of the dead woman from earlier arose and she swayed before sucking in a fierce breath.

The dark man stood beside her and took a good look.

"He's alive," the kneeling man announced after what seemed an everlasting pause.

"Reckon you're right," Savior said to Jacoba. "It is a good thing you didn't listen to me."

Chapter 3

Jacoba studied the rents in what this morning had been a stylish hobble-skirted walking dress. No longer. Now the dress's deep green color was painted with the red splotches of both her own and Charlie's blood. There were grass stains and oil stains, myriad rips, tears and burned spots. The fabric carried the rank stench of sweat and fear. So did she.

Her brown hair hung in lank, straggly lengths. She'd lost her hat, a perky concoction with feathers and flowers, probably when the man who'd saved her forced the jump from the train. The right hand seam had split all the way from hem to knee at the same time, and as she sat in the Deaconess Hospital waiting room, she pinched the sides together between her thumb and forefinger.

Beneath the torn gown, her right leg was bare. Her fine white lisle stocking, ruined beyond repair, had been discarded into a waste bucket when the doctor wrapped her sprained and battered knee round and round in a thick bandage. Another bandage encircled her forehead, covering the neat—she supposed they were neat—row of twelve stitches the doctor had used to mend the cut above her eye.

"You'll have a scar," he'd given warning, his stitches stopping the seeping blood at last. A stern-faced nurse had watched proceedings from over his shoulder. "But you're young," he added. "It'll fade with time."

The nurse clicked her tongue. "You're alive. Many people aren't. Best thank our good Lord for your deliverance and remember that vanity has no place in a godly life."

The doctor ignored the woman. "Keep the wound clean," he told Jacoba, "and when it's healed, you can always pull down a few curls to hide the scar."

Jacoba said nothing at all, afraid that if she opened her mouth it would be to scream. The jab of the needle going in and out of her skin, the tug as the knots were tied off, turned her stomach to jelly.

When the sewing finished and she could trust her voice again, she asked, "Where is my husband? Is there word of him yet?"

But neither could tell her. The nurse pressed a glass of water into her hand and led the way to the waiting room where she indicated Jacoba should take a chair.

"The doctor in charge of Mr. De Groot will come around and speak to you when he's through," she said.

So Jacoba waited—and waited. After a very long time, she began to think everyone had forgotten her.

Charlie and she had come to the hospital together, riding in the same horse-drawn ambulance along with several others of the injured. The journey took hours. Charlie never moved a muscle the whole trip, which had seemed to her never-ending. The spike in his chest quivered with each of his infrequent, shallowly drawn breaths, so long between them that Jacoba believed every one might be his last.

They had separated her from Charlie at the ambulance entrance, with Charlie loaded onto a stretcher and immediately borne away to the operating room. The nurse had escorted Jacoba to a curtained alcove and, while they waited for the doctor, uttered not one word of sympathy.

"Catch that blood in a wipe," she said, handing Jacoba a clean square of cloth. "I don't want it contaminating the floor."

Blood.

It was the dark man, Jacoba's savior, who'd insisted they leave the spike in Charlie's chest when one of the train officials, reacting much like Jacoba, wanted to remove it. He'd stopped the official in mid-reach.

"No," he'd said. "Pull it out, who knows what damage you'll do. Least this way he isn't bleeding. The spike might be what is stopping it. Once I saw—"

But then he had glanced at Jacoba, and never did say what he'd once seen.

Gagne. His name was Gagne, Jacoba remembered suddenly, as she sat alone in the waiting room taking tiny sips of water. She'd heard one of the men call him that. French.

The waiting room, large and cool, had ceilings that soared high above her head. Jacoba thought there must be a reason for the formal architecture, because surely it was expensive to build and maintain such an edifice. But the cries of the bereaved and the suffering were muted here, until it was possible to feel alone in the quiet even though surrounded by people.

How odd, she reflected, to wish to provide for such aloofness at a time like this. Didn't folks who were hurting crave the solicitude of their loved ones? A few chairs over, she recognized a couple from her passenger car on the train. The man and woman huddled together on a bench, holding hands. They'd had a child with them, she recollected, but he wasn't with them now. From the haggard tiredness on the man's face and the copious tears running down the woman's, Jacoba assumed their child had fallen victim to tragedy.

But at least they had each other to cling to. They had that much luck anyway. Jacoba, separated from the only person in the world she trusted, envied them in a way. If something happened to Charlie, she had no one. No one!

"Charlie," she whispered, and stilled her trembling lips with a dirty forefinger.

***

Three hours later a different nurse came to the waiting room entrance and beckoned to her.

"My husband?" Jacoba asked, lurching from her chair, heartbeat accelerating.

The woman shook her head.

With no further words spoken between them, Jacoba, her knee now swollen beyond the wrapping and barely able to bear her weight, followed the woman down a long cold hall.

Jacoba lagged, unable to keep up with the other's long, brisk strides, and when the nurse paused, waiting for her at the entrance to another room, her steps faltered. There'd been a sign on the wall, *Chapel—this way*. She hoped the door didn't lead to the chapel. If so, it must mean Charlie was…gone.

Eyes averted, she halted beside the other woman, who, though wearing a spotless white uniform, strangely enough did not smell of sanitizing agents or of medicine, but of blood and vomit.

The nurse opened the door. "In here," she said. "Dr. Libby is waiting for you."

No. Not a chapel, Jacoba's dizzied mind saw, but a large plain office where the doctor pushed forward a chair.

"This young woman shouldn't be walking. She looks like she could use a hospital bed almost as badly as her husband," he told the nurse who suddenly became solicitous enough to lend Jacoba an arm.

Jacoba needed it, too, as she sank like the shell of a rag doll onto the unpadded oak straight chair.

Could use a bed almost as badly as her husband. That meant Charlie lived. Jacoba gulped and lifted her head.

"How is my husband?" she asked. "He's...he's...all right, isn't he?"

Dr. Libby, frowning, sat down, picked up a pen and tapped his teeth with the capped end.

"Mr. De Groot is in serious condition," he said, his manner somber. "Critical condition. We'll know more by tomorrow, as long as he makes it through the night. The broken leg is the lesser of his injuries. But his chest— another hour and we wouldn't have been in time to save him. The truth is, whoever said not to remove the spike has as much to do with his survival as I do. It just missed his heart. He's been bleeding internally."

Gagne again. It seemed both she and Charlie owed him.

She hadn't realized she'd murmured the name aloud.

"Gagne? Is he a doctor, I wonder?" Dr. Libby's ears seemed to perk with interest. "Sounds French."

"I don't think he's a doctor." Jacoba shook her head. "Just wise. Charlie—my husband—may I see him?"

The doctor nodded. "Briefly. He's still sleeping off the ether. He may not know you're there, and of course, when he does awaken he'll be sick and in pain. You're from the lottery train, are you not? Have you a place to stay while your husband is recuperating?"

"We took a hotel room yesterday," Jacoba said. What did it matter? *Charlie recuperating.* She hugged the words to her. "I'll sit with Charlie tonight."

"Better not." The doctor eyed her. "You look, if I may say so, a bit the worse for wear yourself. Get some rest, help yourself. Your husband will need you later on."

"I expect you'll want to take lodgings in a respectable boarding house quite soon," he added, not unkindly. "The expense, you know. Unless, of course, you needn't worry about that. Perhaps you have family who will put you up."

Jacoba gave an almost imperceptible jump. "No. No family. Neither of us."

"I see." The doctor rose and came around the corner of the

desk to help her to her feet. "Well, try not to worry about it tonight. Perhaps in a day or two your husband will be able to tell
you what he wants you to do."

"Yes," Jacoba said, grateful for the strength of his arm as they
walked to the end of this hall and entered another much noisier
and busier. A few doors down, they turned into a ward crowded
with extra beds. Dr. Libby ushered her over to the middle bed
in a row of five. The man in the bed moaned and muttered but
did not awaken. A construction of wires held the covers tent-like
over one of his legs.

"We've had to make space for more patients than this room
should hold, I'm afraid," he said. "The hospital wasn't prepared
for a major disaster like this train wreck. A couple of these patients
are due to be released soon."

His comment never registered on Jacoba's brain. She stood at
the end of the bed while Dr. Libby raised the blanket drawn up to
Charlie's chest and peered under the loose bandage. But was this
Charlie? Or was this some horrible mistake with a stranger put in
the bed in her husband's place.

The name on the chart clipped to the end of the metal bedstead
had his name on it, but the face on the pillow held barely more color
than the bleached pillowslip. His lips were dry and narrowed to a
thin slash, the cheeks hollow beneath a prominent bone structure.
Surely Charlie had never looked so colorless and drawn.

Her Charlie's fair skin blushed easily over rounded cheeks, his
lips full and soft as a girl's. He'd been growing a mustache lately
in hopes it made him look older than his twenty-five years, and it
stood out in sharp contrast against his bleached skin.

Right now he got his wish, for he did look older than twenty-five. Jacoba recognized him as a pale shadow of his father, and
of a like age. The resemblance to his parent is what convinced her
this was indeed Charlie. That and the mustache.

Dr. Libby finished his examination and laid his fingers over
Charlie's wrist for a few seconds. "You may stay for an hour," he

said. "No more. If your husband wants to sleep, let him. Don't sit on the bed, don't excite him if he wakes up, and don't make him talk or you talk too loudly. You might worry the other patients."

Jacoba nodded. "He's going to be all right, isn't he?"

The doctor screwed up his mouth. "Of course. It's going to be a battle, though, and slow. You mustn't expect him to spring from his bed a week from now and go out to plow a furrow."

She limped past the doctor, going to Charlie's side. "No plow. My husband is a builder," she said. Her pride—his pride—swelled within her. "A master builder."

**

Charlie didn't awaken anytime during the allotted hour, although he moaned and cried out. Jacoba, with tears welling in her eyes, clasped his hand to her heart and stretched to two the hour Dr. Libby had said she could stay. When she finally gave up hoping Charlie would come to himself, a sympathetic volunteer, one of the patronesses of the hospital come to lend her assistance during the crisis, helped her outside to the streetcar stop and showed her which route to take back to the Holliday Hotel.

"Come back tomorrow, my dear," she said. "Try not to worry. We'll take good care of your husband."

Jacoba could only nod mutely, too tired, too anxious, in too much pain herself to clear her head and think. Once at the hotel, a middle-aged bell boy saw her up to the third floor, unlocking their room door for her because the key had been in Charlie's pocket and she had no idea where his clothes might be. She must find that out. Tomorrow. Weariness struck too deeply for now. To her surprise, within fifteen minutes a knock announced the bell boy's return. He bore with him a roast beef sandwich, lettuce peaking from between the layers, and a tall glass of buttermilk.

"News of the wreck is hitting folks pretty hard," he said, his wizened face full of concern. "Lots of folks killed, I hear. I met your man last night. Pleasant young feller. I hope he'll be all right."

Jacoba summoned a tired smile. "Thank you. The doctor said he will recover." *But had he?* Suddenly, she didn't know. All she knew for certain was that she didn't want to remember the "lots of folks" who'd been killed. Charlie had come much too close to being one of them.

Nevertheless, she fished a dime from her pocketbook to reward the helpful bell boy.

Without Charlie, the room echoed with emptiness, the ornate furniture a caricature of good taste. She and Charlie had laughed, bouncing on the big bed where tonight she would sleep alone. With a sense of shock, she realized that had only been this morning. It seemed a lifetime ago.

At first, she eyed the sandwich with distaste, until the scent of the horseradish dressing reached her and the fresh texture of the lettuce triggered a response so strong her mouth watered and her stomach rumbled. Without regard for proper manners or daintiness, she sat down at a small table and ate like a ravening wolf, chewing big bites of bread and beef with the horseradish stinging her nose and bringing healthy tears to her eyes. It had her licking the last taste off her fingers when the sandwich was gone.

She had a difficult moment as she removed the ruined walking suit, tearing two buttons from their moorings and not caring a whit, because it had struck her she didn't even know how to finish undressing herself. She missed Charlie already. *What if he never came home?*

She and Charlie had been married seventeen days, and on every one of those days, morning and evening, Charlie had played maid to her. Each morning he laced her corset strings and, while she held onto a chair or once, braced herself against a wall, pulled them tight. Each evening, before they crawled into bed together, he reversed the process.

Although she'd grown used to his presence now, the first morning after they'd run away his presence had been painfully embarrassing. Now, despite her shyness, she was learning to like the way he looked at her with his eyes dark and slumberous, and she liked the way he touched her, too. Having a man around was quite a different thing than having Matilda, the maid Jacoba had shared with her sisters ever since Madame declared her adult enough to put up her hair and require a corset.

Charlie, Jacoba recalled, struggling now with an unreachable knot in the laces, said she didn't need any such thing. Charlie, bringing a blush to her cheeks, said he preferred her without. Then he had added, "But I can't say as I mind the work," and planted a kiss on the soft spot at the back of her neck and trailed the kiss down and down and around to her throat.

Jacoba shivered, thinking about his kisses, about the texture of his mustache against her skin, about his hands going to her secret places, caressing, exciting.

Come to think of it, their goings on had made them late in catching the train west the morning after they eloped. Just as well, too, because when they did get to the station, they had caught sight of Dietrich, Madame's most trusted cohort—whom she called an assistant—on his way out, alone and wearing an expression of utter disgust.

With a little shrewd probing, her new husband had questioned the ticket agent and discovered Dietrich had been looking for them, although Charlie had let on like his only interest concerned the fellow's foreign accent. But just in case Dietrich came back later and inquired again, Charlie gave her a handful of money and sent Jacoba to buy her own ticket from a different agent, and so they escaped St. Louis with no one the wiser. Or so they believed.

Madame had made a mistake in sending her underling to search for a couple instead of two single people. How she and Charlie had laughed, euphoric at getting the better of Jacoba's mother for a second time, the first being their elopement. It must, they concluded, have shocked Madame to her core. They considered it a triumph.

Jacoba finally cut her way out of her corset, taking her long-bladed sewing scissors and somehow managing to snip the knotted laces. It added another task to the list she once would have given Matilda without thinking twice, that of replacing the tapes. Such chores would belong to her in the future, she admitted ruefully, but for tonight, weariness kept her from worrying about it.

She went to bed, only to have nightmares haunt her when she dropped off to sleep at periodic intervals. Then she would start awake with the imagined sound of train whistles, the harshness of a man's scream, and the clash of steel meeting steel resounding over and over in her mind. She thought she heard Charlie's voice and tried to answer.

Had Charlie screamed? In pain and restless, she tossed from side to side on the too soft mattress, unable to stop thinking of his ashen face, or of that awful thing stuck in his chest.

Gagne. Gagne had saved him. A good Samaritan come into their lives. Shudders shook her, alone in the bed when what she wanted most was to rest in Charlie's arms. Charlie's strong, warm arms. Against his broad, unblemished chest.

Her knee throbbed with every beat of her heart and her head, resting against the firm pillow, felt sore enough, and heavy enough, to sink right through the layers—bedding, pillow, mattress—all the way to the unforgiving floor.

***

In the light of morning, with Jacoba's waking thoughts centered on her husband, she dragged out of bed only to cry aloud the moment her foot hit the floor. For the moment, thoughts of Charlie went right out of her head, forgotten as pain flooded through her. Shocked, she found that under the bandage binding her knee, her leg had turned black and blue all the way to the foot.

To make matters worse when, clenching her teeth, she hobbled over to the basin to wash her face, she discovered her eye below the swollen line of stitches in her forehead rimmed with dried blood, a circle of red layered in the roots of her lashes. The water in the basin turned a streaky pink as she bathed her face, careful to avoid the bandage. Even combing her hair hurt.

She would use a sturdy umbrella as a cane today, she decided, one that Madame had imported from England for her own use, remarking that Britain was a civilized country where they knew the importance of quality.

Wryly, Jacoba remembered something else Madame often said—that America was the only country she knew of where one could get rich not only within one's lifetime, but while still young enough to enjoy it. Madame certainly enjoyed her money. And more than money, her power.

But she lost her power over me. I escaped. Yet, as Jacoba, twisting her body and yanking her new corset strings snug, she was stricken with the thought that Madame's money had bought the full-skirted, blue silk moiré dress she donned. Not the proper dress to wear to a hospital where she would sit beside her injured husband, but at least the full skirt would hide her knee.

Too bad she hadn't worn it yesterday. Perhaps then she could've managed the jump from the train with enough grace to avoid hurting herself.

Pointless to think of the what ifs and perhapses. She and Charlie were alive. *As long as Charlie survived the night.* She shook the thought aside. Of course he had. If anything awful happened, they would've sent for her.

Dr. Libby had said he was seriously injured, that's what. She remembered now. But he'd implied Charlie would be all right, and that's all that mattered. The memory of her rescuer's dark face swam into her thoughts again. She and Charlie both owed their lives to him, a stranger named Gagne. Who was he, really? Had Madame sent him, after all, only not to take her back, but to watch over her?

Chapter 4

The white walls of the Deaconess Hospital sparkled like angel's wings in the early morning light, promising hope to all who entered. Though bright enough to cause the ache pounding behind Jacoba's squinted eyes, but she suspected the walls were not to blame. Her own pain, anxiety and lack of sleep were more likely culprits.

Assisted by a handrail, she pulled herself up the steps to the front entrance. There she put the sturdy umbrella to use as a cane, its ferrule tapping a counterpoint to the heel of the one low-heeled shoe she wore. With her injured leg swollen from knee to ankle, a knitted bedroom slipper covered the foot—the only thing she'd been able to stretch over the hideously painful appendage.

The lobby, as she limped through on the way to Charlie's assigned ward, was empty this early. She smelled food and heard the rattle of metal on metal in a corridor to her right, but more disturbing, off in the distance came the sound of two people weeping.

The probable cause for this sorrow stabbed her with a spasm of fear. It created a set of questions she didn't want to think about.

One nagged at her most, refusing to leave her alone. *What if Charlie had died during the night?* More than once she assured herself the hospital would have sent for her had that seemed likely, but would they really? Or would they wait until she showed up outside the door of his ward, waylaying her then with the bad news? And who would be the one to tell her? Please God, not the woman whose uniform crackled with starch, but who smelled of blood.

Sweat trickled and stung in the cut on Jacoba's forehead. A little short of breath, she trembled as she arrived at Charlie's ward. The intimidating nurse, she saw, feeling slightly reassured, was nowhere in sight. The hall, both up and down, was empty of people and quiet as a tomb.

Tomb. Not a reassuring word to have in mind.

Shivering, and with the odor of antiseptic stinging in her nose, she tiptoed in. A swift glance told the room's occupants, reduced by one to four men, remained asleep.

Charlie's eyes were closed, sandy brown lashes fanned onto a colorless face. That face seemed old and sunken, almost unrecognizable as her healthy young husband. Heart thudding hard enough to break through her chest wall, she crept forward, forgetting to be strong. Why was he so very, very still? She reached out, touching his cheek with shaking fingers. He was warm. Oh, thank God! His skin was warm.

His eyes opened. "Jacoba," he breathed, so faint she could barely hear him. "Jake."

"Yes, Charlie. It's me." Leaning over, she pressed a kiss onto his brow, discovering he not only was warm, but hot. Running a fever, she thought. Did the doctor know? "How are you? Has Dr. Libby been to see you?"

As though too heavy to remain open, Charlie's lids fluttered shut over his lake-blue eyes. "Don't know," he whispered. And just like that, he fell asleep again.

Jacoba knew she shouldn't allow herself the luxury, but when she'd drawn the spindly visitor's chair close to the bedside and taken her husband's hand in her own, a few tears spilled down her cheeks.

Was Charlie going to die? Her Charlie, always so strong? Fear sang along her nerves. No. Why would God be so cruel? And yet, although she closed her own eyes and whispered a desperate plea, she knew God could be pitiless sometimes. Hadn't she seen as much for herself yesterday? The young family losing their child. The man losing his wife. Did God even care about Charlie?

She was still holding Charlie's hand to her heart and trying to pray when Doctor Libby strode into the room. The starched nurse accompanied him, her white uniform skirt pristine and, mercifully, not yet smelling of blood but of soap and alcohol. She wore a name tag today with her name, Nurse Richards, neatly printed on it.

"Mrs. DeGroot," Dr. Libby said. "Here already? You hardly look able to rise from your bed."

Jacoba shrugged. "My husband? How is he?"

The doctor bent over his patient. At a gesture, Nurse Richards thrust a thermometer between Charlie's lips while Dr. Libby drew down the blanket and peeped beneath the dressing covering Charlie's wound.

Jacoba saw his mouth tighten and her heart seemed to almost stop beating.

"Is he worse?" Her voice trembled.

"Another day or two and I'll be able to better tell." The doctor moved on to the strange metal apparatus that held the blanket off Charlie's leg, while at the same time providing tension on the pulley holding his shattered bones in alignment. He reached over and adjusted the pulley, drawing a moan from Charlie. The doctor's expression was unreadable.

"His leg," Jacoba faltered. "Will he lose it?" She forced the words out.

"No. Given time, it will mend." Dr. Libby wasn't looking at her, but at the thermometer Miss Richards had pulled from Charlie's mouth and handed wordlessly to him. "He may walk with a limp after this, but the leg will function. He won't want to dance."

Dizzy with relief—*Charlie would keep his leg!*—she forced a smile. "He never danced much anyway."

"Well, then," the doctor said. With something very like relief, he turned to his nurse. "Nurse Richards, please see this man takes in plenty of liquids and that his chest wound is irrigated every three hours. Looks as though a little infection is setting in. I'll write a prescription for what I want you to use. Bathe him with cool water. If his temperature rises any more, you might try packing him in ice. Keep a close check on him. I know the hospital is busy. Do your best."

"Of course, Dr. Libby." Nurse Richards took the thermometer and shook it down.

"I can do that," Jacoba said. They both turned to her in surprise. "I can monitor his temperature and bathe him with cool water. Please. I'll do it."

"You have no training." It sounded as though Nurse Richards was jealously defending her territory. And yet, Jacoba wondered, how hard could it be to bathe a man's body and read a thermometer?

"I am his wife," she said.

Dr. Libby put his hand on the nurse's shoulder to steer her out. "Stay, then," he told Jacoba. And then, to Nurse Richards, "Mrs. DeGroot's presence will free you to tend other patients. Just don't forget to irrigate his wound and keep an eye his temperature. As helpful as she is, that procedure is beyond this lady."

"Of course, Doctor." Nurse Richards, appearing slightly mollified by this pronouncement, went on her way.

Dr. Libby winked at Jacoba. "She's a managing kind of woman, but a good nurse. You'll see."

Jacoba tried to smile, an actual impossibility. Unable to ignore her own pain any longer, or to stay on her feet, she sat down again and, dipping a cloth in the basin of water on the bedside table, wiped it across Charlie's forehead. By the time she'd done his face and neck, her touch featherlight, Dr. Libby had gone. She started over on Charlie's forehead, his cheeks, his neck, both back and front. Down his arms, his wrists, the bend of his elbows. Begin again, forehead, face, neck, arms, and later on, carrying the pre-scribed course of action to his legs including the one in traction. Except for breaks long enough to go to the bathroom and six hours rest in her lonely hotel room at night, she kept to this ritual until on the third day, Charlie's fever broke.

His eyes opened as she was dabbing at his neck, and he made a noise she interpreted as a pained grunt.

"Charlie!" she cried, dropping the cloth into the basin and in the process, splashing water down the front of her skirt. "You're awake. Oh, thank God!"

Charlie stared at her blankly. "Jake?" he croaked. "Is that you?"

Dr. Libby had warned her not to embrace him or put pressure on his chest. Nurse Richards, who Jacoba admitted had treated Charlie with gentle dedication, said the same. So, although she wanted above all things to fling herself into his arms, she settled for taking his hand and pressing several fervent kisses upon it.

"Of course it's me, you silly." She smiled past welling tears. "Who else?"

He blinked. "For a minute . . . I thought it was Madame." He trailed off.

"Me? I looked like mother?"

His gaze sharpened. "Just for a minute. It's gone now."

"Oh," she said. Truth to tell, Jacoba hardly felt flattered. Madame had a hardness about her, except when enticing yet another husband into her clutches. Each of those gentlemen had been wealthier than the last, although she'd been known to forego great wealth if the suitor bore a title. An implacable pride manifested itself all too readily to her children, as it did to those she considered her inferior. And this, as Jacoba—and Charlie—well knew, was most everybody.

So no, she was not flattered, even though she had inherited Madame's slim, elegant figure, small bones, rich flowing mahog-any brown hair and slightly slanted hazel eyes. Men considered

Madame exotic and beautiful, and if Jacoba was not quite in the same class as her mother, she didn't care a whit. She only wanted to be beautiful to Charlie.

"Your forehead, Jake. What happened? Where..." Although he was watching her, he touched his chest as if to stop the pain there. His gaze went to the pulley device holding his leg. "Wait. The train. The special to Coeur d'Alene. It wrecked, didn't it? I don't—"

"Don't what?"

"I don't remember exactly. Just that the car rose up. I lost my feet, and then I was thrown to the end of the car. People were screaming."

"Yes." Jacoba nodded. She kissed Charlie's hand again. "Sixteen people were killed. A great many, they're not yet sure of the count, were injured. Some as badly as you. Some like me, hardly worth mentioning." She dismissed her cut and bruised forehead, and her aching knee as though they were nothing.

Shock turned Charlie's already pallid complexion whiter. "Sixteen died? My God, Jacoba! That's awful. They kept you from seeing, didn't they? The railroad people?"

Slowly, she shook her head. "I saw, Charlie. One could not help but see." He must have forgotten her finding him, the memory lost within his own injury.

Her reply seemed to trouble him more than anything. "Dammit," he said. His hand slapped weakly down on the coverlet. "Somebody should've protected you. A girl like you, so sheltered all your life. Jacoba, I'm sorry. I should've been with you."

Sheltered all her life? She almost laughed, and for the first time in days spared a thought for the man who'd saved her. He'd wanted to protect her, too. His arm. She'd seen enough now to know it had been broken. The break no doubt happened when he jumped, carrying her with him to safety, and yet afterward he'd kept right on working, helping others, helping Charlie. She hoped he was all right, and wished she'd heard all of his name and where he lived so she could send him a note of thanks at the least. Gagne. It was all she knew.

Laughter rose in her throat. A note. What could she say?

Dear Mr. Gagne: Thank you very much for saving my life and my husband's life. Without you, we'd both be dead. Sincerely, Jacoba Ludke DeGroot.

"And done what?" she said after a moment. "There was nothing you could do, Charlie." She closed her eyes against the remembered scene. Of course, it didn't do any good. The sight would haunt her dreams for a very long time, she feared. Like one of the new moving pictures, but etched on her brain instead of on film.

"What are you thinking about?" Charlie interrupted what had become a waking nightmare.

She forced a smile. "I'm thinking I'm utterly relieved you've come to yourself and have all your wits. I'm wondering how you feel, and if there's anything I can do for you." And she prayed the train wreck hadn't ended their dream.

"All my wits? Well, sure," Charlie said, as though insulted. "Why wouldn't I have my wits about me?"

He was apt to find out tonight, Jacoba thought grimly. When the man who lay in the bed nearest the wall began his nightly screaming. Apparently the man had no family although he kept hollering for "Josie," and with only ten dollars in his wallet and nothing to identify him, nobody knew who he was. Including himself. The nurses or the policeman in charge of investigating the accident repeatedly asked him his name, but all they did was agitate him and came away no wiser. Lost wits, indeed.

She shuddered. What if that had been Charlie, or her, or worse, both? They'd been so careful to cover their tracks on the way out west. What if they'd both died? What if they'd been laid in their graves unidentified, and Madame never discovered what happened to her middle child? What if Charlie's dad lost his second son? Sometimes she felt like screaming herself.

She looked up to find Charlie sleeping again. Regular sleep though. Healing sleep. She didn't realize she was weeping until Nurse Richards, coming on shift for the evening hours, peeped into the room.

"Oh, goodness!" Nurse Richards entered with a rush. "Is he…" Her hand reached for Charlie's wrist as she spoke, checking for a pulse. Upon finding one, she stared at Jacoba as though at the village idiot.

"No, no." Jacoba couldn't seem to stop the pesky tears running down her face. "He woke up, Mrs. Richards. He's better. He knows me, and knows who he is, and he remembers the train wreck."

"Then why are you crying?"

Jacoba laughed. "Because I'm so happy."

The nurse's plain face lit. "As am I, Mrs. DeGroot. As am I. Pat yourself on the back. You've brought him through."

"Thanks to Dr. Libby and to you." Jacoba believed in giving credit where credit was due. Her first impression of Nurse Richards had mellowed over the past few days. Yes, the woman was jealous of her job. But along with it, there was no one more dedicated to the welfare of her patients. Once the nurse had seen Jacoba's entire focus was upon making her husband better, they had worked in concert to this end. Friends? Not quite, although certainly allies in this instance. But Jacoba didn't think she'd ever get used to the smell of blood that clung to Nurse Richards.

"Dr. Libby will be most relieved." Mrs. Richards, having earlier admitted she had a husband of her own, buzzed about busy as a hornet, noting Charlie's pulse rate, his temperature, the look of his wound which, as her first duty, she irrigated once again. Finished, she relaxed into a smile. "In fact, I believe I'll telephone the doctor at his office right now. He'll be pleased as punch."

And so he was, as Charlie's condition stabilized over the next few days. Jacoba took to eating twice a day instead of once, and sleeping an hour longer before hurrying to the hospital. Her own stitches were removed, with the doctor warning that she would always carry the scar. And finally her leg, knee to ankle, slowly—oh, so slowly—returned to something near normal in size, although it remained painful.

But not everything was turning out so well. Jacoba paid a dollar for a room at the Holliday every day, plus the cost of her meals, which caused the supply of cash money hidden in Charlie's satchel to shrink alarmingly. Although she tried not to let on to Charlie, worry gnawed at her, especially at night when she was in bed.

Charlie had planned to obtain work in the days before the land lottery, paying their expenses as they went. And then, even when they'd drawn their one hundred and sixty acres as he was certain they would, he counted on working for others along with building his—their—home. Some of the money in the satchel they'd declared sacrosanct, essential to building and holding the land. A team of horses, tools, food, building supplies. Jacoba counted the items off on her fingers. And she counted the days, the weeks. Perhaps even, as Dr. Libby warned, the months until Charlie was on his feet again.

Charlie hadn't given up the dream. She knew that. But for her, it had all but faded. Then, this morning, he startled her once again.

"Jake," he said before she'd as much as had a chance to remove her hat and gloves. "How long until the lottery. I've lost track."

"Good morning to you, too." She only sounded snappy. In truth, hearing the enthusiasm back in his voice and seeing the color in his thin cheeks raised her own spirits no end. Taking her time, she pulled up the visitor's chair and sat. They were alone in the room, the last of the other patients having been released the previous day. "The drawing is tomorrow. I'm so sorry, Charlie. All your plans, the accident, all for naught."

"You'll have to go." It was as though he only heard what he wanted to hear.

"Go? To the lottery drawing? Charlie, why? I'm afraid our plans are out of the question for now. "

A gesture took in the leg pulleys and moved on to cover his chest. It was as though he hadn't heard her. "They won't let me out of here. It'll have to be you."

"But Charlie, you can't—"

"Can't what?"

She saw she'd offended him.

"I know what you're thinking, but I won't always be crippled or laid up," he said. "We still need a place to live, no matter what. I want it to be on my own land. I want to work for myself. For us."

She thought of the rapidly diminishing supply of cash. He hadn't thought how much it was costing her to live now. Or of his hospital bills, although there was mention the Spokane and Inland Empire Railroad would have to pay them. Or how much it would take to last them through the winter. As badly as his leg had been broken, it might be months before it fully healed. And that discounted his chest. She, who'd been raised in a home in the wealthiest section of St. Louis, who had never in her life had to count the cost of anything, whose mother bore two separate and imposing titles in front of her name, couldn't get money—or the lack thereof—out of her mind.

But how to convey this to him without hurting his feelings. She fell back on what he regarded as her fragility. "But I don't want to get on a train, Charlie. Never again, if I can help it."

He shifted in bed, making the wires to his leg creak and his face crumble into lines of pain. "You aren't scared are you, honey?" A dare from way back when they first met on the stairway leading down to the ground floor of Madame's new mansion. Charlie had caught her sitting on the bannister as if thinking of sliding down. As she had when, in a teasing tone of voice, he said, "You'd best not. You might get hurt."

She took his words as a challenge. Madame's daughter was not allowed to be frightened of anything. Or if she was, not allowed to show it.

So she'd slid down. And she hadn't been hurt. Or only a little when she landed at the bottom on *her* bottom. Oh, how Charlie had laughed.

"Of course, I'm scared," she retorted now. "Aren't you?"

"Maybe a bit. But you have to do this for us, Jake. And if the drawing is tomorrow, you'll need to catch the morning train. You need to be there to pick a site."

She still had doubts. "Are you sure you want to go ahead? Maybe this isn't meant to be. Besides, we don't know that your name will be drawn."

"Yes it will. It's our destiny, Jake. You'll see."

"Charlie, I don't see how . . ." she started, but her protest died half-formed. How could she be the one to shatter his dream? And as he grew more upset, she knew this was something she'd have to do. So why did fingers of unease crawl up her spine? "All right, Charlie. I'll do it. You'll draw the best piece of land on the Coeur d'Alene reservation." She forced enthusiasm into her voice. "I'm sure of it."

He smiled and leaned back into his supporting pillows. "Damn right, I will. We will."

***

Later that morning, taking a short break while Charlie slept, she crept down to the almost deserted lobby of the hospital and found the current Spokane Chronicle, searching through the wrinkled, well-handled pages until she found an advertisement for single rooms.

Fifteen dollars a month, it said, breakfast included. Twenty-two dollars for two. Clean, but not fancy. Although not certain of the address, she thought that while not in the best part of town, it wasn't in the worst either. One thing for sure, she couldn't stay in the hotel any longer, no matter how safe and comfortable she felt there.

Looking around and finding herself unobserved, she folded the paper and carried it with her when she went to search out the rooming house.

***

When Charlie awakened, Jacoba sat perched in her usual chair at his side reading a newspaper. If her face appeared a little flushed, he made no comment on it.

"Did you get your train ticket?" he asked as soon as he opened his eyes.

Jacoba fanned her hot face. It was warm and close in Charlie's hospital room, the window tightly shut against the summer air—and she'd been hurrying.

"Yes. I'm on the first one in the morning."

"If the drawing runs too late, you may need to stay in a Coeur d'Alene hotel tomorrow night," he said, as if she didn't already know. "Depending on how long the lottery drawing takes, you might need the room for two nights."

"I know."

"Well, do you know how to sign in at the hotel?" Now she'd made the plans, he began worrying. "You won't be too bashful to order a meal, will you? And there will be filing fees in connection to the lottery. Don't let anybody overcharge you, Jake, but be sure you have all the correct paperwork done. I don't want any slip-ups when it comes to my land title. I'm pretty sure when they find out I'm a train wreck victim they'll mail the deed papers to me for signature. Just don't..."

"Charlie!" Jacoba smiled a little at his excitement and laid a finger over his lips, stilling the flow of words. "I know what to do. I've read all the lottery instructions, same as you. I'm Madame's daughter, for goodness sake. When did anyone ever get the best of Madame in a business deal?"

Plus, he seemed to have forgotten she'd been taking care of herself for almost two weeks now.

At this, Charlie leaned more comfortably against his pillows, his blue eyes glinting. "You might look like Madame, Jacoba, but you sure in hell don't act like her. You're nothing like her, honey, and don't you forget it."

But Jacoba, although she gave her husband a quick peck on the cheek for the encouragement, wasn't so sure. She wagered Mrs. Griswold at the rooming house might not agree either.

It never crossed her mind that Charlie's name might not be drawn in the lottery. And Charlie had no doubts at all.

Chapter 5

Jacoba had learned her lesson. Denying her fear of the behemoth, she boarded the train early, while the day still smelled fresh and clean and before the heat began building inside the car. Birds trilled energetically in the lone tree standing sentinel beside the brick station.

Instead of a smart traveling costume—hers having been destroyed in the wreck ten days ago—she wore a simple, light cotton dress, one that in her previous life she saved for at home days. Her hat was simple, too, a cool straw designed to shade her eyes. But as before, she took a seat by the window. If trouble came, she knew what to do this time. Run and jump—the mere thought of which made her knee throb.

Once underway and thundering across the flat prairie toward Coeur d'Alene, her heart pounded in time with the wheels clacking rhythmically on the track. Although full, the train was nowhere near as crowded as on the previous run, with passengers packed in like fish in a tin. Men still stood in the aisles and outside on the platform, but not on the roof. One could at least breathe, although with the sun blazing through the windows, heat soon began building.

Gradually, as the ride proved uneventful, her fear abated under the other passengers' high spirits. No one mentioned the accident and soon she found her eyelids drooping. She'd gotten very little sleep the night before.

She hadn't told Charlie yet about moving out of the Holliday, since she knew he wouldn't approve. Another reason for the omission, or so she excused herself, was because he'd been so excited, so full of advice, so full of plans, she hadn't the heart to bring up as mundane a topic as money. That Mrs. Griswold's boarding house lay only a couple streets away from an area rife with saloons, gambling establishments and cheap flop houses she planned on keeping to herself for now. And she'd certainly never mention that she knew about the brothels. No, Charlie wouldn't like it one bit.

Although clean, the living quarters's main attraction was price. Otherwise, the pokey little room in Mrs. Griswold's establishment grew hot enough to bake bread without an oven, and with the one window open, noise from the streets kept her nerves on edge. Every single night! Jacoba hadn't expected so much noise, being used to the solid, quiet comfort of the Holliday.

Late last night, after finally dozing off, she'd been awakened by gunfire that sounded as if it were right beneath her window. Most probably some out-of-towners on a bender, celebrating who knows what, according to Mrs. Griswold's light comment this morning. Or perhaps someone shooting someone else. After that, she remained awake for several hours, relieved when dawn drove away the shadows. But for now, she only wanted to sleep.

If, she reflected after a moment when her eyes had glazed over and drifted shut, anyone would let her.

"You don't look like a homesteader."

Jacoba heard the words, but didn't realize they were intended for her until a sharp elbow in the ribs demanded her attention. Her eyes blinked open and she met the piercing, rather steely gaze of the elderly woman next to her.

"Nor do you," she said after a moment's worth of examination. The woman, though thin and spry looking, seemed too old and far too frail to be clearing new land. And apparently, she was as alone as Jacoba.

"Hah! See these?" The woman held up her hands, big for the rest of her diminutive size and clad in old-fashioned fingerless mitts. "Strong. Got calluses from chopping wood, scars from cooking, fingernails broke to the quick from working in soil. Not to mention chapped skin from scrubbing clothes on a washboard. I know how to work."

A moment passed as they both stared at Jacoba's small, smooth hands, gloveless in this heat, folded in her lap. Like the other woman, she took pride in what they showed the world—a testament to the standard of her work. Soft, clean, white, with the nails shaped into ovals and burnished to a shine. Appropriate indeed, for Madame's daughter.

"I see," she said, just a touch of distaste in her voice. "You flaunt them as a badge of courage, I assume."

The woman cackled merrily, beady dark eyes snapping with glee. "Found me out, didn't you?"

Jacoba couldn't stop her smile. "You should use a good lotion every time after your hands have been in water or soil," she advised, "and try a milder soap. Also, wear gloves as you work."

This time the little woman belted out an infectious laugh. "Soap—lotion." She smoothed her half-mitts over swollen joints. "It'd take more than that to make my hands as pretty as yours."

"But those things would make you more comfortable." Jacoba's tone was serious. "And your facial skin if it is dry, too."

The shake of the woman's head was not entirely one of disagreement. "Those things come too dear for me, I'm afraid. Why, I wouldn't know what to do if I started pampering myself. Face lotion! What next? Silk unmentionables?"

Jacoba smiled, wondering what would be wrong with that until the other said, "But you still don't look like a homesteader."

"What does a homesteader look like? I'm ready to work. Isn't that enough?"

A sigh replied. "Let's hope so, my dear, because I'm afraid most of the women you'll meet on the reservation will look more like me. I'm Mrs. Thomas Merrimont, by the way. Opal Merrimont." She offered her hand to shake, taking Jacoba's, which came out to meet it.

Mrs. Merrimont had a grip, Jacoba found, like being clamped in a vise. "Jacoba DeGroot. Mrs. Charles DeGroot. I'm pleased to meet you, Mrs. Merrimont."

"And you, Mrs. DeGroot. Newly wed?"

She felt a blush rising in her cheeks. Surreptitiously, she worked her fingers. "Yes. We've been married for about a month now."

Opal's eyebrow arched and she peered about. "Where's your husband? He shouldn't leave a pretty girl like you alone in a coach full of men."

And yet, Mrs. Merrimont had no husband dancing attendance on her. Jacoba's thought must have been evident on her face, because Opal said, "My Thomas don't need to worry any about me. I'm not a lovely young girl." She laughed. "In truth, I never was. Lovely, that is. Mr. Merrimont can stand out on the platform and smoke his pipe to his heart's content."

If only Charlie were well and able to lend him company. Jacoba overcame her natural reticence in defense of her spouse's seeming neglect. "My husband was hurt in the train wreck ten days ago. He's still in the hospital, although getting better. He insisted I come to Coeur d'Alene for the drawing."

Opal pursed her mouth sympathetically. "I see. I'm sorry to hear that. Such a terrible tragedy. You're fortunate you weren't with him. Mr. Merrimont and I, too. We took an earlier train, praise the good Lord."

"Oh, I was with him. But with the terrible heat in the coach my husband went to find water. He got caught in the first car when the trains struck. Someone else helped me jump from the train before the collision." The Samaritan's action still bewildered her. Why had he bothered with her, a stranger? This, she realized, was the first time she'd spoken to anyone about the wreck, about her fear and the horror of finding Charlie with a spike through his chest. She relived that every night in her dreams—no—in her nightmares.

As Mrs. Merrimont probed for details, her eyes bright with curiosity, Jacoba's story poured forth, a rush of words she couldn't seem to stop. Even the part about the man who'd saved her life. Somehow, sharing the ordeal of the past ten days with a stranger made everything easier to bear; a catharsis of sorts. If only she could have talked with her mother. If only Madame would have cared like this work-worn old lady seemed to do. An empty feeling knotted her insides, which she did her best to ignore.

She became aware of Opal asking her a question. "Pardon me?"

"I asked if you ever learned the man's name." Opal yawned a little and without giving Jacoba a chance to answer said, "I'm afraid the heat has made me sleepy. I believe I'll take a little nap before we reach Coeur d'Alene. You should do the same, dear. It's going to be a long day."

Since she'd been trying to nap before this conversation started, Jacoba nodded. At first it wasn't so easy to put Charlie from her mind again, but then she closed her eyes against the glare outside and the next thing she knew, the train had reached the end of the line. She opened heavy eyelids to see they were on the Coeur d'Alene terminal docks. Instead of flat prairie, the view out the window revealed dark blue-green water capped by a foamy white chop, and nearer, people who'd already alighted from the car. She started to her feet, suddenly afraid of being left behind.

Mrs. Merrimont stood blocking the aisle in a flurry of drawstring reticule, lunch basket, and askew bonnet.

"We're here," she announced, as though Jacoba couldn't see for herself. Excitement rippled her voice. An older gentleman wearing a dark woolen suit, an obviously new celluloid collar poking into the folds of his chin, and stiff shiny shoes clutched a small suitcase and tried to hurry her along.

Mr. Merrimont, or so Jacoba assumed. She picked up her own small traveling case—upon which she'd been resting her feet—checked the slant of her hat, made certain her purse dangled securely from her wrist, and slid across the bench seat to join her new acquaintance.

"Why don't you walk along with us?" Mrs. Merrimont looked to her husband, whose nod showed barely stifled impatience. "Really, you shouldn't be alone in this crowd. A gathering like this...well, it's hard telling who might be on hand. Pickpockets," she explained. "Riffraff." Darker still, "Drunken riffraff."

"Now, Opal," said Mr. Merrimont, his voice a reedy baritone. "Don't start with that. There's nothing wrong with a man having a drink for medicinal purposes—or after a hard day's work. Or for a little celebration, for that matter."

"Well, and what do you suppose they're celebrating this early?" Mrs. Merrimont gave a grudging sniff. "Best to wait until they find they have cause."

Jacoba, hardly listening, glanced warily around as they alighted. She hadn't given the crowd, already unruly, much thought before. Now her mouth opened in amazement. "I will walk with you, if you truly don't mind," she said. "Thank you."

"Think nothing of it, my dear." Opal Merrimont chuckled. "We may be neighbors one of these days. Neighbors look after each other."

To Jacoba, raised under Madame's philosophy, the concept sounded like something out of a storybook *Neighbors look after each other?* Charlie was the only one she could depend on. Why should anyone else care? But what a relief, a lovely surprise, that someone else did seem to care, if only a well-met stranger on a train. Make that two well-met strangers on a train, now.

***

Willy nilly, Jacoba allowed herself to be swept along in the tide of passengers all rushing toward a large open spot not far from the train depot. Even so, she and the Merrimonts were among the stragglers, partially due to Opal suffering from a hitch in her side and needing to slow down.

"Go on," Opal urged her husband, who valiantly supported her on his arm while visibly restraining himself from surging ahead. "You don't want to miss the first pick. It might be your name."

But Thomas, wise after many years of marriage, held back. "A runt like you is apt to get lost in this crowd. No, Mother. We'll stick together. The drawing won't start for another quarter hour. We'll get there."

Jacoba, dodging a boy rude enough to shove her in the back, was quite charmed. Would she and Charlie still care for each other like that when they were old? Or would they go their separate ways, together, yet apart, like so many of the older couples she knew? No. She answered the voice in her head quite firmly. Never. She and Charlie were mated for life. Not like Madame, many times married, then as many times divorced as widowed.

Her train of thought disappeared as the heavy brogan worn by a bruiser of a man jockeying for a better position crushed her foot. Pain shot through her leg, aggravating her barely healed knee. She staggered, almost falling as bodies streamed into the space opened between her and Opal and Thomas Merrimont. The older couple didn't notice, their attention now on an important looking man stepping onto a wooden platform set in the middle of the open area. Someone else held a bullhorn to his mouth and made an announcement lost to her in the distance from the stage. Clutching her traveling case, Jacoba limped on, trying to see either of the Merrimonts and finding herself stymied.

The heat generated by the large group of people packed closely together almost overwhelmed her. Sweating humanity mixed with the turf trampled beneath hundreds of feet sent an odd, unpleasant smell into the air. Her mouth was dry as a southwestern sidewalk in July.

Except for a low background hum that sounded like the drone of worker bees, the shouting abruptly stopped. The man with the megaphone bellowed into the mouth of the instrument, making an announcement that mixed in a bit of political grandstanding.

"Ladies and gentlemen, please welcome Judge James Whitten. Judge Whitten has traveled all the way from Washington, D.C. to oversee what is likely to be the most important land lottery ever held in the United States of America. The Homestead Act of 1862 . . . ."

Momentarily, Jacoba lost track of his speech. She stood on tiptoe, searching, to no avail, for sight of Mr. and Mrs. Merrimont. Lost in in the crowd somewhere, they might as well been on another planet.

". . .introduce little Miss Helen Hamilton, niece of our esteemed Mayor Boyd, who with a couple of her friends is going to draw the first envelopes. For those of you in back who might not be able to see, we're opening the barrels right now, and men are on hand with shovels to mix this grand pile of yellow envelopes together. We're told there are more than 105,000 entries, and we're only drawing 1500. What you see is what you get, folks. Entirely random. If your name isn't drawn, you'll have to see if you can buy a homestead from one of the lucky winners."

Jacoba jumped up and down on one foot, the one that hadn't been crushed, squinting and trying to see over the shoulders of the men in front.

"Are you ready?" the man continued. A huge roar responded. Sounding giddy as a girl, the man laughed. "Here we go. Thank you, my dear."

He must have been speaking to the child, of whom Jacoba caught a brief glimpse as the man in front of her bent sideways to speak with the man beside him. Total silence gripped the crowd as though each person there drew in a breath. Then a new voice, which Jacoba presumed belonged to Judge Whitten, announced, "First pick goes to Mr. H. F. Wright, of Linneus, Missouri."

The crowd emitted a collective gasp, and then a man hollered something indistinguishable, something jubilant.

"Next envelope, please," the announcer said, and so the drawing proceeded, name after name after name shouted out to the crowd. After a couple hours, Jacoba heard Thomas Merrimont's name called, whereupon she discovered her new acquaintances hailed from Illinois. Although happy for them, she wished it had been Charlie's name she'd heard called. What if she never did? She felt ill at the thought, although she told herself the sudden roil of nausea came from standing in the direct rays of the sun. It made her feel dizzy as a whirligig.

A quarter of an hour after the Merrimonts won a place, she heard another familiar name. Somehow, it took her by surprise, and then she couldn't think why.

"Ruel Gagne," the announcer had called—a new announcer, after Judge Whitten had grown too hoarse. He spelled the name, then waited for the owner to come forward with a proper pronunciation. There was a confab near the stage. "Mr. Gagne is from our own neck of the woods."

"What's Gagne doing, signing up for the lottery?" a man in back of her grumbled. "Ain't he already got some of that land?"

"Dunno," another answered. "Might not be enough Indian. Or the wrong kind."

Without bothering to puzzle this out, Jacoba slipped through a slight gap in the crowd, thinning now as the drawing neared its end. The few extra steps allowed her a better view of the action, including line of sight to the newest winner. It was he. Her savior.

Today, instead of the ill-fitting suit she'd last seen him wearing, he had on workaday jeans and a dark-colored shirt. A broad-brimmed hat shaded his face. Hardly appropriate for such a momentous occasion, she thought, although the garments did make him appear thinner than the first time they met. As she remembered, his suit had been as utterly destroyed as her own on the day of the wreck. Perhaps he had no other.

Impossible to think of him as a gentleman, she concluded apprehensively. He looked quite rough, today. And strong, except for the plaster cast and a sling holding one arm immobile. The arm broken in saving her life. Guilt wriggled her conscience, battling a natural reserve over approaching him, yet she still owed him thanks.

As though drawn by something in her thoughts, Gagne's dark eyes met hers over the mass of bobbing heads. Holding some paperwork in his free hand, he stepped down from the platform and headed towards her, pushing with effortless ease through the men — and a few women — separating them. He stopped in front of her, a slow smile warming a rather austere face. In the background of noise, the announcer called yet another name, stuttering a little over the pronunciation. "Klingensmith."

"Patched you…" he started, just as she said, "I never had the…"

They both stopped, Jacoba feeling all the awkwardness Madame despised so heartily in her offspring that she often refused to claim her second child.

"You first," Gagne said.

She tilted her chin up and smiled tentatively. "I'm so glad to see you again, sir, and be able to say thank you. A thousand times, thank you. Without your help I — my husband and I — would both be dead." She gulped. "The doctor said Charlie would've bled to death had anyone removed the spike from his chest. You stopped those who wanted to do that."

A ruddy flush climbed his high cheekbones, although he looked at least a little pleased. "No thanks due. Every man able stepped forward to help others. You happened to be handy when my turn came around."

Jacoba, remembering the man with his three children who had ignored her pleas, knew differently.

"You helped me twice, Mr. Gagne. It's as if — " She stopped, unsure if her regard for him as her special savior was either polite or diplomatic to mention. He might read too much into it, or try to take advantage.

He saw she wasn't going on, shrugged his unharmed shoulder and said, "Think no more of it, missus." He hesitated in his turn.

"I see they patched you up pretty good." At her blank stare, he pointed, almost touching her. "Your forehead. Nice row of stitches. You were bleeding something fierce, last I saw of you. And barely able to walk."

A wave of her hand dismissed these trivialities as beneath notice. "But you. Your poor arm. Are you able to work?" She had the horrible, sinking feeling that if not, Charlie and she owed him the means to live until he could. "Your homesteading claim, will you be able to take it up? Congratulations on your name being drawn."

As she paused, she heard another name called: Parsons.

She was afraid her relief showed on her face when he said tautly, "I'm fine. I've got other means of support. Besides, it will be spring before I can start work on the claim, at best."

Since she hardly knew how she and Charlie were to get by, his reply lifted a heavy weight off her back. Certainly Gagne's broken arm proved not to be as severe a curtailment of activities as Charlie's leg and chest injuries. Even now, using his one free hand, her savior rolled his precious lottery document into a thin tube in fine fashion. Still, fair was fair. Her acquaintance with the DeGroot family had taught her that much, even if Madame Ludke would've scoffed at such sensibilities, accepting the sacrifices of others as her due.

Gagne looked around. "Guess your name has not been called?"

His accent, which she still hadn't placed, made it into a question.

"My husband's name," she corrected. "Charles DeGroot. No. I'm afraid not." She tried to smile. Charlie would be so disappointed. She thought she might break into tears, embarrassing as that might be. Worry gnawed at her. All their plans come to naught, and what were they to do now?

"It looks like they're almost done. Charlie—my husband—counted so much on the Coeur d'Alene lands. He didn't particularly care for the Spokane or Flathead areas." *And how can I break the news to him? How?*

"I'm partial to the Coeur d'Alene allotment myself," Gagne

said. "You can be sure there'll be some of these parcels up for sale within a week. Maybe your mister can buy one of those."

"Yes, maybe." A pipedream, Jacoba knew. It would take most of their savings just to live until Charlie healed enough to work again.

People had begun drifting away from the staging area. Officials on the platform checked their lists. One man had a wide broom, wielding it to sweep wildly scattered yellow envelopes into a pile, ready to be put back in the barrels and disposed of.

The auction had ended. So had Charlie's dream. Their dream.

Jacoba didn't know what to do next, where to go, or if a return train to Spokane had been scheduled to leave soon. She dithered, a heavy, hopeless feeling weighing her down.

"Well," she said at last, looking up at Gagne and trusting none of her doubts showed. "I'm happy to have seen you again, and my congratulations on the lottery. Perhaps we'll meet sometime in the future." Words. She doubted their paths would cross a third time.

In the background, the man on the platform seemed to be making an announcement, causing the remaining lottery hopefuls to pause their exodus.

Gagne cocked his head to one side, listening. "They found they were short one name. Somebody's luck turned up after all." One of the little girls sprang into action, diving into the swept pile and selecting an envelope. The announcer took his time opening it.

Jacoba, shrugged, bent down and picked up her train case. "Again, my thanks, Mr. Gagne, for everything." She said goodbye, turned, and took two decisive steps before the name the announcer blared out reached her brain. Spinning, she looked back. Gagne stood there, watching her and smiling.

"What name did he say?" she asked. Blood pounded in her veins.

"Jacob DeGroot." His eyebrows shot up. He pronounced it as the other had done: Deegroot, with an emphasis on the dee.

"Jacob? Why, he must mean Jacoba. Jacoba DeGroot." Incredulous, she laughed. "That's me! Oh, my word. Not Charlie's name. Mine!"

Chapter 6

"You'd best go and get your allotment number from the official,"
Ruel Gagne advised. "They'll tell you what to do next. Where to
go, who to see."

His dark eyes glinted, most surely with amusement, as Jacoba,
flustered by the sudden change of fortune, stood frozen with her
mouth very slightly agape. Then, becoming conscious of ridiculous
she must look, she snapped it closed.

"Yes. All right. I will." Feeling like a ninny, she started forward,
afraid there'd been a mistake made. What if she hadn't heard—
Gagne hadn't heard—correctly? She'd be too embarrassed to hold
her head up when they turned her away. She went forward anyway,
a tide of hope rising inside her, aware of him watching.

But she hadn't misheard. It had indeed been her name they'd
called, the fellow apologizing for not seeing the A at the end of
her name which, as they both looked at her application document,
plainly stood out.

Her name. Not Charlie's. Oh, dear, she thought in wonder. What
would Charlie think? What would he say? They'd been so certain

his application would be the one chosen. In a daze, she accepted her allotment number and stepped away from the stage. Only then did she become aware of a familiar voice calling, "Yoo hoo, young Missus. Here you are. I thought we'd lost you."

Mrs. Merrimont, appearing none the worse for the long siege under the hot sun, trotted forward with a broad smile crinkling her face. Mr. Merrimont trailed along in her wake looking far more worn, perspiration pouring from beneath his hat band and soaking into his high collar. Nevertheless, his faded blue eyes were triumphant.

"They drew our entry," he announced, as proud as though it had been his doing and not pure luck.

"As they did yours, I see," Opal added. "And in the bare nick of time, too. I imagine you must almost have given up. See? I told you we'd be neighbors. What a climactic end to the lottery!"

Jacoba, hardly knowing how to reply, smiled, nodded, and said nothing. A moment later, her manners recalling themselves, when she turned around meaning to introduce Mr. Gagne to these people who would be his neighbors too, she spotted him some distance away striding off across the open grass in the wake of the winners. An odd feeling of puzzled hurt shot through her. Why had he been so abrupt?

"Shall we go?" Mr. Merrimont was saying, flapping his arms about as though hurrying along a flock of chickens. "Best follow the crowd, I guess. We don't want left behind. Everyone is heading for the land office and I want to get my bid in for a particular quarter section I've got my eye on—if somebody else doesn't claim it first," he added as though suspecting some dark plot afoot.

Jacoba, aware that as the last name called she'd have to take whatever piece of land was left, retrieved her case and tried to tell herself it didn't matter. Charlie wouldn't care. He'd said it himself, more than once. *It's all good.*

"I'm ready," she said.

***

Hours later, head abuzz and too exhausted to sleep, Jacoba lay between the stiff sheets clothing a saggy old bed in a not-so-cheap hotel room. This pokey hole, no larger than her dressing room at home in St. Louis, turned out to be the only place available at the end of the day. Competition had been fierce for any bed in this small town. Unfortunately, the celebration still taking place down on Sherman Avenue came clearly to her ears. The saloons, from the sound of things, were doing a booming business and she, all too aware of the thin door and inadequate lock of her room, hesitated to close her eyes. Instead, she stared blindly at a bar of light shining through the gap under the door and thought back over the day.

It had been nine o'clock in the evening before her allotment number came up and the recording clerk looked at it. The Merrimonts, exhaustion claiming them both, had long since abandoned her, but Opal said they'd reserve a room for her at this hotel. Right now, somewhere on the hotel's two floors, they were sleeping the sleep of the just, for when she finally got here, she discovered they'd kept their word.

Bless them, she thought, pushing the sheet aside and freeing her swollen feet to the surrounding air. The room, stuffy and stifling hot made her feel like an over-extended balloon.

"This isn't a good number," the land office clerk had told her when she'd finally stepped up to his table. Bags, like tea-stained pouches, swelled beneath his eyes and quivered when he talked. Fascinated by them, she wondered what he'd say if she recommended a good cucumber poultice followed by a soothing lotion.

"There's only one parcel left on the Coeur d'Alene reservation and between you and me," he was saying, "it isn't the best if you want farmland. You can transfer this number to the Flathead reservation, if you want. Or the Spokane."

Perhaps he'd meant to be kind, Jacoba thought now. On the other hand, he was probably just as tired as she and wanted as badly to get home and rest. She didn't think he'd even had a break for supper but then, neither had she.

Her stomach rumbled, reminding her that as of now, 1:30 in the morning, she still hadn't. There'd been people bringing carts of sandwiches and coffee to the recording office round about five o'clock, peddling the food from trays. She'd bought a cheese sandwich from one, choosing the cheese because with the heat, who knows whether the beef had soured. She'd deemed the ham too salty, considering the lack of water on hand. But that had been hours and hours ago.

What would Charlie say when he found out what she'd done? Because after thinking the clerk's advice over, she'd ignored it and signed for the Coeur d'Alene parcel. The huge map pinned to the land office wall showed the location; right down by a place called Amwaco landing on Windy Bay. It was quite a distance from the town of Worley, which had been platted just last year in anticipation of the lottery. She'd heard no one actually lived there yet, but some folks had already spoken of building a store and a bank and a blacksmith's shop and of course, a saloon or two.

They'd need a school, too. She had a good education. Perhaps she could be a teacher if money became a problem. She'd have to ask Charlie what he thought. On this bright resolution, Jacoba fell asleep at last and didn't wake up until she had to hurry to catch the train back to Spokane.

***

Whatever Jacoba had expected, it wasn't Charlie turning his face away when she broke the news to him that the little girl had drawn her name in the lottery. That her name appeared on the homestead papers.

As soon as the train pulled into the station, she'd hurried over to the hospital. She admitted to feeling trepidation when telling Charlie about the acreage she'd selected. In fairness, he seemed to understand that. But she hadn't anticipated the way his lips, only now regaining a bit of color after the trauma his body had endured in the wreck, flattened into a thin line.

"Your name, Jacoba? They called your name?"

She'd hoped he wouldn't mind—but he did. His emotions showed all too clearly.

The pleasure she took in telling him about the lottery proceedings evaporated. She unclasped her purse, drew out the papers folded inside and held them out to him. "As you see." And then, since she wasn't one to hold back—not when it came to Charlie—she asked, "Why? It doesn't make any difference, does it? You or me. It's for both of us. The name on the claim shouldn't matter. That's why we both signed up, isn't it? So our chances would be better?"

"Yeah, but, Jake. I'm the head of this household. I'm supposed to be taking care of you."

"You are. We're taking care of each other." She put enough warmth into her voice that he couldn't mistake her intentions—if he'd only believe.

But Charlie's face turned red and wore what she'd come to recognize as his mule-headed look. Flat on his back in bed, he determined he should have the last word, either not knowing or not caring if he hurt her in the process.

"Yeah, Jake?" he said. "Damnation! Here I am in a fix just because you had to have a drink of water."

She froze, her eyes widening. Did Charlie really blame her for what happened? How could he? He'd been the one to insist on fetching water. She'd said no. She'd asked him not to leave her.

For a long moment she stared at him, the scene from that day unfolding before her eyes. Then she blinked, swallowed hard, and came back to the present to hear him still talking and working himself into a tizzy.

"Do you think you're going to clear the land and build the house, and put in a crop while I'm laid up? Somehow, I doubt it."

Her innards gave a little lurch. He used pretty much the same tone Madame often took in speaking to her. She touched her lower lip, stilling its tendency to tremble. "I never said I could do those things, Charlie. We both know I can't. But I thought I could cook your meals and wash your clothes and help make it possible for you to do them. When you're back on your feet, of course."

"Oh, hell, Jacoba! You can't even cook. You can't do the wash. Do you even know how to start a fire in a wood stove? There isn't any gas down there on the reservation. Can you even chop wood?"

She bowed her head and lowered her eyes, trying to hide the quick tears that welled up. This didn't seem like her Charlie, saying these wounding things. One of the reasons they'd eloped when they did was because he couldn't abide the way Madame spoke to her.

Anyway, she thought, her temper flaring just a little, why blame her because she didn't know how to cook or chop wood. For all her life servants had performed these everyday household chores. Madame had seen to that, even when she cried out that she was too poor to live decently. And they lived in the city, for pity's sake. Why would she know how to farm? She knew how to raise flowers and herbs, though. Was it really so different, except perhaps the scale? All plants had basic requirements. One had only to become acquainted with growing habits and vagaries of climate. And she did know how to do practical things. She could make soap. The very best soap! And lotions and perfumes. Some medicines.

She raised her head and frowned at her husband. "I'm not stupid, Charlie. I may be small, but I'm strong. And I can learn to do anything I'm required to do. You know that. Why are you being so disagreeable?"

Charlie, who'd been told numerous times by Nurse Richards that he shouldn't do any such thing, jerked the leg still in traction, then yelped with pain. "Disagreeable, Jake? Me? I'm not being disagreeable. Is it so wrong I wanted my name to be on the land?"

Jacoba sighed and said, "No. It's not wrong. I'll turn the land over to you, Charlie. Just as soon as I can."

Now he pouted. "You don't have to do that."

"I want to. Really I do."

"It wouldn't be the same." Charlie, determined to sulk, closed his eyes. "I'm tired, Jacoba. I'm going to rest now. Doc is supposed to come sometime this morning and take my leg out of traction. Maybe in a few days I can get out of this stinking bed."

Jacoba took a sustaining breath and jumped to her feet. "Releasing the traction? Why didn't you say so before, silly? This is wonderful. You'll be back up on both feet in no time, Charlie. You're so strong."

She acted, as she feared Charlie would easily guess, a touch more excited than she'd normally be over the news which, cued by Nurse Richards, they'd all been expecting. But, whether he did or not, he accepted it all at face value.

At least her enthusiasm had the effect of bringing Charlie out of his doldrums. By the time Dr. Libby came in with his tools and shooed Jacoba away, his mood had turned a great deal more cheerful.

Hers? Well, maybe not so much.

***

"Attention, everyone . . . ." Mrs. Griswold, seated at the head of the table, took a good-sized dollop of oatmeal, plopped it into her bowl, and covered it with sifted brown sugar and cream. "Mrs. DeGroot tells me her husband will be released from the hospital at the end of the week. I'm sure we'll all be happy to have a new resident join our little group. Are there any special needs your husband will require, my dear?" Passing the bowl of oatmeal to Mr. England, seated at her left, she motioned for Bettina, the hired girl, to pour coffee for everyone.

"No, ma'am," Jacoba answered from her seat halfway down the long, handmade pine table. "Not as regards his diet. He'll be on crutches for some time, however, so he may need a little extra time to get about."

"Indeed," Mr. Howard said. "My uncle broke his leg a couple years ago and I remember stairs set him back for two or three months."

Charlie had been warned about stairs, Jacoba remembered, and that he'd have to approach them with caution.

Jacoba, when the groats, as Mrs. Griswold called the oatmeal, came to her, eyed the grayish-brown mass distastefully. Served at least three times a week, as she'd ascertained in the two weeks she'd been here, she couldn't exactly blame Mrs. Griswold for watching the budget, and no doubt oats were cheap. But why would anyone wish to have groats for their breakfast when toast with jam and a boiled egg would be so much better? So far, the only alternate to the groats had been bacon and biscuits. To be fair, Mrs. Griswold didn't exactly cheat her guests at the table. She ate the same food she set before her boarders. Nevertheless, Jacoba admitted, apprehension not far behind, to being concerned about what Charlie would have to say about the frequent oatmeal. Not that he was a picky eater, but still. Oatmeal was oatmeal, not what fancy name one gave it.

Sighing, she sipped the rather weak coffee Bettina, a German girl who preferred to be called Betty, served breakfast to the group of boarders. It splashed into her white porcelain cup in a pallid brown stream. Beggers, she reminded herself, couldn't be choosers. She and Charlie needed to guard their remaining money oh, so carefully. In the spring, there'd be a team of horses to purchase, along with various farming implements. A plow, for instance. Saws, axes, hammers and drills and all sorts of things she didn't know the names of. Charlie had had to leave his carpentry tools behind when they eloped. Just to build their house—and a mansion like Madame's was most definitely *not* in the plans —he'd have to acquire new ones. He hoped to find good used tools and had told Jacoba to start watching the want ads in the newspaper.

"Mrs. DeGroot!" Impatience in the male voice indicated Jacoba had been woolgathering.

Not woolgathering, she denied as, attentive now, she tilted her head toward the speaker. *Worrying*. About money to see them through. About what Charlie would say to living in this boarding house. About the other people living here. Some of the boarders were a little . . . rough.

"Yes, Mr. Finley? I'm sorry. I missed your question."

He'd rented his room three weeks ago, only days before her, but so far he'd pushed himself into every mealtime conversation. She didn't like him, although her face reflected only pleasant inquiry. She'd practiced the expression her whole life and knew she had it down pat, as her poker playing brother would say.

Anyway, she knew there'd been a question, although it had flown right past her. Mr. Finley always had a question, the problem being that he never listened to the answer. As likely as not, he'd ask the same thing again next time they met, sometimes even stopping residents coming down or going up the stairs. It struck her that he posed a sort of test to see if people answered the same each time.

"I merely asked if you've heard how much your husband will be reimbursed by the railroad for his injuries." Finley leaned forward, greed oozing from every pore. "You must be anxious."

Hiding a shudder, Jacoba, who just yesterday had told him that since Charlie had not yet been released from the hospital they'd not been eligible to apply, gave him a cool stare and shrugged. Even if she'd known what the final charges would be, she'd never tell him. She felt certain he'd try to somehow wrangle a part of that reimbursement for himself. Although how he'd manage that, she hadn't the faintest idea.

Anyway, Mrs. Griswold banged her coffee cup down and said, her Scottish brogue strong, "That most certainly is none of your concern, Mr. Finley. I hope everyone will agree it's much too personal for public discourse." She looked around the table.

"I should say so!" Jacoba said.

Heads nodded, Mr. Howard snorting his disgust at such ill manners.

Finley smiled. "Can't blame a feller for being curious, now can you?" Across the table from him, one of the other female boarders, a woman who worked at the Palace Department store, winked. She apparently approved his curiosity. If that's what it was.

Anyway, Jacoba thought, *she* could blame him. Because in her world, one only asked questions like this if a scheme, most likely an unethical money-making scheme, was in the works. Its aim? Ensuring money changed from one party's hands to another party's, most likely not in a legal fashion. It could include outright robbery.

Convoluted? Yes. No less in the explanation than in the commission.

What did Mr. Finley have in mind? That's what she wanted to know. Whatever, she'd never fall for it.

Breakfast, after choking down half her *groats*, finally ended without further remarks. Not a moment too soon in her opinion.

Chapter 7

Mr. Finley's unwelcome interest in the DeGroot finances, and Jacoba's offhand rejection of his curiosity, came back to haunt her the very next day.

This being Wednesday, it was a bacon and biscuit morning at Mrs. Griswold's boarding house. The aroma of frying bacon and boiling coffee, a not unpleasant way to greet the day, wafted up the stairwell to creep under Jacoba's door.

Taking in the scent, she thrust aside the single sheet she'd used as a blanket, all she could bear in the little third-floor attic room's stifling heat. She stretched arms above her head and shifted her hips to counteract the sag in the bed's middle. How she and Charlie, with the impediment of Charlie's cast, were to accommodate each other in this bed remained an open question.

And, for about the thousandth time, she wondered what Charlie would say about living here. Nothing good, she'd be bound.

Sitting up late last night, she'd done her best to figure their finances to some kind of advantage. Charlie had a habit of treating her like a delicate flower to be protected at all costs, but he sometimes forgot that, much as she might reject the premise, she was still Madame's daughter. Which meant she knew about money—and even the lack thereof.

All her life she'd been subjected to Madame's monetary schemes. The almost constant harping about money. Or mainly, what Madame considered too little money, which, as far as Jacoba could tell, meant any amount. That's why all her mother's marriages, the divorces, and once, the extraordinarily convenient death of one of Madame's husbands loomed over Jacoba every day.

She'd seen Madame's accounts. Helped with them actually, as Jacoba had a knack for both organization and mathematics. She knew about taking all costs under consideration when running a highly profitable cosmetic business. Then there were the personal expenses, from a nickel for streetcar fare, to dollars for coal delivery, or a tip to insure prompt service, up to several thousand for another of Madame's diamond parures, for which she had a fondness.

Therefore, yesterday evening, seeing that only two days remained before Charlie's release from the hospital, she'd made out a strict budget as well as an accounting of their assets. Neat columns ran down a sheet of paper regarding the budget. Rent, food, medicines, all the items they'd need on the homestead.

Their assets took only a few lines. First she'd counted the money Charlie had secreted in one of his boots, then all he'd had in his wallet and his pockets. Next, she added in what she had in her reticule and the extra little bit she'd saved from the allowance Madame used to give her. This, on Charlie's recommendation, she'd been keeping tucked away in her riding skirt's pocket to keep it safe. Then there were her pearls, to be sold only as a last resort. They'd been a gift from her father's mother, now deceased.

But when she added the sums up three times, to ensure no mistakes, the balance sheet disappointed. Not enough. No way would she and Charlie make it through until spring. They'd been counting on Charlie earning a paycheck during the winter, but Dr. Libby said he wouldn't be able to work for several months yet.

And that, Jacoba knew, meant she had to find a way to keep body and soul together. She needed a job. A job with a salary.

What would Charlie say?

The worry still with her this morning, she shuddered at the thought then, yawning, got out of bed. She dashed water over her face at the commode, brushed her cloud of dark hair before twisting it into a knot atop her head, and donned one of her simple morning-at-home dresses. If she didn't get to the table before the rest finished eating, there'd be nothing left. And really, Mrs. Griswold did make excellent biscuits, light and fluffy as any Madame's highly paid Parisian chef had ever managed.

But before leaving the room, she made certain the bulk of Charlie's money was safely hidden. His wallet with the extra cash resided between the springs of an old upholstered armchair, its cover tatty and worn. The sacrosanct homestead money went in a different spot altogether. The pearls were interwoven into the lace of the curtains, half hidden behind a dresser so worn it tilted on a back leg. Her own money, a solid one hundred dollars, she hid in her riding skirt pocket. Planning ahead, she set aside enough for streetcar fare and perhaps, a sandwich at one of the department store lunch counters, leaving it on the commode. Hurrying now as someone, Betty, she thought, called her name from the bottom of the steps, she closed and locked the door behind her.

The other boarders were at the table, as she'd expected, most eating quickly before going off to their various jobs. How would it be, she wondered, when she joined their ranks of employed persons. Though a part of her quivered, terrified at the thought, another part anticipated.

"I'm so sorry to be late." She made her apologies to Mrs. Griswold who nodded forgiveness. The others paid her no mind. One, Mr. Finley, had finished with all but his coffee.

He grinned at her. "Bad night? I expect you're missing your husband."

Although the words were innocuous enough, his leer said something else. The store clerk lady giggled, earning a sharp look from Mrs. Griswold.

"I do miss my husband," Jacoba said, her voice chilly. "Naturally."

Sighing, she poured her own coffee and nabbed a biscuit from the basket Mr. Howard passed to her, adding a thick slice of bacon to her plate. What she wouldn't give for a dish of fresh strawberries. But that would, no doubt, be an extra cost if the berries could even be procured. The meal she had was included in the boarding fee.

"Take no notice of him," Mr. Howard whispered to her. "He's a lout."

Jacoba flashed a small smile at him.

With a slurp, Finley finished his coffee and rose from the table to bound up the stairs to his room on the second floor. The clerk, who at least had the manners to mutter, "Excuse me, please," to her table mates followed him.

Mr. Howard rose as well, but he, without further ado, headed directly off to his work as a meat cutter at a butcher shop.

Jacoba, relieved to see him go, gave a sigh and reached for another bacon slice. Although he'd been very kind and mannerly, the smell of blood always seemed to cling to him. An odor that reminded her all too vividly of the hospital right after the train wreck.

It took a moment to clear her nose and her memory of that time. About as long as it took for the rest of the boarders to finish breakfast and take their leave.

"Have you finished, Mrs. DeGroot?" Barely waiting for Jacoba's nod, Mrs. Griswold rang the little bell that sat at hand to call Betty, and rose to her feet.

"May I use the laundry facilities today?" Jacoba asked quickly, before her landlady could escape. While bed linens and some community towels were supplied, clothing and personal items were not. Most of the boarders sent these things to one of the many Chinese laundries around town. Jacoba had decided she could use the practice of doing the wash herself. After all, there'd be no Chinese on the reservation when Charlie and she took up their homestead.

"Of course," Mrs. Griswold said. "I'll tell Betty to put the water on the stove to heat."

"Thank you." Stretching her fingers, knowing her hands would be dry and sore before she finished with the strong lye soap, Jacoba sighed. At least she had a good supply of lotions and cremes from Madame's store. Her mother had never quibbled about supplying her daughters with the same beauty aids her company sold to wealthy women for astonishing prices. Quite the contrary. Jacoba and her sister Amalie had been expected to perform as models for the luxuries. But now, when those were depleted, there'd be another route to follow.

She sighed again. She had the recipes. She'd need to perfect the process on a much smaller scale. A few ideas perked in her head on how to improve the creme used around the eyes. For instance, the addition of ultra-purified olive, or, by her personal preference, avocado oil. That, she felt certain, would do the trick. It all depended on if one could acquire these exotic oils on the western frontier. Or lacking oil, if she could get hold of avocados, at all. If she could even afford them.

Oddly enough, she and the repulsive Mr. Finley met on the stairs leading to the third story. He was descending and grinning like a loon as she ascended. Only two attic rooms up here, her own and that of a man attending Gonzaga's law college. The rooms' under-the-rafters location was the reason they were cheaper than those on either the second or ground floor.

So what, she wondered, frowning after him, had brought Finley up here? He'd ignored the studious law student previously so she doubted they'd been visiting. In fact, the student had no doubt already departed for his regular early morning class.

In an odd panic, she bounded the final few steps to the landing.

Her door stood ajar although she distinctly remembered locking it. Yes. Locking it with the key she held between her fingers at this very moment. Not that it would ever work again. The lock had been forced, as the bent metal clearly showed.

Finley, with his audacious grin. Had he been in her room?

Reaching out a forefinger, she pushed the door all the way open and stepped inside.

Yes. The answer came on a wave. She smelled him, the odor of stale sweat with an overtone of some cheap scent that clung to his skin and clothing.

Her stomach churned.

At first glance, nothing seemed amiss. Except . . . her bed, originally only a little rumpled from her restless night, now had sheets pulled all the way from their tuck beneath the mattress. *As if someone had been feeling beneath.* The pillow she'd used, quite flat to begin with, had been shaken enough to plump the feathers.

Hah! There'd been nothing for anyone to find there. Not in either place.

Trembling now, panic making her dizzy, she tipped the old armchair to see the underside. She pulled Charlie's wallet out from its hiding spot and looked inside. Froze. Her dizziness grew.

The money was gone.

Blinking back horrified tears, she went next to the closet cupboard.

One of the closet's two doors hung open. Oh no, she thought. *No.*

Rising on tiptoe, she felt above the open door, shaking fingers finding the two tacks she'd used to hold the small pocketbook containing their homestead savings on the inner side of the cupboard. Reaching the pocketbook down, she pressed the snap closure apart.

"Thank God." She didn't realize she spoke out loud until her own voice echoed in her ears.

But her relief soon faded.

He'd found her stash. Emptied her riding skirt pocket of her hard-won savings. Not only that, but also the money she'd planned to keep them through the next week or two, as well as the coins she'd left sitting on the commode.

Anger coursed through her in a red hot wave. She'd thought she'd been oh, so clever in putting the money in a pocket. Charlie had declared no man would suspect a riding skirt as a hiding place. After all, no one had seen her wearing the garment. Why would he even think of that?

Moments later, it struck her. Finley probably hadn't. The lady clerk had followed him when he left the table. They seemed close. More than likely, it had been she who suggested where to look if he found nothing beneath the mattress.

A woman's cunning, Jacoba realized. She blamed herself with scathing disgust.

Now what? Her best bet seemed to be to tell Mrs. Griswold. Then the police. Could they, perhaps, get her money back? But would the police even believe her? Was it safe to put her trust in the local police? She'd heard some uncomplimentary things about the Spokane bluecoats. They might not be interested in helping a now penniless couple staying in Spokane only long enough to participate in the land lottery.

Another thought occurred to her. Unless she used Madame's name. Madame. Rich, famous, a country-wide celebrity. If the movers and shakers of this city had never heard of Madame Ludke, most certainly their wives had. And surely she and Charlie were beyond Madame's anger, her reach, by now. Her mother would know she and Charlie were married, all legal and tight. There would be no need to hide anymore.

Would there? Had there ever been? Charlie had thought so, but sometimes she wondered if all the subterfuge, if their elopement, had truly been necessary. Perhaps . . .

She cut the thought off. This was now. Ought she to bank on her family name?

No. Jacoba couldn't bring herself to do it.

What would Charlie do? What would he tell me to do?

Her heart almost froze in her chest, each beat harder than the last.

She couldn't possibly tell Charlie they'd been robbed. Not, at least, until Dr. Libby released him from the hospital and he felt stronger. Bad news might set his recovery back another week. A further look around showed her pearls were safe. She felt a tiny rush of pride, one which quickly faded. If only she'd been as clever in hiding Charlie's wallet.

Jacoba collapsed onto the worn stuffed chair, where a sprung spring—the alliterative sound struck her fancy—poked her in the derrière while she sifted through the wallet again. There, tucked into an almost hidden slot, she found a five-dollar bill, overlooked no doubt, in Finley's haste. Small consolation.

What, she wondered, should she do next?

"Mrs. DeGroot!" Betty's hail came from the landing below. "Your wash water is ready. I've set the tubs out on the back porch." The hired girl's accent turned wash water into *vash vater*. Another alliteration.

"Thank you," Jacoba called back. "I'll be right there."

She rose and tossed the wallet into a dresser drawer. No need to hide it now. In fact, why had Finley replaced it in the springs when he'd taken the money?

Only one answer occurred. Perhaps she'd been too open in her dislike of him. Perhaps this was a taunt, meant to show her up. Thinking the theory over, she felt sure of it. Resolve struck. She must learn to hide her feelings better.

"Mrs. DeGroot." Betty's call came again. "This here wash water is getting cold."

"Yes, Betty. I'm coming."

Three minutes later, laundry collected, she descended the steep stairs, careful not to stumble as she peeped over the top of the pile. She had to talk with Mrs. Griswold right away and persuade the landlady to report the theft. She didn't look forward to it. The landlady wouldn't either. A rooming house robbery wouldn't do

Mrs. Griswold's reputation any good, but she must be informed that one, maybe two, of her tenants were thieves.

Setting her laundry to soak, Jacoba went to beg a few minutes of her landlady's time.

At first Mrs. Griswold had nothing to say, although her face slowly drained of color as Jacoba's tale unfolded.

"No," she breathed then. "No, indeed. Thieves are not allowed in my house."

Thieves, as Jacoba well knew, could be found anywhere.

"Why do you think it was him? Them? Mr. Finley and Miss Cronk. Could you," Mrs. Griswold asked hopefully, "simply have misplaced your money?"

"No, ma'am. I know there's no mistake." Jacoba spoke more sharply than she intended, but really, did people think her so backward, so hysterical and ineffectual, that she would be mistaken about such a thing? Or did her landlady think she was lying? "I met him coming down the stairs from the third story as I went up. My door had been locked. The lock is broken now. And then—" she hesitated.

"Then?" Mrs. Griswold looked a bit ill.

"I smelled him. Quite plainly. He had definitely been inside my room."

The landlady made no attempt to gainsay the evidence of Jacoba's nose. Mr. Finley's odor had been remarked on by more than one boarder, especially by anyone unlucky enough to be seated next to him at the dining room table. Except, that is, for Miss Cronk.

"Maybe he . . ."

"He stole my money," Jacoba said fiercely. "Either you or I must call the police."

Mrs. Griswold, in the end, believed her no matter how much she railed against having harbored a thief in her home. With obvious reluctance, the landlady did call the police. Perhaps they felt the message non-critical as Jacoba had managed to finish her wash, soaking herself in the process, before a blue-coated officer turned up at the boarding house door two hours later.

Betty, who had been on the lookout, caught her on the doorstep as Jacoba entered the house from hanging out her laundry. Betty had a warning.

"This Detective Hansen is a bugger," the maid said, peering over her shoulder and whispering. "Don't let him throw you off, Mrs. DeGroot, or bully you like he's trying to do with Mrs. G. He just got here himself a few minutes ago and he already has Mrs. G in a dither. Here it is time to start the pies and he's got Mrs. G panicking for fear meals will be late. He hasn't finished talking to her yet." Her voice dropped even lower. "I heard him. It sounds like he is accusing *her*!"

A shiver ran down Jacoba's spine. "Thank you for the warning, Betty. I'd best do what I can to rescue her."

Betty nodded, showing her the way into Mrs. Griswold's private section of the house. She cracked open the door to a back parlor where a tall, blond-haired and rather cavernous-appearing policeman stood in front of a cold fireplace. He rocked on his heels, his expression annoyed and impatient. Jacoba thought Mrs. Griswold also looked impatient and perhaps a little frightened. Definitely put upon. But who did she blame, Jacoba or the policeman?

"Ah." Her relief plain, the older lady waved Jacoba forward. "Here you are at last, Mrs. DeGroot."

Jacoba forced a small smile, but said nothing. She stood straight, posture perfect, her expression as calm as she could make it, and waited for the detective to speak first.

To her surprise, he feigned not to notice her as he pored over a small tablet. Licking the pencil he'd been writing with—completely souring any hint of professionalism as far as Jacoba was concerned—he made a 'hurry up' motion at Mrs. Griswold.

"You were saying?" he said to the woman. Pencil poised, he deliberately left Jacoba standing.

Having caught the quick flick of his eyes toward her, she recognized his ploy. For whatever motive, he was trying to rattle her but it wouldn't work. She had a lifetime's experience with a master intimidator. No one was better at it than Madame.

Turning her back on him, she wandered over to the parlor window and looked out. This view of Mrs. Griswold's backyard, which overlooked a fragrant bed of herbs and flowers, calmed her. She didn't mind waiting her turn.

Chapter 8

Mrs. Griswold aimed a burning glance at Jacoba, relief plain on her face. "I was saying," she said, "that I only know what Mrs. DeGroot told me. She reported a theft by one of my boarders and I called you. Called the police station, I mean. I've told you all this before."

"This Mrs. DeGroot, she seem trustworthy to you?" Detective Hansen, speaking as though they were the only ones in the room. He still hadn't acknowledged Jacoba.

"Yes. Of course."

"What about this Finley and his girlfriend? They trustworthy too?"

Mrs. Griswold wrung her hands, which she'd clasped across her stomach in a nervous gesture. "I thought so when I allowed them into my house. But after a week he, at least, seemed rather unsavory. I've considered asking him to leave, especially since he has been late on his rent every week. As for Miss Cronk, well, she may be a little flashy, but she does pay on time. And by-the-by, I don't know that she's his girlfriend. They act friendly toward each other, is all."

"She laughed at everything he said," Jacoba added. She often noticed when her friends indulged in excessive laughter around men, it meant they had their sights set on some fellow. Which probably, she privately thought, was often more annoying than enticing.

Once more, Hansen ignored her. "Unsavory how?"

The landlady tapped her toe. "Pushy. Overly nosy. Crude. And as I said, neglected to pay his rent. He is behind again for three days right now."

Flipping his tablet to another page, Hansen wrote something before nodding toward the door. "Got it. You can leave. I'll need you to let me into this Finley's room after I talk to the victim. Supposed victim."

Mrs. Griswold's eyes narrowed. "Into his room? I shall accompany you, of course."

Hansen shrugged. "Yeah. Whatever you say. Won't hurt to have a witness." He waited for Mrs. Griswold to leave before shifting his hard stare to Jacoba. He pointed at her and then to a chair. A hard chair, an extra from the dining room.

"You're this Mrs. DeGroot?"

Tilting her head in a manner of which her mother would've approved, Jacoba said, "I am." She seated herself, feet precisely placed, on the edge of the chair and folded her hands.

He examined her, his blue eyes cold and calculating. "You don't hardly look old enough to be a Missus Anybody. You look like a girl who'd fly off the handle and bust out bawling if a man said boo."

Drawing dignity around her like a shawl, Jacoba had a flash of recall. The train wreck with the dead, the dying, and the lost. And suddenly, of her savior, Mr. Ruel Gagne. "You would be mistaken," she said coolly. "On both counts."

"Is that right?"

"Yes."

They stared at each other.

Hansen's gaze fell first, to the tablet with his notes. He licked his pencil lead and wrote down one word.

What had that word been? Jacoba wondered. Something uncomplimentary, she'd be bound.

Now, at last, the policeman drew a chair up across from her. A book lay on a tiny nearby table. He sat, took up the book and set it on his lap as a makeshift desktop. His pencil touching the paper, he said, "Tell me what makes you think this Finley stole from you?"

"I don't *think*. I know he stole from me." Taking a deep breath, she began. "I arrived late to breakfast this morning. Consequently, all the other boarders left the table before Mrs. Griswold and I. But as I went back upstairs, I met Mr. Finley coming down from the third floor."

The policeman shrugged. "So?"

"So, he had no cause to be up there. There are only two attic rooms, mine and one other. I found my room door open, its lock broken, and my money gone."

"How much money?"

"Two hundred and sixty-seven dollars and forty-seven cents." Jacoba's mind quailed over repeating the number out loud.

A whistle escaped Hansen's pursed lips. "That's a lot of money. Interesting that you had so much. Interesting you know how much down to the last penny. Most women leave finances to their husbands."

"Except women who know how to make their own money," she said. Credit Madame with that much. "And yes. It is a lot of money." *Pin money to mother, although surprisingly hard for me to save. But that was a different life.* "Almost everything my husband and I had." Her voice, despite her best efforts, broke on the last part. It earned a deeper look from the policeman, as if he were truly seeing her for the first time.

"Where is your husband? He oughta be here. You sure he ain't run out on you with the money?"

A smile twitched at Jacoba's mouth. "Trust me," she said. "My husband hasn't run anywhere, nor will he anytime in the near future."

Of course, she had to explain her statement, not that Detective Hansen appeared impressed, or even sympathetic.

Upon the policeman's demand, Jacoba accompanied him and Mrs. Griswold to her room. The landlady exclaimed at the door's broken lock, the bed with only one side disturbed by a sleeper, but both sides by a searcher, and tsked as the full story of Charlie's and her problems came out.

Detective Hansen seemed quite unmoved by the evidence, showing more interest in the DeGroot's misfortune.

"Read in the *Chronicle* about a feller with a spike sticking out of his chest," Hansen said. "The reporter said him and his wife was living at the Holiday Hotel."

"My husband is still in the hospital," Jacoba said. "And I moved out of the Holiday to save money. A mistake in retrospect."

"Yes. Looks as if."

Relieved the policeman apparently believed her now, Jacoba trailed along with him and Mrs. Griswold when Hansen demanded a view of the man's room. "In case he left a bunch of money laying around," he said.

The air, when the door opened, carried a fetid stench. Even Hansen waved a hand under his nose and sent a sharp look at Jacoba. "Guess I can't disbelieve you. Reckon you could've smelt him. Pretty strong stink."

"Indeed," Mrs. Griswold said.

Vindication, she thought as she and Mrs. Griswold shared a look.

But that turned out to be the only good thing, as if such low evidence could be ever be considered good. Immediately obvious was that Mr. Finley had fled. He'd left a dirty—disgusting, actually—set of underwear, a ragged shirt, and half a bar of soap behind.

Jacoba had to wonder when he'd used the first half.

"Now, how'd he get out of here with his things and neither Betty nor I see him?" Mrs. Griswold wondered.

"I'll ask him when I catch him," Hansen said.

As it turned out, they found Miss Cronk had departed as well, although in an altogether tidier fashion in that she left nothing behind. Including, something the two miscreants had in common, no clue as to where they might have gone.

Jacoba faced the fact, in the face of Detective Hansen's uninspired investigation, that their, her's and Charlie's, money was truly gone. Poverty stared them in the face.

* * *

That afternoon, during her daily visit with Charlie, Jacoba found herself unable to tell him about the theft. The words sat on the edge of her tongue, almost more than she could do to restrain, but really, what purpose would it serve? He'd be so shocked at the revelation. He'd think her careless. Neglectful. Stupid. It would break his mood, better at his imminent release from the hospital than it had been in the past couple weeks.

He hadn't been shy lately when it came to saying those hurtful things. Although yesterday he had watched what he said. She'd still been able to tell what he thought. His eyes and mouth couldn't hide from her scrutiny.

In any case, he must have guessed she had something on her mind. "What's up, Jake? You're not worrying about taking care of me when I get out of here, are you? The doc says I'll be scooting around just fine on my own in another month. I'll be a good patient. I promise."

"I'm sure you shall be. I'm not concerned at all." Oh, she was worried all right, which made her a liar as well as all those other things.

"I'm not helpless anymore, Jacoba. I can do for myself, mostly. And the hotel has an elevator, which I'm glad about. Stairs are hard to navigate on crutches."

She wished he hadn't mentioned that. The beginnings of panic set in. Coughing a little, she steadied her voice. "Have you been doing the strengthening exercises the doctor set for you?"

He frequently complained about hobbling around the halls, a nurse hovering at his side as if he were a toddler or worse, a senile old man. And the halls were flat. How on earth was he to manage two flights of stairs?

What had she been thinking? She should at least have found something on the ground floor. Stupid indeed!

Grinning, he gave the hand he clasped a little shake. "Your skin feels a little rough, honey. Did you forget to rub in some of that nice lotion your mother makes?"

Jacoba pushed down the pique the small criticism raised. She forced a smile and said, "I guess I did forget." *No. What she'd done is used a scrub board and that horrible strong soap like the rest of the hoi polloi, as Madame dubbed regular folk.* And he hadn't even asked what she'd been doing, as if he thought she only sat on her behind and ordered minions to do her bidding.

Walking home at the end of visiting hours, dire thoughts ran through her head. Soon, very soon, they would have to ask for support from the railroad since Charlie couldn't work. Others, she'd heard, were doing so and Charlie's injuries were worse than most. Who could tell, however, when the promised money would come through? If ever. What then, should she do in the meantime?

Her lips, which had been trembling, firmed into an uncompromising line. Theft or no theft, she had to find a job. A paying job. Today. Well, not to start before Monday. She couldn't leave Charlie on his own on his first day out of the hospital. But make a job a fact before Charlie got home and tried to dissuade her. He would, of course. Try to dissuade her, that is. She could almost hear him now.

"Jake," he'd say, and there would be some truth in his argument, "you've never worked. Why, you even had a maid to help you dress. Your mother is very likely the richest woman in St. Louis. Maybe the whole country. You can wear diamonds, if you want."

He'd made the same assertion when she told him 'yes,' that she would elope with him. So humble, he'd been, in suggesting they get married and make their own way together far from their controlling families.

She couldn't help wondering where Charlie got the idea she'd ever worn diamonds. Some of his preconceived notions were funny. Young women didn't wear diamonds, or at least not until they were engaged to be married. And then only if she obeyed her mother and became engaged to a cruel man old enough to be her father. *A fate I escaped, thanks to Charlie.*

Lips twitching in sudden amusement, she mashed down that line of thought although her lips quirked enough that a man walking toward her smiled back.

Anyway, she thought, Madame kept the sparkling gems for herself. Pearls were for young women. And, thanks to a grandmother she'd never met, the only item of value she owned. Remembering, the quiver in Jacoba's stomach stilled, although Charlie's voice echoed in her head.

"You don't have a trade," he would say to her. "Unless it's looking pretty."

He'd said that once, and added that he'd take care of her.

But now he would ask, "What can you *do*?"

I've had this discussion with myself before. What can I do?

Maybe she should make a list this time. A serious list. This was serious, after all. A matter, almost, of life and death.

At least, the life and death of Charlie's and my dreams of independence.

Charlie, although he'd nominally been added to the "DeGroot and Sons Construction Company" when his father added the *s* to Son, still hadn't much hope of being more than his father's and his older brother's lesser satellite. Yes, even though they were, all three DeGroot men, master builders. That expertise is why she'd met Charlie in the first place. His father had been Madame's contractor of choice to construct her new cosmetics factory and built the addition onto her own mansion. It had been Charlie, relegated to work inside the mansion, who toiled over a particularly elaborate stair railing. It had been Charlie's first solo endeavor and occasionally, all didn't go quite right. Once, purely by chance, Jacoba's math had saved him from a costly cut on some imported tropical wood.

They'd first met on the stair itself, Charlie barking at her to "Watch your step. Don't, for God's sake, break that bullnose trim piece. It took me an hour to fit in place."

Jacoba remembered she'd been a little offended at his accusation of clumsiness.

Only age and seniority separated the DeGroot men. Incompetence certainly didn't hold Charlie back. She didn't think so, anyway. But why did he feel she had no talents.

Beyond looking "pretty."

Scornfully, as she walked, she began her mental list, going on from where those earlier thoughts left off.

Organizing. Accounting. Knowledge of cosmetic formulas.

All very well if she were going into competition with Madame. But she wasn't. She hadn't time. She needed money now, before Charlie's wallet grew too thin.

Gardening of flowers and herbs. But regardless of the plant, for now the season was wrong and their land, from what she understood, filled with timber. She had no proper spot for her special garden.

Teacher? Except teachers for the school year had all been hired.

Washerwoman? Surveying her roughened hands, she thought not. Even the Chinese employed mostly men in their laundries.

What did that leave? She just didn't know.

Somewhat to her surprise, Bettina, Mrs. Griswold's hired girl, provided a possible answer to the conundrum.

It started at the dinner table, where the landlady eyed Jacoba with an unsettled expression. "Mrs. DeGroot, I need to talk with you after dinner, if you would be so kind as to stop by my parlor."

Jacoba, spooning a tasty fresh corn chowder into her mouth, looked up, arrested by the lady's tone. "Of course, Mrs. Griswold." Then, on a rush of hope said, "Have you heard if the police arrested Mr. Finley?"

"No. I haven't heard a word. I'm sorry. I wouldn't get my hopes up, if I were you," she added dryly. The lady then turned her attention to another of her boarders, a woman who'd arrived in town from the coast who'd landed a teaching job at the new high school.

Jacoba envied the woman.

Betty, undercover of setting a basket of fresh bread rolls on the table, bent to whisper in her ear. "She wants to see if you can pay your rent. I hope you can." The girl had, for some reason, taken a shine to Jacoba.

"Oh." Jacoba gulped. "Thank you." The topic almost spoiled her appetite, since it was exactly what she'd been brooding over all day. The need for a job loomed ever larger.

She tarried as the other diners left, including Mrs. Griswold who generally made it a point of being last to leave the table. To check if Betty nibbled at the leftovers? And who could blame her if she did? Except tonight there were no leftovers. Finally, Jacoba, finishing her piece of custard pie, spoke as Betty cleared the dishes.

"About Mrs. Griswold's rules," she said, "she didn't toss Mr. Finley out and I heard her say he was behind on the rent."

Betty, her face hot and red as she struggled with a heavily laden tray of soiled china, scoffed. "But he's a man. For some reason, she's always comes down harder on women. Seems to me it ought to be the other way around."

"Yes. To me, as well." Jacoba paused. "I'll need a job. I wish I knew . . ." Lacing her fingers together in her lap, she looked up at the maid. "I've never had a paid job. I don't even know where to look. Or how."

Swiping some crumbs from the table into her hand, Betty made a face. "I have. Lots of times. Been in service since I was twelve and I'm twenty-four now. Half my life."

She sounded woebegone, not that Jacoba blamed her. "Can't you find something you'd like better?"

Betty, glancing over her shoulder as if to see if Mrs. Griswold might be lurking, plumped onto the chair next to Jacoba. "I would if I could. I'd dearly love to be a telephone girl. Sit all day and just plug lines into those little connection holes."

Connection holes? Jacoba smiled. The job sounded boring to her, but certainly better than being a washerwoman. Or a maid of all work. "Why don't you become one then?"

"Because of my German accent. They won't hire anyone who doesn't talk pure American. Like you do. You could be a telephone girl." Betty sounded wistful. "And besides, I don't write so well. Or read. It's hard, and I had to find work before I had much schooling."

"I'm so sorry. But . . . one would think that being bilingual would be to your advantage."

"Bi what?" Betty's eyes opened wide. "I'm not bilingual!"

"Oh, but . . ." Suddenly understanding, Jacoba smiled. "You speak two languages, don't you? German and English?"

"Yes."

"Then you're bilingual. That's what the word means." She wondered what Betty would say if told Jacoba spoke five languages fluently and read a couple more. English, Hungarian, French, Spanish, and even Betty's own German. Those were accomplishments, weren't they? Perhaps marketable?

"Huh," Betty said. "Anyways, the telephone company is hiring. Mrs. Griswold spoke of an advertisement in this morning's newspaper."

Excitement lit a small flame in Jacoba's breast. "Do you know how much a telephone girl is paid?"

"Forty-five dollars a month to start." Betty's lips turned down. "I make thirty dollars and found."

Not what Jacoba had hoped for. But enough to pay the rent and maybe leave enough for Charlie to have some money in his pocket. As for landing the job, well, how hard could it be?

Jacoba went to meet Mrs. Griswold in her parlor a few minutes later, her outer confidence covering the fact she was quaking in her shoes. Having Madame for a mother had paid some dividends. It meant she'd been taught by the best to present calm equanimity. And, in difficult situations, to take charge of the conversation with a bit of flattery and go from there.

When the interview ended, Jacoba retained her room and Mrs. Griswold her peace of mind. A draw, in sportsmanlike terms. For Jacoba, a success and good practice for reacting to potential employers.

Chapter 9

The next morning at 9:15 precisely, Jacoba walked out of the Home Telephone and Telegraph office with instructions to begin her new job the following Monday. Truthfully, she didn't know whether to be happy or terrified.

As it turned out, her fluency in several languages indeed proved a marketable commodity, but only since she spoke English without a trace of accent. Although she could, if she wanted, sound exactly like a member of uppercrust English society.

She'd been shown around the facility, eyes wide as she observed the row of women, some of them only in their mid-teens, with the sound receivers clamped over their ears as they plugged and un-plugged wires out of connection receptacles. *Little holes,* as Betty called them, *jacks* according to the employer.

The process didn't appear difficult to understand, only fast-paced enough Jacoba worried a little that she'd be able to keep up. And a job where one would be required to keep one's temper. Some of the patrons were less than polite.

Yes, and she'd been told what to wear, as well. She wasn't at all sure she liked that, either, her ingrained fashion sense offended by the edict. But it would only be for the winter months, she consoled herself. Come spring, she and Charlie had promised one another, they would move onto their homestead even if they had to live in a tent. If they could afford a tent.

Pausing to smooth her gloves, the male supervisor's hand when they'd shaken had been sweaty and she couldn't wait to get home and wash, she made an inner vow that every week she would save a little something out of her pay envelope and put it aside to purchase ingredients for her soaps and lotions, even it meant walking to her place of employment every day rather than paying to take the street-car. Not that she was at ease with the idea of traversing the streets by herself. Spokane was a bit wild, with out-of-work men who had joined the Wobblies, men who wanted to create a union to work for more honest employers and better pay, overtaking the streets. Mostly, they seemed to spend their time drinking and carousing.

But she didn't want Charlie commenting on her "rough" skin again. Although surely he must know pioneer women were often forced to go without amenities they were accustomed to having.

Was she a pioneer woman? Right now she felt like one. Excitement rose like water bubbling through a percolator coffee pot.

She found Betty scrubbing the front stoop when she arrived back at the boarding house. Just to be on the safe side, she had timed the walk between there and the telephone company. Her aim was to never be late.

"Did you get the job?" The hired girl looked up from her work.

"I did, thanks to you." Jacoba smiled at Betty. "Without your help I'd never have known to apply. Or how."

Betty flushed, a return smile curving her lips and making her almost pretty.

Noticing the hired girl's hands were red from the harsh treatment they received, Jacoba instantly resolved to present her with a jar of Madame's finest creme, the kind with purified lanolin. It was the least she could do to show her gratitude.

The next day, Charlie came home.

Unwilling to risk his skill on the crutches, Jacoba hired a cab for transportation. He had yet to become expert in their use, and would find it difficult to manage the step up into the streetcar. As they kept to a schedule, streetcars waited for no man or woman. Besides, upon alighting, they still had a block and a half from the corner to walk. Too far. Protest as he may, her husband just wasn't up to it yet. Even the hike down from his second floor hospital room to the sidewalk had taxed him.

The thought of the boarding house stairs made her queasy with apprehension.

Charlie settled back on the cab's seat while regaining his breath, frowning as he surveyed the streets they passed through. "I don't remember these buildings. Where are we going, Jacoba? Are you sure this the way to the hotel?"

She'd hoped to start an explanation before he noticed. She forced a smile. "It's the way to our temporary home. The hotel was much too expensive, so I found a boarding house. The landlady is a very good cook."

He seemed not to hear the last part. The positive part, since Charlie was generally a bit fussy about his edibles. "A boarding house? What kind of boarding house? Where is it?"

"It's the kind of boarding house you live in when you don't have a house of your own." She winced. That had come out a little sharp. Rushing on, she softened her words. "It's a clean, respectable house I assure you. For instance, a schoolteacher lives there and you know how strict school boards are about their teachers' reputations. Let me see . . . there is a bookkeeper who is employed at the Exchange National Bank; a man who works in a butcher shop; and . . . and a couple of other clerks. I don't know where they are employed. Oh, and a couple who may be retired as they appear quite old."

Charlie's frown turned thunderous. "A schoolteacher? Clerks? A butcher? Good grief, Jacoba, you can't associate with these people. What would Madame say?"

Clasping her gloved hands tightly in her lap, Jacoba sought to control the wave of pique. "What Madame would say doesn't matter, Charlie. Not to me. Why would you even think of her? Isn't she the reason we've come so far west?" She thought a moment. "Aside from the fact the west is where the open land is. Have you forgotten we are to become homesteaders, Charlie? Homesteaders!"

Her set face must've cued Charlie that he'd overstepped. "Well, sure. It's just that I want to protect you, Jake. Now a man, he can live anywhere. A boarding house sounds just fine. But a girl like you, you're used to better things."

Jacoba's irritation melted like butter on a hot summer day. That was Charlie, always concerned for her welfare. Still, what did he think she'd been doing these last three and a half weeks? She'd managed just fine to discover a decent and *affordable* boarding house on her own. Even liked living there, the fly in the ointment being Finley and the robbery, which she now had to explain. Oh, and one other thing, the lack of a private bathroom.

Given Charlie's outburst over simply moving from an expensive hotel to a respectable boarding house, how on earth was she to tell him about the robbery? It all seemed beyond her. Rather than her best friend, her husband felt like a newly met stranger to her now. Sometimes she thought the accident and his brush with death had changed him, a change she regretted.

And the job. What about the job? She most certainly didn't look forward to breaking this news given his soured attitude.

It was almost a relief when the cab pulled up outside Mrs. Griswold's house. Thank goodness the pine needles had been raked from the yard, the stoop swept and tidy. Charlie had nothing to complain of there.

Thankfully, the cab driver climbed down to help Charlie from the vehicle and lifted down his duffle with the items Jacoba had taken to the hospital over the last few weeks.

Betty must've been on watch for them, for she ran out of the house eager to help. "*Guten Morgen*, Mr. DeGroot. I am happy to meet you. Let me get your luggage."

Jacoba seized on Betty's presence with relief. "This is Betty, who works here. She's been a good friend to me, Charlie."

Her words drew a sharp look from her husband, but he smiled his thanks at the girl.

"Hello, Betty," he said. "I appreciate your help."

It struck Jacoba that his face turned even paler than blood loss and his days in the hospital accounted for when he learned he'd have to climb the stairs leading to their room. Although not so steep as some stairways due to the taller than average ceilings in the house, there were two flights. The steps up appeared endless.

Guilt gnawed at her as he turned to her with a disgruntled look. "Really, Jake? We're on the third floor? Why on earth—"

He stopped himself, although she knew it cost him. Inwardly, her stomach clenched.

"I'm sorry." She gulped, her voice dropping lower. "This is what we can afford for now, Charlie. You'll be all right. I'll help." Although how much help she'd be when working as a telephone girl remained a mystery.

He collapsed onto the bed as soon as they reached the attic room, too exhausted to complain. Jacoba scurried about the single room, doing this, doing that, plumping pillows and talking in a quick, high voice until he begged her to stop.

"Leave it be, Jacoba." He threw his arm across his forehead and closed his eyes. "Come Monday, you can start looking for a different place. The Holiday may be expensive but at least it has an elevator. I'll use my savings and find work when I can, even if it means a late start getting out to the homestead."

Here it came, Jacoba thought. Confession time much too soon. "That's not a good idea. If you start late, you come in last. My mother says that, your father says that. I've heard them. And they should know."

He pulled his arm back to stare at her. "So, Jacoba, am I to be a prisoner in this pathetic little room? Because I'm not traipsing up and down those stairs four or five times a day."

"I know. And of course you're not a prisoner. What a thing to say! You will do only as much as you want to do. Otherwise, I'll bring your meals up to you. Me or Betty. I've already asked her and she says she'll do it for a dollar a week."

"A dollar a week? Why pay her when . . ."

She cut him off before she lost courage. "Because I won't be here. I have a job, Charlie. I start Monday." Arms stiff at her sides, her hands clenched.

For a moment she thought he quit breathing.

"You have a job? You? Without asking me?" He sat up, his face turning from sickly pale to blotched red. "Doing what?"

"I'll be a telephone girl. An operator for Home Telephone and Telegraph. Six days a week with hours from ten in the morning until eight in the evening. At least until I can get more accommodating hours."

His mouth opened and closed, sort of like a guppy fish she'd seen in an aquarium. "A hello girl?"

"Yes."

"I don't like it," he said. "You'll have to tell them you can't do it. I won't let you."

"Won't let me, Charlie?" Her voice came out thin, like steel wire. "You should think twice about that. My wages will pay the room and board for both of us here, plus a little extra. If we're careful, we'll still have the stake to begin on the homestead in the spring. If I don't work, we won't have anything left. It's as simple as that."

"I heal fast. We'll live on my wallet money until I can replace it when I find a job."

"There's not much construction here in the winter. I've already been told that." Mr. Howard from the butcher shop had been careful to explain the local economics to her. "And loggers and sawmill people coming into town for the winter fill what job openings there are. Times are bad. I'm told there are ten applicants for every job."

She had yet to force word of the robbery past the lump in her throat.

"I'll find something," he said stubbornly.

"I'm sure you will when you're able. But Doctor Libby said you'd be laid up for some months, that you need to take the time to heal properly if you don't want problems later on."

"You sound just like your mother." It wasn't a compliment. "I won't have my wife working as a hello girl. And that's that."

Flinging himself flat on the bed again, he closed his eyes, refusing to speak further.

"According to my mother, everyone has to start somewhere." Jacoba gave a flounce, one Charlie didn't see. "Madame gave her children good advice sometimes, you know. She wouldn't be the richest woman in St. Louis if she weren't smart. A millionaire on money she made herself. By working."

"In her own business. Not for the telephone company." Charlie snorted. "And she got her start by marrying rich men. Men who had a habit of dying off when they became inconvenient."

Jacoba felt the blood drain from her head as she caught the allusion to Madame's most recent husband less one. "Are you calling my mother a murderer, Charles DeGroot?" Her voice turned dangerously quiet, she stood stock still in the middle of the room.

Shooting her a wary look, Charlie fumbled for an excuse. "That's nothing more than what we've both thought, Jacoba. Remember when Count Emrys got shot and we caught Madame lying about where she was that night."

"I'm quite certain I know where she was, and it wasn't lying in wait for her husband to pass by the entrance to a dark alley." *No. She'd been entertaining the man who became her seventh husband a few weeks later.* "Count Emrys had been cheating at cards. The man he cheated was arrested and sent to prison for his murder." Jacoba knew it for an overly quick denial. Yes, the man had been convicted, but was he guilty? It wasn't so difficult to find someone willing to pull a trigger for a set sum.

Regardless, what Madame did or did not do should not reflect on Jacoba. And most certainly not on whether she took a job to pay their bills. Shouldn't she be commended for wanting to lighten her husband's load?

Arms akimbo, she fixed her husband with a level stare. "Also, you may be interested to learn that we have been robbed. A thief broke into my room a few days ago, which is what precipitated my hurry to find work. He didn't get the homestead savings, nor the cash you have reserved to buy tools. He did, however, get the money in your wallet as well as my savings, which I'd counted on to pay current expenses."

Charlie sat up, his eyes a little wild and snapping. "What?" The word was a barely restrained shout. "I suppose you ignored what I told about hiding our money. I said you should shove it down in one of your dress pockets. A man would never think of looking there."

"Well this man did. That's exactly where I had it."

"And my wallet?"

"Deep in the chair springs, like you said."

Charlie glared. "If you'd stayed at a decent hotel, this wouldn't have happened. This is your fault."

Fighting angry tears, Jacoba refused to take the blame. "My fault? Don't be ridiculous. Anyway, hotel rooms are broken into every day. And at least the thief didn't find everything." Charlie hadn't asked for any particulars, she thought, but simply gone on to fault finding. What if she'd come up when Finley was in the room? What if he'd hurt her? Killed her? Would Charlie be happier then, proven correct about her ineptitude?

An angry turn around the small room did nothing to assuage her feelings. Her voice had turned from cold to husky by the time she stopped and added, "The police are investigating. I hope to get the money back."

Charlie's scoff proved police involvement hardly mollified him. "That'll be the day. If they find him they'll probably take what's left of the cash themselves and let him go free."

Unable to tolerate quarreling any longer, Jacoba turned to the door. "I've got things to do downstairs. There's a cowbell on the table beside you. If you need anything, ring it. I'll hear and come help you."

"A cowbell," Charlie said, as if it were the silliest thing he'd ever heard. "Your idea?"

"No. Mrs. Griswold's. She said it worked very well a while back when she had a sick lady in one of the upper rooms."

Speaking of sick, Jacoba's stomach churned as she made her way down the two flights of stairs. She sat alone in the darkened parlor for the rest of the afternoon, rising only to pace when sitting became intolerable. When it was time to take Charlie's supper to him, she found his foul mood had lightened. Or if not his mood, at least the tenor of his conversation. They didn't speak of the robbery, nor of Jacoba's job. Apparently, he'd decided if he ignored these events, they'd go away.

Sadly, Jacoba came to the realization that she had more of her mother in her than she either liked or wanted. And that it was all too easy to carry a grudge.

No matter how much she'd longed for Charlie's arms around her, when she lay down beside him that night on the all too narrow bed, she claimed only the farthest edge. Sleep came slowly.

Chapter 10

On Monday, Jacoba arose early, unable to sleep longer due to Charlie's sprawled limbs and heavy plaster cast taking more than his half of the already narrow bed. Though much too early to leave for her job, she felt as nervous as though forced to sing at a dinner party for a hundred of Madame's high-society guests. Excitement whipped through her, mixed with equal parts of apprehension. Her stomach churned in a most uncomfortable way.

What if Charlie was right? What if she wasn't capable of holding down a real job? What if the telephone company fired her for incompetence and sent her home in disgrace on her first day?

Resolution stiffened her spine, fortified by the cup of pre-breakfast coffee Betty passed to her when Mrs. Griswold wasn't looking.

"You will do well," Betty whispered. "Don't worry."

The hired girl's confidence buoyed her, and Jacoba forced a shaky smile. Betty was right. She could do this. Lots of girls with less worldly experience than she managed to succeed. She would too.

And, as it happened, she did.

The girl who showed her how to listen in on calls was fired a month after Jacoba began working. Which meant that she moved up one seat to have only nineteen girls in front of her for the lead girl position. When or if she ever became number one, it would mean a two-dollar raise in her weekly wages.

She sincerely hoped she wouldn't be there that long, tethered by cords as she plugged prongs into jacks. Sometimes almost as fast as she could move her hands.

The work, beyond the first couple of weeks, did not prove onerous. Simply mind stultifying and boring unless, of course, vilified by patrons of the service. Some of them seemed to believe they were paying for the privilege of berating the girl on the end of the telephone line. She proved adept at acting as though she didn't hear their remarks. As though she didn't care. And truly, after a while she didn't, even though her feelings were ruffled at the time.

Evelyn, Jacoba never learned the girl's last name, told her how easy it was to get the last laugh. All one had to do was to keep saying, "Number, please" as though deaf until the caller hung up. As one might expect, between the 'number please' charade and inattention to the whereabouts of the overseer at any given moment, Jacoba soon moved up to Evelyn's seat, putting her only eighteen from the top.

Nevertheless, for most of the girls, their curiosity got the best of then whenever a panicked customer requested the police. They frequently managed to linger on the line long enough to hear at least part of the call. Which is how Jacoba, giving in to that curiosity one day when calls were slow, overheard the dialogue between the proprietress of Bird's Boarding House, and the same Detective Hansen who had taken the report of the theft at Mrs. Griswold's.

The woman, Mrs. Bird, had asked for the police, a call Jacoba promptly put through. On the verge of disengaging, she heard the woman say, "Officer, I wish to report a theft on the behalf of one of my boarders."

A familiar situation. Curiosity overcame her and she hesitated.

To her surprise, Jacoba recognized Detective Hansen's voice on the line. Unable to resist, she listened in. After all, she excused herself, how could she *not* be interested. Hadn't the very same thing happened to her? *A case still with no resolution.* The thought of her missing money, never far from her mind, rose yet again.

Mrs. Bird and Detective Hansen discussed the particulars of the theft, short and swift. One of the boarders, a lone female, had allegedly had her room broken into and her savings, a matter of twenty-one dollars, stolen from under her mattress.

Jacoba heard the loud snort Detective Hansen emitted and a derogatory exclamation of, "Mattress, huh?"

Well, she had to agree. Not a very innovative hiding place. Not that riding skirt pockets or the springs of an old chair proved any better.

"Anybody there see any strangers? Any locks broken? Anything else taken? Anyone other than the single lady admit to being robbed?" Hansen's questions were like the staccato tap of a hammer.

"No strangers. Just the one lock broken. Nothing else taken. None other of my boarders fell victim that I've heard of." The landlady's answers were just as short.

"Got any ideas who mighta done it?" Hansen asked.

"A suspicion. Another of my boarders." Mrs. Bird spoke as though the words were dragged out of her. "A man named Finley who lives on the same floor as Miss Harris. By the way, Miss Harris told me he's been bothering her."

Jacoba barely muffled her gasp in time to keep from being heard.

"Bothering her? Bothering her how?" the detective demanded.

"Not attacked, if that's what you're asking. Just accosting her, trying to get her alone. Even knocking on her door late at night when everyone else is in bed. Their rooms are next to each other, you see. And he asks a great many questions that are none of his business." The woman made it plain she didn't approve. "You will most likely find him at home after five o'clock. He lives in the Quail room."

"The what room?" Hansen said.

The rooms at the boarding house all had bird names, the explanation of which threatened to become lengthy as Mrs. Bird expounded on the variety.

But any connection as to the suspected person's name and the mode of theft apparently flew right over Detective Hansen's head like a bird on the wing.

He ended with an excuse. "Well, ma'am, I'm busy today and tomorrow, but I'll be along the day after to see what I can see. Meanwhile, have this Miss . . .whoever . . . bunk in another room until I can get there. This Finley know you're calling the police?"

"No. I haven't confronted him."

"Well don't. Let me catch him at home. Understand?"

"Yes. But . . ."

He disconnected before Mrs. Bird could say more.

Jacoba unplugged a few seconds before the landlady, but not before she heard the woman say, "I never! How rude."

Worse than rude, in Jacoba's opinion. Sloppy and incompetent were among Detective Hansen's more damning traits. But now she had something to look out for.

There might be a way of getting her money back.

As though ordained by angels, that way opened up not an hour later. When one of the girls told Helene Marie, a recent hire taking Evelyn's chair, that Jacoba spoke Hungarian, she begged for help. She had a "friend"—the word bore quotation marks around it— who spoke very little English. Helene Marie, like Jacoba, was of Hungarian descent. However, unlike Jacoba, she had never learned the old language. Mr. Kovacs needed an interpreter in order to rent a room he'd just found available at Bird's Boarding House. Mrs. Bird, it seemed, required a strict interview with her potential boarders.

"Bird's Boarding House?" Jacoba repeated, striving to keep the incredulity out of her voice and expression. She couldn't help wondering what kind of impression Finley had made at his interview.

"Yes. That's it. Can you please go with us to inquire?" Helene Marie asked. "Please. I promised to help him but I only know three or four words in Hungarian."

"When should we go?" Jacoba asked, trying not to appear too eager. *It must be soon.*

"Tomorrow." Helene Marie clasped her hands under her chin. "Oh, Mrs. DeGroot, does this mean you will help us?"

Jacoba, almost giddy with the opportunity and her mind racing, could barely contain her glee. A few minutes by herself and maybe she could find a way to search the place. If only she could find his room. But wait. Mrs. Bird had told the detective the victim and Finley's rooms were side-by-side. Chances were, the available room belonged to the victim.

"Of course," she told the other girl. "I'll be happy to help you." What would Charlie think when she told him? Probably scowl in disapproval. So, she thought, backtracking her first idea, she just wouldn't discuss her plan with him.

Charlie, as he frequently did of late, showed his displeasure when informed that instead of staying in and playing games with him on her day off, Jacoba meant to spend the morning running unspecified errands.

"It's your only free day. I thought we might take a buggy ride. I'm sick of being penned up in this one room, Jacoba. I need to get out."

Jacoba did her best not to mind that almost every sentence had begun with *I*. And really, he was healing well. Dr. Libby encouraged him to get out and take some exercise, but Charlie resisted the advice. She longed for the day he got back to his old generous, loving self.

"I know," she said, arranging her countenance into a properly sorrowful expression. "I'm sorry. But maybe we can go for a buggy ride in the afternoon. As long as it doesn't rain," she added. It looked to her as if a storm was brewing, dark clouds rolling in from the coast. She hoped it would blow out overnight.

"A little rain never hurt anybody. Anyway, if it rains on you while you're running errands, a little more wet won't matter. At least it'll be fresh air to breathe."

He had a point. She didn't care for being trapped inside for days on end, either. "Don't you go into the back yard during the day?" Jacoba thought to mention. Her forehead wrinkled. "That's why Mrs. Griswold keeps tables and chairs out there, so that the boarders may enjoy the sunshine, or shade. Although it is too bad frost has killed the flowers and the vegetable garden now."

"Why would I want to sit outside by myself? There'd be nobody to help me if I needed something. That old woman is the only one I've ever seen out there. Yesterday, I asked if she'd bring me a glass of water and she acted like I'd asked for the moon."

She flicked him a glance. The old woman was not a servant, but another boarder. "Charlie, if you mean Mrs. Bishop, she's as disabled as you are. She has to use a cane to walk." Charlie had been very rude to her last week with a comment about not moving out of his way fast enough.

Anyway, it had been two and a half months since the train wreck. Dr. Libby said Charlie should be doing these things for himself, strengthening his muscles for the day he gave up the crutches, which, the doctor said, was no more than a week to ten days from now.

"And that is why she should stay out of people's way," he said. "She wasn't the one almost killed in a train wreck. I was! By the way, have you heard anything from the railroad about when our bills will be paid?"

She sighed. "Not yet."

"You should stop in at their office as long as you're out. See if there's any news."

She nodded. "All right." The task suited her. It sounded like the makings of an excuse for however long it took at the boarding house, no questions asked.

* * *

In case Finley remained at the boarding house, Jacoba dressed with care the next day. Wrapping herself in a long, heavy coat that added ten pounds to her slender frame, she perched a wide-brimmed hat with a filmy veil on her head. As a disguise, she hoped it would be enough.

Charlie blinked at her as she headed out the door. "Isn't that your winter coat? Won't you be too hot? The sun is shining."

She found herself wishing for the rain to come back. Or even snow. She shrugged. "I'm feeling cold this morning, is all."

"Hope you're not coming down with something."

It was the first utterance of concern to issue from his mouth in a while. Quite a long while.

"I don't think so." She smiled. "I'll be fine."

"As long as you're not contagious then. I don't want to catch a cold."

Jacoba met Helene Marie and Lajos Kovaks at the streetcar stop a block from their target. Lajos, she found, was a young man who spoke with such a heavy accent that even she had trouble understanding his extremely limited English, as he speckled it with Hungarian words. Also, he came from a different region than Madame, so even the accent was difficult. She couldn't help wondering how Helene Marie and he communicated since Helene spoke only English.

Kisses, she decided, after a time of watching them together.

Their little group approached the Bird Boarding House where Lajos knocked on the door and stepped back. Jacoba tucked herself in behind him while Helene moved forward to do the talking.

A serious little girl opened the door. She asked them to wait in the foyer while she went to fetch her mother, presumably Mrs. Bird. Quiet voices sounded from what Jacoba discovered to be a spacious parlor opening off the foyer. Peering around the corner through a doorway, she spotted several people taking their leisure, older men reading the newspaper or with writing equipment in hand; women with sewing or knitting on their laps. Unlike Mrs. Griswold's house, where children were not allowed, two boys and a girl played quietly in a corner set aside for them.

The room was clean, with draperies drawn back to allow in light provided by the weak sunshine. The furniture looked comfortable.

A woman with a splotch of flour on her cheek, her hair done up in a neat bun, and wearing a green gingham apron over a plain gray dress, came hurrying to greet them. The little girl trailed behind her.

"May I help you?" the woman asked cordially of their group at large.

A discussion followed, which Jacoba, true to her word, translated to Lajos when the English spoken left him appearing bewildered. Which, in all honesty, wasn't often.

"How much does he understand?" Mrs. Bird peered at him with a doubtful, nearsighted stare. "I don't know. It could be difficult if"

Lajos answered for himself. "I speak some. Speak . . ." he made a patting motion as though pushing something down, slowing the pats.

Mrs. Bird nodded. "I see. Well, the children probably . . . they seem to understand when adults never do. I think—"

"How much?" Lajos asked, drawing the lady from her stammering.

Jacoba began to think she'd wasted her time coming here as Lajos nodded as though agreeing to the sum Mrs. Bird mentioned. Less, she noted, than she paid Mrs. Griswold, even when it had been just her before Charlie got out of the hospital.

Panicking a little, she decided to take a hand. "Excuse me, please, ma'am, but are you troubled any by crime here?" She looked around, hoping the lady would be honest and not take offense. "It does seems very open and comfortable."

Mrs. Bird's mouth twisted. "There was a theft. At least, I *think* there was a theft. One of my ladies said she was missing some money." She frowned. "But the man she accuses, he denies it and I have no way of being sure. The police haven't come, so. . ." She stopped. "So I've warned everyone to put their valuables in the safe I keep in the office. Just in case."

Lajos frowned as Jacoba translated.

"I see. You didn't believe the woman then?" Helene Marie thoughtfully asked the question Jacoba hesitated over.

"Well, she . . . had a tendency to be excitable. Anyway, she moved out. It's her room that is now for rent."

Although Lajos nodded, Jacoba spoke quickly, before he could form the correct words of agreement—or of denial. "May we see the room?"

"Yes. Of course." She looked down at the little girl. "Mable, go fetch the key to the Grouse room and show these people where it is, please."

"Yes, Mama." The little girl, obviously delighted to be entrusted with the chore, skipped off.

"I'll be in the kitchen," Mrs. Bird said. "Please call for me when you decide, whether for or against."

"Thank you," Helene Marie said as Lajos echoed in Hungarian. "*Köszönöm szépen.*"

Following Mable single file, the four of them trouped up a rather narrow stairway, Jacoba deliberately trailing. There were five doors opening off a short hall. A plaque adorned each door, all of which had a bird of some type painted on it. One, The Nest, was ajar, showing a bathroom. The little girl stuck the key in the lock of Grouse and pushed open the door.

"Here we are," she said importantly. "Come in."

Jacoba, meanwhile, tried the door next to the Grouse room. Although she didn't expect it to be unlocked and she'd come prepared with a fine crochet hook and hairpins as tools, it opened. She slipped inside as the others vanished into the room next door.

One inhalation and she knew the room's occupant. It smelled, stunk really, of Finley. She spared a thought for Mrs. Griswold who'd complained of how difficult it had been to eradicate the odor he'd left behind.

The room, untidy in the extreme, drew her eye. At least she wouldn't have to fear disturbing anything, but she hadn't much time. A few minutes at best and her companions would begin to wonder where she'd gotten to.

So where would Finley hide his money? Her money!

She whirled around, looking.

Not in a pocket, for sure. But there, a trunk half open with some tools exposed. Not woodworking tools like Charlie used, but wrenches, screwdrivers and the like. A lot of them. Stolen goods, she wondered? Finley might hide the money in with them. Or, it struck her, rig up a secret hiding place within the trunk itself. *Might?* As though she smelled the money, Jacoba honed in on it.

She listened a moment. Still talking, she heard the child's piping voice and Lajos' deep halting rumble of reply.

The trunk, Jacoba found, contained not a false bottom, but a false lid, with a tiny, clever latch she broke a fingernail opening. Her money—hers and Charlie's—was there. Five twenty-dollar gold coins wrapped in the bills taken from Charlie's wallet. All the money was in the small bag she'd kept the coins in, her name embroidered in purple silk on the black velvet bag.

Careless. Sloppy. Confident. Finley, she thought, smirking a bit, was not even a *good* thief.

Breath coming in spurts, she stuffed the bag in her pocket and dropped the lid down. Darting for the door, she eased it closed behind her just as Helene Marie, Lajos and Mable left the Grouse room.

"It's nice, isn't it?" she said to Lajos. "Will you take it?" There, she thought in satisfaction. That sounded calm and in control, didn't it? And like she'd been with them the whole time.

"Yes," Lajos said, although Helene Marie looked at her askance.

"What did you do to your hand?" she asked.

For the first time, she became aware of pain. Blood from the finger with the broken nail, torn to the quick, dripped to the floor. She found a handkerchief in her pocketbook and bound the finger.

"It's nothing. I'm not even sure how it happened."

A panicked thought ran through her mind. *Did I leave a trail of blood?*

Not, she told herself, that it mattered. What could Finley do about it, anyway? Complain that he'd been robbed?

Glee rose inside her although inwardly, she trembled.

Chapter 11

Spring approached in a rush of chinook winds. Snow melted, turning streets and roads to muddy quagmires. Skirts were splashed to the knee, trouser legs laden with muck. Boots and shoes had to be left at the door. Then the days grew longer, the sun finally came out, and buds on trees swelled with life.

Over his sulks at last—for the most part, at least—Charlie swelled with new purpose. Limping only slightly, toward the end of February, he had begun his search for a team of horses. He figured, quite accurately as it happened, the end of winter was the best time to buy, when folks sometimes ran out of money to feed themselves, let alone a couple draft horses who stood around eating their heads off.

Jacoba, when he told her about the search, blinked at the prodigious amount of feed necessary for the giant horses.

"I'd rather invest in a couple extra months care than pay top dollar when spring work starts." Charlie made it sound as if he'd been a farmer all his life, causing Jacoba to secretly smile. Not the best judge of horseflesh, his biggest problem lay in finding a team

that suited him. That and money. More than once he mentioned to
Jacoba that maybe it was time she contacted Madame and asked
for a loan to see them through. They'd pay it back, he assured her.
As soon as the homestead produced an income.

Jacoba, clamping her lips shut, didn't answer. Nor did she write.

Mr. Howard, the butcher, proved to be an odd go-between to
a deal when it came to finding a team. After several days where
Charlie rushed from one stable to another, always one step behind
an earlier purchaser or only to find what even he knew was subpar,
one of Howard's customers had the answer. Accustomed to procur-
ing pot roast or chicken for his family's Sunday dinner, the man
had found work scarce, which reduced him to buying soup bones.

"He's put his horses up for sale," Mr. Howard reported. "He
can't find work for them and can no longer afford the hay, let
alone the grain, they need. They're good horses, too, a fine team.
It's a damn shame."

Charlie, barely restrained from leaping up from his supper, went
out later that same night to look at them. And lay down his cash.

"Bought them," he announced proudly when he returned to the
boarding house. "Tope and Pym."

"Tope and Pym?" Jacoba smiled.

"Their names. They're Shires. Well, a mix."

Tightening their budget, she made do, and discovered she
loved accompanying him to the livery where the horses were
stabled. Giants of a sweet nature, their withers rose taller than she,
their backs broad, their shaggy winter coats making their beige
hides appear mangy and worn. She helped Charlie prepare them
for spring work with curry comb and brush until, with warmer
weather, their coats shone.

Due to Jacoba's connection with Helene Marie and Lagos Kovaks, Charlie had, by this time, also bought a good set of carpen-
ter's tools, stating they were all he needed to build a fine house.
The money saved to begin work on the homestead was depleted
and Charlie grew impatient, chafing at the delay when a late March

snowstorm put off his first trip to the reservation. He chafed at her, too. At the world in general.

"Hasn't your mother written back yet?" he asked after the postman failed to deliver the letter—or any letter—postmarked St. Louis.

Jacoba hadn't quite worked up the nerve to tell him she hadn't written.

"No," she replied.

Charlie needed work to do.

* * *

They hadn't gotten around to changing the owner's name from Jacoba De Groot to Charles De Groot on the homestead paperwork, as yet. The fee to do so seemed an unneeded expense. Even so, Charlie had begun calling the land 'his,' and if Jacoba's forehead puckered into a frown at times at the lack of sharing implied, for the most part it didn't seem to matter.

Another thing she hadn't gotten around to was telling Charlie about the recovery of their money on that day in October. She had an idea eking it into their budget in case of vital emergency might prove a wiser plan. She'd discovered Charlie was not always as provident of their finances as he should be, especially on days he spent time at one of the many downtown saloons.

Anyway, Charlie would be sure to disapprove of the way she'd gotten the money back. She thought it as well she kept the recovery to herself judging by the way their homestead savings disappeared so quickly. Her husband seemed to think three hundred dollars would multiply on its own and last forever.

She'd heard through Helene Marie that Finley had been arrested for stealing. The police had found a good many possessions belonging to other people in Finley's room, including the tools Jacoba had seen in the trunk. He was serving time in the county jail. The thought brought a smile to her lips at the most inappropriate times.

Her smile faded on the first fine day of the spring when Charlie announced he was going to Hawkesford to stake out his land and make a start on clearing it.

"I'll give notice." Weary of what had become a boring, routine job, thoughts of packing up cheered her.

"Better not," he said. "I'll be living in a tent until I can get a house built. This little job of yours will give you something to do while I'm gone."

Jacoba's hazel eyes flashed fire. Little job? They'd been living on her wages. How else did he think they'd gotten through most the winter with his savings intact? "I'll live in the tent with you," she said.

Charlie's laugh struck her as a bit offensive. "Live in a tent? You, Jake? It's camping out in the elements. You know, like mountain men." He'd admitted to her once that he'd been enthralled by those stories as a youngster.

"I know." She forced a smile. "We talked about it on the way west."

"Yes, well, I've more experience now. I know better than to think you could survive out there in the wild."

She didn't try to hide her hurt. "But . . . but what about our plans. And who will cook your meals?"

He laughed again. "Not you, Jacoba. You don't even know how to cook."

"Do you?"

"How hard can it be?"

"Exactly," she shot back. Did he really think it would be easier for him to learn than for her? Although it was true his culinary tastes were less . . . refined . . . than hers.

Jacoba realized Charlie had not gotten over having to depend on her. She thought having a brother helped her understand, or at least know about, a male's sensitivity regarding supposed threats to his manhood, which her new independence seemed to be. But why? Did he expect her to melt if he weren't there to stand between her and . . . whatever? Did he *want* her to?

She had begun to see why Madame had been married seven times. She rather thought her mother had been trying to find a man not intimidated by her independent nature, let alone her superior business acumen. A quest less than successful, evidently.

She hated the next thought that flashed through her brain. The one that said, *if Charlie doesn't change his attitude soon, history may repeat itself.*

What was happening to them? To Charlie and to her?

But in the end, she hid her frustration and hurt tears and waved Charlie and the team off toward the rail yard where he and the horses were loaded into a stock car to carry the three of them to the town of Rockford. They'd travel from there by road to the reservation.

Without her.

For now. Plans formed as she trod her lonely way back to Mrs. Griswold's boarding house.

Charlie, as it turned out over the next few weeks, proved an indifferent communicator. His letters, when he got around to sending one, were sparse both in number and in information. Often no more than a couple lines written on a penny postcard.

> *Wish I'd drawn a better piece of ground. Some of this goes down to the lake and is too steep to be of use. Tope and Pym work hard. Me too. I'm learning to log.'*

Log! Logging was so dangerous, especially on one's own. Jacoba prayed he took care.

His next card proved just as worrying as the first, though in a different way.

> *Met some other homesteaders, he wrote. We played cards in my tent the other night. I won two dollars. Ha, ha.*

Charlie gambling? Small stakes, granted, but what, Jacoba wondered, was she to make of that? A little bitterly, she determined he didn't seem to be missing her. What had happened? The accident had changed him so much she sometimes hardly recognized him.

What she did recognize was that he never forgot to ask what she'd dubbed *the question*. Had she received anything from her mother?

When she wrote back, she soon realized her small doings didn't interest him at all. Not even the promotion she got at work, except for the two dollars and fifty cents a week raise she received. All due, as it turned out, to her ability to speak more than just pure American English.

Jacoba's hard-earned raise came about because of an incident involving Eileen, a stolid seventeen-year-old girl seated some distance away from Jacoba at the telephone switchboard. Late on a busy Friday afternoon, when the telephone exchange was at its busiest as businessmen finished up their week's work, a short break at her station allowed Jacoba to hear a sort of rising panic in the generally unflappable Eileen's soft voice. That it came from six seats away drew her attention. She peeked around the other girls to see what was happening.

"I am sorry," Eileen kept repeating, more and more loudly, as if volume compensated for clarity. Each of the girl's round cheeks bore a bright crimson splotch. "I do not understand you. Please, do not hang up. I will get my supervisor."

Every girl within hearing understood the implication behind Eileen's stilted diction. It meant she was speaking with someone lacking fluency in the English tongue. Or maybe the American tongue. Unfortunately, their supervisor, Mr. Lehman, was nowhere to be found, which, to the girls on the line, came as no real surprise. He took frequent cigarette breaks outside the building. Not that his presence would do much good. He spoke no other language than, as he put it, American.

Jacoba sighed, put her board on stand-by, got up, and trod down the line to Eileen's station. "What language is the caller speaking?" she asked in a whisper.

Eileen turned her head from her microphone. "I don't know. But he keeps shouting. Oh, Mrs. de Groot! Whatever shall I do?"

Able to hear the man, although not distinguish his words through the receivers clamped over Eileen's head, Jacoba thought she recognized the cadence of the man's speech.

She nodded to Eileen. "I'll take the call if you'll sit in my place until this is straightened out." For Eileen's sake, and her own, too, she hoped Mr. Lehman stayed gone.

Snatching the receiver set from her ears, the girl leapt to her feet faster than Jacoba had ever seen her move. "Thank you," she breathed, and fled.

Jacoba seated herself and adjusted the receivers. "Repeat your question, sir," she said into the microphone. Only she spoke in Hungarian.

"At last," a man said in that language, his relief plain. "Please help. I need help."

"Do you need the police?" Jacoba asked.

"A doctor. I need a doctor. At once. A man has been shot. He is bleeding most profusely. I think he is dying. Quickly, quickly."

"What is your location?" *Shot.* Jacoba's stomach gave a lurch as she listened, then scrawled down the address. The best hotel in town. Why hadn't the Holiday's personnel taken a hand?

The man on the phone began weeping, saying, "I'm sorry. I'm sorry," over and over. "It was an accident."

"Stay with the victim." Jacoba leaned closer to her microphone. "Press a clean handkerchief over his wound. Press firmly and hold it there. That will help to staunch the bleeding. If the blood is pumping from his wound, if possible, you must apply a tourniquet between the heart and the wound. I'll call the police and the hospital. Help will be with you soon."

Pulling the key from the jack, Jacoba smoothly changed the connection. She called the hospital first, directing a doctor to the downtown location. Next, although she hesitated, wondering how attentive they would actually be, she called the police station. The man who answered the telephone promised quick action. Whether it happened or not, she had done her part.

And then she was done. Her knees shook as she stood up and went to pat Eileen's shoulder. Without further speech, they traded places again, each to her own station. The supervisor still absent, they both sighed relief.

Leaving one's assigned post, Jacoba reminded herself, was the sort of thing that got a telephone girl fired if the situation reached the wrong ears.

Except, in this case, it didn't. Or it reached the right ears first, at any rate.

The next day, tripping along faster than her normal pace as she was a few minutes behind time, Jacoba approached the Spokane Telephone and Telegraph Company's imposing building. The place seemed extra busy this afternoon, with several men hovering about, one of them pointing an important looking camera here and there.

Jacoba stopped on the boardwalk and caught her breath. Was that the mayor standing at the building entrance shaking hands with Mr. Lane, founder of the company? Two or three of the girls from her shift had been lined up alongside the men, each looking flushed and excited. And why not? It wasn't every day one had one's photograph taken with such important people. Even so, it was the man accompanying the men who arrested her attention.

He most surely was not anyone local if she were to judge by his appearance. He wore an exquisite suit tailored with a vaguely military feel and colored a deep, dark red. A short Van Dyke beard adorned his chin and his dark hair gleamed with pomade. He smiled widely at the mayor and Mr. Lane, while they beamed back, holding the pose for the camera. He must, Jacoba decided, be an important and remarkable personage.

She took note of Mr. Lehman standing off to the side out of camera range, a disgruntled expression clouding his face. Not something that boded well for the girls on her shift today, she imagined. Herself in particular as he always seemed to feel threatened by her.

She stood back, waiting for the steps to clear, when one of the girls pointed at her and said, all in a breathless rush, "That's her. She's the one."

Every head swiveled her way. Nearly a dozen pairs of eyes settled on her.

Jacoba stopped in her tracks and stared back, her mind gone blank. Until she heard the gentleman in the stylish suit speak. He spoke in Hungarian—to her.

"I am Barany István." He announced himself in the Hungarian fashion, last name first, while flashing a smile as though delighted to see her. "Secretary to the princess. When you speak to me, use the language of the Magyar. These people will be impressed."

"As you wish," she replied, although not convinced she wanted to impress anyone.

Smoothly, he broke away from the photograph assemblage and came down the steps toward her. Both his hands reached out to grasp both of her own. He leaned forward to murmur in her ear.

"Follow my lead and do not contradict anything I say. A scandal must be averted. You will be compensated."

He may have spoken in a warm tone and been smiling pleasantly, but his grip on her hands hurt.

Her chin tilted upward. It would be gratifying to dig a fingernail into his palm right now, if only she weren't wearing gloves. Her smile turned as false as his. "No compensation necessary. I did my job. Your story is your own."

"Miss, miss," one of the men whom she'd determined must work for the newspaper called to her, "tell us about that phone call. Mr. Barany István says the princess is calling you a heroine."

"Indeed the princess did. And indeed, this lady is." The secretary's smile never wavered, as though pasted on.

"Did you know you were speaking with royalty?" Someone asked her.

Barany laughed. "Oh, we never mention that we're royalty," he said, although of course, he just had. In fact, he'd just said he served as her secretary. So just who was he, and what position did he really fill? Had he been the gunman? Obviously, he hadn't been shot, but who had? Why? And how?

For that matter, what was the princess's name?

"Will you meet with the princess? If so, when?" The question came at her so fast she didn't see who'd asked it

Barany dropped her hands at last and, once again, answered for her. "Princess Hegedus Piroska . . ." he began.

Princess Hegedus Piroska? Shock ripped along Jacoba's nerves. The princess was Madame's cousin, once removed. Well, she wasn't about to mention *that* to anybody, especially not the princess.

". . . and her party are grateful. Thanks to this lady's knowledgeable quick action, the accident, though most regrettable, will have a most fortuitous ending. But this, right here," he made a flamboyant gesture, "will be the end of it."

Except, Jacoba thought, for the big splash in the newspaper. As he very well knew.

A man with a pencil and a child's lined tablet shouted a question. "Miss, about the gunshot wound? We talked to the doc. He said the telephone girl, that's you, gave proper advice. You probably saved the man's life. People are gonna want to know how you knew to treat the wound? Can you tell us?"

A buzz of satisfaction enveloped her, followed by a twinge of something else. Here was a question the Magyar couldn't answer for her.

Two reasons rose in her mind, only one of which she felt able to relate. "My husband and I were victims of last summer's train wreck. I . . ." she hesitated, then went on, "I learned something about wounds from observing the first aid provided by the doctors and nurses and others who came to help. Any credit goes to them."

She didn't want to mention the second reason, because the second of Madame's husbands, a philanderer, although he'd added substantially to Madame's wealth, had been shot by a jealous suitor. It's what the doctor had instructed them to do. Not that the husband had survived, but the correct motions had been gone through and any loose talk about the suitor being a scapegoat in

Madame's plans quickly quelled.

Oh, yes. She would keep that to herself.

Another flurry of questions arose, some she barely heard. Mayor Pratt, aided by Mr. Lane, took over the podium, releasing Jacoba and the other telephone girls into the building to take up their jobs.

Jacoba discovered, as she unpinned her hat and set it aside, she'd fallen victim to a bad case of the shakes.

Meet Princess Hegadus Piroska? She guessed not! Because most certainly, it would get back to Madame. What's more, her curiosity as to who and why a man had been shot had faded. She no longer had any desire to know.

Nevertheless, the next morning she went out and bought two editions of the morning paper. Clipping the article with its rather grainy photograph, she tucked a copy into an envelope with her own short explanation of events and sent it off to Charlie.

She couldn't wait to hear what he made of this piece of news.

Chapter 12

If Jacoba expected praise from her husband regarding her supposed heroism—especially with her photograph being splashed
on the front page of the newspaper as news— disappointment became her lot instead.

At least Charlie cared enough to send an actual letter for once,
instead of his usual penny postcard. Or maybe he just felt he needed
more space in which to chastise her.

Dear Wife,

*You should have avoided this embarrassing noto-
riety. You should have taken care to cover your face
and hide your name. My name. We can only hope this
doesn't make it into the St. Louis papers. I don't want to
give my father or brother any line on me. Not until I'm
good and ready. As for your mother, I doubt she will
care, if her tardiness in sending any money is an indication. But at least you're making more money as a result.*

Did Charlie really still worry what his family would think if
they knew what he was doing? At first Charlie had been afraid the

DeGroots would think his foray into homesteading to be a major societal step down. But on second thought, wouldn't they admire his initiative? Besides, the reporter had misspelled the DeGroot name. Made it almost unrecognizable. And this wasn't really a *big* story, worthy of getting into newspapers far and wide. Jacoba felt certain no one even remembered it by the next day.

Meanwhile, we've had a lot of rain here.

As if Jacoba hadn't noticed the rain. One would think that in his mind they were hundreds of miles apart rather than thirty-five or forty.

It's a good thing you're not here. You wouldn't like it at all, Jacoba. It's quite primitive and there's not much for entertainment. Good thing we all like to play cards. I'm helping a fellow by the name of Jim Ledger clear a few acres, and in return, he's going to help me. Give us each enough land for a small crop as long as everything goes like it should. It may be getting a little late in the season for me. I'll have to find work again this winter, I'm afraid.

We all? What we all did he mean?

And *Find work again*? Maybe she was being unfair but it seemed he'd taken an awfully long time to heal and so avoided the problem of non-employment for more than half a year. As for her not liking to live primitive, well, she didn't like the way he discouraged her from joining him, either. Why did he? This wasn't what they'd planned in those exciting, loving days when they first eloped. Exactly what kind of deal had he and this Jim Ledger made?

Forcing these disgruntled thoughts away, she continued with the letter.

Meanwhile, ratty little dwellings are springing up all around. Log cabins, no less, if you can believe it. I should soon have more work than I can handle, building and rebuilding for folks who want something better. You'll see. A village, which right now is more like a few

*buildings thrown together in a haphazard way, has been
platted out near a year-round creek. Not too impressive
at the moment, but everyone is talking about growth
and schools and whatnot.*

*Seeing as how you got that raise, you need to send
me another ten dollars as soon as possible. I plan on
getting some seeds in the ground soon.*

*Hang on, Jacoba. Everything will work out fine. I've
got to go now. Jim is waiting on me.*

Your husband, Charles DeGroot.

Not one word about missing her. About loving her. About coming to see her. About her coming to see him, or even wanting her with him so they could build a life together. And ratty little log cabins . . . what did that mean? A school? A school meant children and women. Mrs. Merrimont came to mind.

Bitter thoughts flooded to the fore. Thoughts she tried to force down. One kept coming. Charlie had every concern about keeping this Jim Ledger waiting, but not her.

And really, the best way to ensure other homesteaders wanted his building services would be to erect their own house as quickly as possible and use it to demonstrate the standard of his work.

Jacoba had to laugh. He should take Madame as an example. A good example. She told everyone she owed her youthful looks to the creams and potions her cosmetic company created, although Jacoba was certain it owed more to her mother's excellent heritage. And, of course, she did take good care of herself. Her cosmetics truly were of superior quality and fortunately for Madame's profit and loss statement, they made scores of other women believe that through regular use they'd become as beautiful as she.

Charlie, she thought, could learn a thing or two from studying Madame's success.

The month turned, then another. Jacoba drudged on, enduring Supervisor Lehman's glowering looks when he was certain Mr. Lane wouldn't see. In mid-June the weather finally warmed, turning fine.

She hadn't heard from Charlie for at least ten days, and admitted to periods of worry. Even Mrs. Griswold mentioned the dearth of letters or postcards. Betty's expression showed commiseration. Jacoba just plain got angry.

Ten days? Yes. And the last time she'd heard from him he'd demanded twenty dollars. He had debts of honor, he said, that must be paid.

Heart heavy, she mailed the money.

While Charlie may not have suspected it of her, Jacoba knew exactly what the euphemism "debt of honor" meant. One of Madame's husbands had used the term. Often. Too often, in the end, for Madame to countenance. The end came in divorce.

And it meant Charlie had gambled and lost.

With Madame's example, Jacoba hadn't forgotten Charlie's mention of card playing. Or of his glee at winning a mere two dollars. Or of the smug closeness she sensed with his friend Jim Ledger.

It was time, past time, she paid her husband a visit. And, not necessarily of secondary importance, had a look at what one of these days would be her home.

Accordingly, Jacoba arranged to take the following Saturday off from work and give herself two full days away from the switchboard. Excitement trilled through her as, carrying a satchel with a few items necessary for an overnight stay, she rushed to catch the early train to Rockford. She wasn't exactly sure how she'd get to Hawkesford from there, but thought there must be a stable where she could hire a riding horse, if not a buggy.

After all, she was a homesteader now— or at least a homesteader's wife. She must be capable and resilient, and, yes, hardy. She'd always known how to ride. The rest she might have to learn.

* * *

Jacoba, much to her own astonishment, found mounting the steps and entering the railroad car to be more nerve-wracking than entering the telephone exchange the morning she'd applied for a job. In a word, difficult. She felt quite dizzy as she traversed the aisle and dropped gracelessly into a seat. The sun blazing through the grimy windows; heat already building and making the stale air hard to breath; the loud chatter of excited travelers; all combined to bring her back to the day of the train wreck. Would it would always happen, the fear and dread?

She closed her eyes to block out the scene and wished she could stopper her ears as well. A failed exercise, as it happened. The lurch as the train wheels caught and began to move almost made her cry out. Metal clacked on the track. She sat frozen, or perhaps she meant melted,into her seat as they gained speed.

The city disappeared behind them. Her eyes blurred. The countryside hazed into unformed flashes of green and brown. Her hands clenched and unclenched. Finally, after what seemed like hours but truly was less than one, the train slowed. It stopped beside a small building almost hidden amongst a stand of tall pine trees. Wobbly though she might be, Jacoba joined the other passengers who quickly disembarked. Within moments the train began moving again, a rush of black smoke and cinders billowing into the vivid blue sky as it continued on.

Jacoba, trying to compose herself, stood stock still and looked toward the town. She supposed she'd better follow the others— when her legs felt a bit stronger.

A woman wearing a concerned expression on her face stopped beside her. "Are you all right?" the woman asked. "Do you need help? I noticed you on the train and thought you seemed a little pale."

Drawing a deep breath, Jacoba felt some of the built-up tension roiling her insides release. The train had remained upright. She was alive.

"I'm fine, thank you for asking. Just glad to be on solid ground." She forced her fingers to relax and gave the woman a shaky smile. A middle-aged and prosperous appearing matron, she wore an ankle-topping dress that, though quite plain, was of a fine cotton material.

"Although," Jacoba added, while she had someone helpful at her side, "I do need to find a livery stable."

"A livery stable? Then let me be your guide." Suiting action to words, the woman took her arm and walked with her down a set of steps to the dusty ground. Piles of horse manure, wheel ruts and flattened weeds indicated this to be the thoroughfare into the town proper. "I am Mrs. Mitchell," she said. "My husband owns the machinery and feed store. The livery is right down the street from there. May I ask your destination?"

"I'm going onto the reservation. My husband, Charles DeGroot, is there. We're new homesteaders."

"Homesteaders?" Mrs. Mitchell eyed her. "If I may say so, my dear, you're not really dressed for it. I believe conditions are very rough on the reservation, at present. Folks there come here to buy their goods and groceries. Those," she added wryly, "who have the money."

Jacoba looked down at herself. She'd known not to wear one of her telephone girl outfits, as plain as they were. And also that, as Mrs. Mitchell indicated, conditions were a bit hardscrabble at the moment. But, since she planned on hiring a horse, she'd thought her attire of a riding skirt that ended at mid-calf and just covered the tops of her shiny brown boots, a pale green shirtwaist, and a light jacket, perfectly appropriate. "Not dressed for it?" she repeated.

Mrs. Mitchell laughed. "I imagine you will be a sight for sore eyes, as these westerners say, when your husband sees you. Although, if I may speak plainly, I'm quite shocked he isn't here to meet the train."

It seemed to Jacoba she heard a question at the end of that sentence. Should she have told Charlie she was coming? "It's to be a surprise," she said, wondering now at her own intentions.

The woman, pointing at a slurry of animal waste in their path, guided her around it. "As I'm sure it shall be." She delivered the comment in such a dry tone of voice as to make Jacoba wonder at it.

At the Rockford Livery, even upon Mrs. Mitchell's vouchsafing of her, the proprietor seemed a little leery of providing her with a horse, several of which drowsed in a corral in back of the barn.

He studied Jacoba, his set of woolly eyebrows drawing together. "You ever ridden before, missus?"

"Of course." She'd seen women in Spokane riding about wearing outfits much like hers, and yet, these people appeared to think her gear either inappropriate or outlandish. She wasn't sure which.

"Ridden across country?" he pressed on. "Wouldn't want to lose my horse if you got dumped."

Dumped? "Do you mean unhorsed?"

Mrs. Mitchell and the hostler shared a meaningful glance.

"I do," he said.

She shrugged. "I've been trained to never drop my reins. I assume your horse has been trained to stand."

At this, he laughed out loud. "To stand? More'n likely, he'd run off and leave you the one standin'. Coz, if you ain't in the habit of of being *unhorsed* I'd bet you'd drop your reins."

"Well," Jacoba started, fighting to keep her voice level, "I believe that remains to be seen."

Mrs. Mitchell, standing in a position to see out into the street, broke in on what seemed on the edge of becoming a contest of some sort. "Sarge, is that the LeTevere family's wagon I see going by?"

The proprietor, Sarge, peered out past Jacoba's shoulder. "Yep. Appears so."

Clearing her throat, Mrs. Mitchell said, "Perhaps they would be willing to take Mrs. DeGroot onto the reservation. Maybe even to her husband's homestead." She turned to Jacoba. "For a small fee. I'd suggest a dollar."

"DeGroot, you say?" Shaking his head and muttering indecipherably, Sarge clomped out past the women and gave an ear-splitting whistle. "Hey there. You, LeTevere, got a little favor to ask."

Turning, Jacoba spotted a tall-sided farm wagon driving down the street. Or what passed for a street, it being the main road through the countryside on the way to Idaho, as well. There was an automobile parked in front of a store, a rare sight outside of Spokane given the state of the roads.

The wagon, to Jacoba's dismay, was driven by a brown-skinned man wearing a high-crowned black felt hat. A couple feathers stood up from an intricately beaded hatband. On the seat beside him, a short woman with a brightly colored shawl wrapped around her shoulders—how she kept from sweltering Jacoba couldn't say—shook her head. In the wagon bed, a trio of children, all who kept moving around like restless puppies and were all nearly the same size, watched with wide dark eyes.

The team of four horses, each of a different size and color, stopped altogether at some unseen signal.

The man, LeTevere, gave Sarge, Mrs. Mitchell, and, most of all, Jacoba, the once over. "Whaddya want?" he asked. Not unfriendly, but not friendly, either.

Sarge's thumb jerked toward Jacoba. "This woman needs to get to the settlement on the reservation. She was gonna hire a horse but I think a ride along in your wagon would be better. She's apt to get lost, otherwise."

The Indian's dark eyes studied Jacoba. His mouth thinned as he caught the glare she shot at Sarge. "Don't think she wants to ride with us."

"He," she said, meaning Sarge, "seems to think I'll fall off any horse I get on. But I won't. Anyway, I don't see a single horse in this corral that would be any great loss if it did succeed in unseating me." Her hands landed on her hips. "Which it wouldn't."

The Indian woman's lips moved, although Jacoba defied anyone of the white people to hear a word. However, the man nodded. "Interesting idea to test," he said. "But not today. She may climb up."

At this, the woman scooted closer to her husband, making room.

"One dollar," she said.

Mrs. Mitchell smiled. "Told you," she said. "Better take the deal seeing that Sarge has his mind made up."

Indeed, the liveryman's jaw clamped tighter. "Welp, I don't want any of those . . . fellers . . . coming over here and ripping our town up. Which someone would be bound to do if anything happened to this lady."

Fellers? What had he meant to say. And just who did he mean? Chastened by his tone and intention, Jacoba picked up her satchel, which she'd set on a handy bag of feed where it wouldn't be dirtied, and nodded to Sarge. "Thank you for your concern, sir." She forced a smile. "But I would've been fine with your horse."

His face reddened.

Jacoba's smile at Mrs. Mitchell came more naturally. "I thank you for your concern and help, as well, Mrs. Mitchell. I am most happy to have met you."

"I hope to see you again, Mrs. DeGroot."

While the LeTevere horses stood still as planted posts, Jacoba climbed around the wheel and mounted the step up to the wagon seat. When seated, the man whistled to his team. Smooth as silk, surprising given their varying sizes, off they went.

Jacoba waited until they were out of Sarge's hearing before she said, "I would *not* have fallen off that man's horse. The nerve of him."

The Indian woman's laughter pealed. By the time they crossed a clackety little wooden bridge over Rock Creek, the two were chatting like friends.

"I was afraid you wouldn't speak English," Jacoba said. "I speak several languages, but not yours, I'm afraid. Perhaps you could teach me."

The woman's eyes opened wide. "Teach you? Why? Our own children are not allowed to learn their native language. We all, the children all, must speak English. It is the law."

"It is?" Brow puckering, Jacoba considered the idea. "How very

odd. Although I do have a friend who speaks with a German accent. She couldn't get hired to work for the telephone exchange
because of it." She could tell the subject upset Mary, whose name
she'd learned in the first minute of acquaintance. Mr. LeTevere's
name was Louis. The children, two boys and one girl, as it turned
out, had not been introduced, but the little girl was leaning against
Jacoba in a companionable sort of way.

Apparently, Jacoba thought, French names were, if not preferred, at least passable. Mary and Louis, she learned, had been
taught English, along with other subjects, at the Mary Immac-
ulate School, the site of an old Jesuit mission. Their children
would, perforce, follow them there but for now, with the eldest
only five, they were too young. Mary rued the day her children
would be taken away and sent to school. Jacoba felt for her. Felt
for the children too.

When she'd been six, Madame had sent her off to a Catholic
school to be trained in deportment and obedience and religion, among
other things. Sometimes she thought the schooling hadn't taken.

It was when Jacoba asked if Mr. LeTevere had heard of her husband that a silence fell. A silence so leaden as to weigh on her heart.

Chapter 13

A few cleared fields broke through areas of forest as they ranged through the countryside. Hills rose and fell. The road, after the previous days of rain had grown dusty again, a gray powder that rose in clouds beneath the horses' feet. Squawking and calling, birds flew in circles overhead, annoyed at the noise the humans made with their voices and the rattle of the wagon. A deer, fleet and graceful, bounded in front of the team. A second followed, then a third. The horses threw up their heads, with the second, larger pair prancing in place as the leaders came to a dead stop. Louis held off the reins until the last deer fled into the bushes.

"You should have shot the buck," Mary said. "We're running low on meat."

Louis flicked a quick glance toward Jacoba. "Not a good idea. I'll hunt when we get home. Or maybe kill a pig."

Grateful they were speaking again after her question about Charlie, Jacoba waited until the team had shaken out and regained its momentum. Oh, she could tell Louis had heard of her husband, all right. Not being stupid, or even naive enough to know what a sudden silence like that portended, she knew she'd have to follow up on the question. To the end, no matter what. A bitter end. She felt it coming.

Her indrawn breath was deep and loud. Mary's dark eyes flashed toward her, then away.

"What has he done?" Jacoba said. "My husband, Charles DeGroot."

After another of those tight periods of silence, she amended the question. "What has he done wrong? Something, I know. Please, tell me."

The silence held a minute longer, then Louis said, "He borrowed an axe from Vincent Gray Horse. Borrowed it for two days. After four days, Vincent needed his axe and asked for it back. This De-Groot, he got mad and slammed it into a rock. Ruined the edge. A piece flew off and caught Vincent in the leg. Bled for an hour. Then he had to take the axe to the blacksmith, pay to fix it. Had to buy a new head."

Jacoba's eyes closed tight, then she opened them again. She'd have to pay for the axe, the least she could do. "Was Mr. Gray Horse hurt badly?"

"Nah. But money out of pocket. No more favors for DeGroot."

The story worried Jacoba on several levels. "That doesn't sound like my husband. He is always careful to keep his tools in good order. He depends on them to make a living. Besides, he had a new axe when he came to here." Jacoba's brows drew together. "Why would he do such a thing to harm someone else?"

"He was drunk. Him and that Jim Ledger." Louis' blunt words pounded at her.

Jacoba gasped. "Drunk?" The Charlie she knew never over-imbibed, limiting himself to one beer, perhaps two at most.

"Laughing and stupid, both of them." Clearly, LeTevere had no great opinion of either Charlie or this Ledger person and made no bones about it.

Mary had something to say, too. "And Jim Ledger, he put his

hands on Naomi Gray Horse, Vincent's wife. He tried to . . ."

"Woman, hush," Louis said.

"Put his hands on her?" Jacoba forced words between tight lips. "Do you mean he tried to . . . violate her?" Rape seemed too drastic to say. "This Jim Ledger. But not my husband?"

Louis stared straight ahead, seemingly fixed on the road spiraling out in front of them. "Not your husband. But he did nothing to stop his friend."

Mortified beyond saying, Jacoba ducked her head. "Is there no law here? Can nothing be done?"

"Tribal police are the only ones who care and they can do nothing to the whites. The agent ignores all such trouble, coming here only if provoked. The white man's law also ignores all, especially insult to our women. Except maybe murder. Maybe stealing." Louis pondered a moment. "Big stealing, worth many dollars. Horses. Cattle. Small things they call borrowing, only nothing is ever returned."

That Charlie would attempt to permanently "borrow" Vincent Gray Horse's axe made Jacoba's stomach churn. What had happened to her husband in these months they'd been married? She blamed the train wreck. It had done more than break his leg and damage his health. It had done something to his spirit, as well. Made him bitter. Hard. Had she ever really known him at all, or only a facade he put on for her? Sometimes she hardly recognized him for the man she'd married, but *this.* This took an entirely different twist even as a new chapter of their life began. A chapter that did not bode well.

Sitting straighter on the hard, jouncing wagon seat as they penetrated farther into the reservation lands and its poor excuse for a road, she set her lips. This was not the Charlie she knew. It wasn't! On the instant she determined to quit her job at the telephone company at the end of this week, pack up their possessions, and move to the reservation, even if she did have to live in a tent. That's all there was to it.

Eventually, by early afternoon, they reached the LeTevere home.

Mary and the children climbed from the wagon, the children running and laughing as they played with a litter of black and white
puppies that had dashed out to greet them.

Although she'd heard most of the Indian-owned properties
were bare improvements over the native's old days of gathering
roots, shooting game, and living in teepees, she found the LeTevere homestead a tidy place, starting with a well-built two-sto-
ry house. Two barns, a couple sheds, and an outhouse with the
traditional crescent moon cut into the door lay near, but not too
near. Chickens pecked around in a pen, some pigs lolled under a
shade tree, a spotted milk cow chewed its cud, and a corral full of
fat horses neighed a greeting. A field of oats and another of what
she thought was wheat surrounded the place. It looked like any
prosperous mid-west farm.

"You have a nice place," she said.

"You are surprised?" Louis, sober-faced, nodded and flapped
the reins to start the team onward to where he said they'd find the
DeGroot homestead.

"Yes, a little," she said. "I understood this was all virgin territory.
Unsettled and raw."

"It's what the government wants you to believe. My family has
been here a long time."

Well, yes, she supposed so. It seemed obvious.

After a while, he said, "Not far now. Have you been here
before?"

"No." Her voice dropped. "My husband said he didn't want me
to come until he had a house built."

"A long wait for you." The laconic reply could've meant
anything.

Jacoba understood what he meant when, after threading the team
and wagon through forest thick with huge old pines, they came
at last to a clearing. Not a large clearing. Certainly not enough to
qualify as a field. Or, she thought, touching her upper lip to keep
it from curling, even much of a garden spot. What in the world

had Charlie been about, these past three months? A dozen or so medium-sized trees, their branches still attached, lay fallen criss-crossed over each other. A pile of ash and wood cooked down to charcoal showed where someone had made a start at clearing a spot. Close beside the fire's remains, a slightly scorched canvas wall tent leaned northward.

Helplessly, head reeling and dizzy, she turned to LeTevere. "This is it? Are you sure?"

He nodded. Pointing, he said, "We are close to the lake here, just over that ridge there. The DeGroot claim runs right down to the lake edge. There is a nice little bay down below this hill, so you'll have good water here, too, when somebody digs a well."

She saw no sign of one. No sign of Charlie, either. Or of the horses, Pym and Tope. She did see what appeared to be where he kept the animals, a rope enclosure and some hobbles lying on the ground.

Slowly, she clambered down from the wagon and proffered the agreed upon one dollar fare. "Thank you, Mr. LeTevere. I hope we'll meet again. And Mary and the children, too. I appreciate what you've told me, even if . . . if . . . it was unsettling."

An understatement.

Louis stared around, apparently doubtful of leaving her alone at the deserted camp. "You know your way to my place, Missus? In case . . ." He stopped.

"In case my husband doesn't show up here tonight?" Jacoba finished the question for him.

He nodded. "Saturday night."

Her jaw set. "I'm aware." Drawing in a deep breath, she straightened her shoulders. Madame always said one could take attitude from one's erectitude . . . not that there even was such a word, but her daughter grasped what she meant. Something along the lines of the inner self growing to meet the outer self, and by damn, that outer self better look the part one intended to become. Or something.

Forcing a cheery smile, she waved one last time as the Tevere's wagon made a sharp turn and retreated the way they'd come. Then it grew eerily silent, only the susurrant sigh of the forest and the calls of birds to break the stillness. The scent of pine resin rose all around. She smelled barnyard, too, although no animals were in sight. It seemed to her that underneath it all, she detected the slightly fishy odor of the lake, although the trees and verdant underbrush grew so thickly she saw no trace of water from where she stood.

Jacoba had never felt so alone. Shuddering, the hair on her arms rose like the hackles on a frightened dog.

Turning in a circle, she surveyed the camp. Not homesite. Camp. Anger roiled her gut and twisted her stomach into knots. Anger and disgust. Almost three months to cut a dozen trees and drag them here? Or was this where they'd grown in the first place? She thought some stumps indicated so. Why, Charlie hadn't even started a rudimentary shelter for those big horses with their demand of quantities of fodder and grain.

And the money she been sending to Charlie for the things he'd listed, what about that? Food for him and the horses. Equipment, including, as her memory dredged up that list, *two* good axes and a used flatbed wagon that he'd said he'd build sides for. Better sides than anything store bought, had been his brag. Where were they?

Where were the panes of glass he'd said he'd soon need for the house? The house that hadn't even been marked out on the ground, let alone started. The nails, lumber, fittings, bricks and mortar, various other items she'd never even known a house required. Where were they? The only thing she found was a large milk can that contained water.

Had those other things all been stolen? Or had they never been realized in the first place?

Evidently, the money had disappeared, but where—no, on what—had it been spent? She thought she knew the answer. Was afraid she knew the answer.

And, most of all, where was Charlie?

At the fire, a few embers were hot enough that when Jacoba built a little tent of twigs and dry grass over them, then gently blew, a flame leapt into being. Within a few minutes she had enough of a fire going that a soot-blackened pot she found soon heated enough water for some tea.

She entered the tent and found, nose wrinkling at the stale smell, not the hoped for glass window panes or paint or any other building supplies stored within, but not even the longed for tea. Only a few tins of food, beans, peaches, tomatoes, along with a couple cots with rumpled bedrolls spread over the canvas. Two cots, both used? Who had been sleeping in the second one?

So, she discovered no tea, but only some coffee. While she waited for it to boil and the grounds to settle, Jacoba stomped around the tent. Out back, a stack of grass hay had been piled along the outside wall of the tent where it served as both fodder for Tope and Pym, and insulation. Farther back, she spotted a rope line stretched between trees making a sort of corral. A galvanized wash tub, rife with green scum upon an inch of water, served as an occasional watering trough. A great deal of manure, clearly not cleared away for weeks, spread a noisome aroma around the area.

A growing rage lent her the strength to tip out the tub. No animal in her presence was going to drink out of such a filthy utensil.

Even to Jacoba's inexperienced eyes, this was a puny effort at homesteading. She figured she could done better all by herself. Certainly no worse.

Her emotions rattling about like marbles in a tin can, she drank her coffee. At some length, when the silence became almost overwhelming, she remembered Louis saying the lake was just over the hill. She might as well take a peek. Catch the lay of the land.

If she had expected a sandy beach and a pleasant stroll along the lakeshore, disappointment lay in store. Oh, she found a path of sorts through the woods, all right. Thank Pym and Tope for that, their big feet having pounded a zigzag route down the steep hill to the bay. Steep? If it hadn't been for the horses' work, she probably wouldn't have been able to keep her feet but instead skidded down on her derrière. As it was, the way suited the horses, but she'd rather had steps. Many, many steps.

And once down, she found a simple drop-off at the lake's edge. No beach. Even the horse's watering spot looked a bit treacherous.

But what she did find was that across the bay, a long dock protruded out into the lake. A tidy cabin sat in a flat spot, smoke curling from a chimney. This place did have a beach of sorts. Not a sandy beach, but nicely mowed grass right down to the water. It appeared that a natural flat area had been enlarged enough for a garden spot, a barn, and a couple small outbuildings. A trail wide enough for a farm wagon to maneuver zig-zagged to the top of the hill. A hill, luckily for the homeowners, not so tall and steep as the one on the DeGroot property.

Jacoba looked landward first, patting the sweat from her face with a hanky. As she caught her breath after the rather challenging descent to the lakeshore, she studied the boat tied up at the dock. A fairly large boat, she saw now, one that could transport heavy goods across the lake to and from . . . where? Coeur d'Alene, she supposed.

Made small by distance, she watched two men, one followed by a large dog, push wheeled carts onto the dock toward the boat. Farther out, where the bay met the broad dark waters of the lake, a flotilla of logs had been bound together. A boom, she believed it was called.

After watching a while, she trudged, panting and legs aching with strain, back up the hill to the camp and waited for Charlie to return.

Turns out she had another visitor first. Or rather, two visitors.

She heard them coming before they came in sight. No voices, but just a rustling of the brush, a tumble of stones, some panting breaths.

Being alone in the middle of nowhere hadn't bothered her before. Now it did. She wished for a weapon and picked up a stick.

The first visitor succeeded in scrambling up the same trail she had taken, burst from the forest and barked a question at her. Startled, she took a long step back.

At least, a question is what Jacoba thought she heard and she replied as if she had. "I'm Jacoba. Who are you?" Not a bear, anyway, she thought. But then, she hadn't really expected one.

On this note, the dog's tail wagged and he, or she, Jacoba couldn't tell through the long hair obscuring such details, bounded over to greet her with a lick on the hand, then raced off to encircle the campsite, stopping to lift a leg and mark territory every few feet.

A male then, Jacoba concluded. One that in color looked remarkably like a relative of the puppies that had been ecstatic when the LeTevere children got home.

"Well," she said, spinning to watch with a smile breaking through what had been her dour thoughts, "make yourself at home."

A second visitor stepped from the shadowed timber. "He will," the man said, "as long as he's not discouraged."

Startled, Jacoba's heart struck a stronger beat, pulsing in her ears. For the second time in an hour, she felt a little dizzy. "Why would I discourage him?" The stick dropped from her hand.

The man grinned. "Because otherwise he's going to mark every single place you've been."

Indeed, the dog did appear to have been tracking her, even into the tent and right back out.

At a whistle, the dog whisked over and sat in front of the man.

In front of Ruel Gagne, her savior from the train, who said, "How do you do, Mrs. DeGroot? Have you come to stay?"

"I do well, Mr. Gagne, thank you. And you? I see your arm is healed." Her voice, despite herself, quavered a tiny bit.

He swung the arm around, causing the dog to jump up and stand at attention. "It's fine."

An awkward pause hung in the air between them, until Gagne moved toward her, the dog with him.

"What is your dog's name?" Jacoba asked.

"Quill."

"Quill?"

At the sound of his name, the dog's ears, which were a funny cross between flapped and pricked, bounded to her and sat. She reached down to scratch his head. "I like your name," she told him.

"He's always been curious about everything. When only four weeks old, he became curious about a porcupine and ended up with his nose full of quills."

"Oh, poor baby."

Gagne stood in front of her, his dark eyes narrowed. "I thought . . . ." He paused, studying her as if she were a puzzle he needed solve. "Are you here to stay?" he asked again.

Chapter 14

"Stay here?" Jacoba's gaze took in her surroundings, eyeing the sagging tent, the piles of slash, and the stinking horse pen. She came to a quick decision. "Tonight, yes. Tomorrow I must return to Spokane and my job."

Gagne smiled. "I see. Coyotes serenade us most every night. Don't be afraid of them, They're just out hunting for their dinner."

Jacoba flinched. "They don't eat people do they?"

Her question drew a full-fledged chuckle. "No. They're more apt to be looking for mice."

"Good. I didn't know I'd have to sleep outside of walls."

His eyebrows lifted.

She shrugged. "I expected to find a more developed homesite here. Charlie . . ." She broke off, forcing back the words that wanted to burst forth. Loyalty demanded more of her. "Have you met my husband?"

"Seen him around, not to talk to."

"Oh." Jacoba stared at the ground. What in the world had gotten into Charlie? He knew the name of the man who'd saved him that awful day of the train wreck, and here Gagne was, right over the hill and come to greet her. He and his dog. Charlie must know where to find him. The least he owed Ruel Gagne was to say thank you in person.

"Do you live down there, by the lake?" she asked.

"My mother does. I built the dock and use it for my boat, so I'm often here for a night or two. I transport mail and goods from Coeur d'Alene to this side of the lake, and ship out produce and other goods to meet the train over there."

"And people?"

"Sometimes people. There will be a train stopping at this landing soon that'll ship logs to the big Coeur d'Alene sawmills. For now, I float the logs across the bay to the mill's pens. That's why you see so many in the bay right now. I'm getting ready to take'em across tomorrow. I'm just waiting for Anderson to skid down his logs."

Jacoba understood only part of this explanation. What she did sense was that he wanted her to know him for a man of substance. A man who had goals and accomplished them.

He smiled at her. "I saw your photograph in the Spokane newspaper. You looked . . . out of sorts. The reporter said you saved a man with a bullet wound from bleeding to death. And you said you could help because of what you learned from people at the train wreck. So something good came of that."

"I said, 'a man at the wreck.' I learned from you." She didn't miss his flush of pleasure. So different from Charlie's embarrassment over the whole encounter. Embarrassed *because* she had helped. "And you're right. I didn't want my picture taken."

"Hmm," he went on, "so, if I ring for the telephone operator and a lady speaks, will she be you?"

Jacoba laughed. "I don't know. Possibly, but there are twenty of us at any single time."

"Then maybe one day I'll try it and see."

"For one more week." Her smile died. "Then I'm quitting. I . . . I need to come here. To help my husband."

Ruel's jaw tightened as he gazed around the clearing. He may not have realized it, but to Jacoba, his thoughts were all too clear. Worse, they jibed not only with Louis Tevere's, but with her own. Feelings she didn't want to have and most certainly did not want to show.

"I don't think he's ready for you yet, Missus. I think you'd best stick with your job in town a while yet." He held out his hand, and unthinking, she took it. His thumb brushed her fingers, her palm.

"Your hand is soft," he said. "Fine. The hand of a lady. Homesteading—" he shook his head. "Homesteading is hard work."

Snatching her hand back, her temper flared. "You think I'm useless? That I can't work hard?"

Quill, the dog, whined and pawed at her riding skirt.

"I think you can." His dark gaze bored into her. "But if you were mine, I wouldn't want you to know the hardship."

His? "I'm . . . I'm . . ." she started, but at that moment, the sound of a wagon rattling over the trail through the woods reached them. Charlie's voice, singing a song bawdy enough to make her blush, cut the forest's stillness. Their stillness, Ruel's and Jacoba's.

"I shouldn't have said that. Forget it." Ruel shook his head. "Come, Quill," he said, and strode off into the timber, the dog, after a moment, following him. Only the dog looked back.

* * *

Ruel Gagne hadn't wanted Charlie to see him. That much was clear. Jacoba could only wonder why.

Motionless, she stood in the shade of a giant pine waiting for Charlie to arrive. So motionless, in fact, he apparently didn't notice her until he'd almost driven past.

"Whoa." He brought the team to a halt and stared at her out of bloodshot eyes. "Jacoba? Is that you?" His bewildered voice belied the proof of her presence, then it hardened. "What are you doing here?"

Did he see her as an apparition?

It was not the welcome she'd hoped for. That she should've been able to expect.

"Hello, Charlie. I came to see how work at the homestead is coming along." An arched brow and her glance around the small clearing spoke volumes. "And to visit my husband. Aren't you glad to see me?" If that last sounded sour, well, maybe that had been her intent.

Charlie made a gesture that set Pym and Tope to shuffling their huge feet. "As you can tell, I ain't exactly ready for visitors."

She almost laughed. Little did he know he'd mirrored Ruel Gagne's estimation. Except she felt they came from different motivations.

Ain't? Her amusement died as his words echoed in her ear. Since when did Charlie speak with low grammar? An answer occurred. *Since his 'friendship' with this Jim Ledger he'd written about. And who the LeTevere's had spoken of, the couple's colliding glances speaking volumes.*

"I'm not a visitor." It took effort, but Jacoba held her voice level and steady. "This is my land, too. My life. I have to tell you, Charlie, I envisioned things a little differently. You've been here almost three months. I saw other homesteads along the way. Most have homes built on them. People have begun clearing their land. They've planted crops, started gardens."

Fiddling the reins, Charlie's face took on that sulky look she'd grown to dread during the past winter. "I've been busy. Those other people have families to help, or they've got the money to hire somebody. I've just got me."

"What about this man, this Jim Ledger, you wrote me about. You said you'd been trading work." An evil demon caused her to add, "When you aren't playing cards and drinking alcohol." Able to smell the stale odor of whiskey, she knew that now, too.

"A man's got to have some fun at day's end."

Charlie's whip lashed out over Tope's back, causing the big

horse to shift in the traces.

Jacoba jumped aside, her eyes narrowing as Charlie and the wagon continued on toward the makeshift corral. She followed him around to where he halted the wagon, dust rising in her face. She couldn't help thinking of Ruel Gagne just then. His dark eyes. His concern. His gentle touch on her palm.

She was relieved he'd gone. She wished he'd stayed.

Although hours of daylight remained, Charlie declared himself done working for the day.

"We should celebrate being together again," he said, his grin both sheepish and meaningful. "It's been a while. Too long."

It took a moment for her catch the insinuation. When she did, it brought a flush to her face. Right now, she didn't in the least appreciate his mode of "celebration."

At least he'd brought some groceries, she discovered, peering into the wagon bed. A relief since she hadn't eaten since a bite at the boarding house before catching the train.

Charlie took his time unhitching the horses and removing the harness. He let it drop where it fell, and instead of brushing the sweat from the horses' neck and shoulders, he loaded some water cans over their bare backs and started them down the beaten trail to the lake.

Fortunately, the horses knew their way and moved slowly, reins tied over their necks, plodding down the slippery slope without guidance.

Astonished at Charlie's lack of attention to the horses, Jacoba didn't know what to think. He'd been so eager when he'd been searching for a team. Then, when he'd first purchased Pym and Tope and paid top dollar, he'd taken every care of them. Jacoba had happily helped. But now, he'd flicked Tope with the whip, cutting hair, if not skin. He hadn't bothered to brush them. He hadn't even picked up the sweat-soaked harness. Worse, she'd spotted a gall on Pym, where the stiffened leather had rubbed a sore spot.

She'd take care of that, herself. She had a healing balm with her, good for horses as well as humans.

When Charlie and the horses returned to the camp, for Jacoba couldn't bring herself to call a tent and a rope corral a homesite, he went immediately into the tent.

"I'm tired," he explained. "I'm going to lie down for a while. It was too hot, working out in the sun. It's drained me dry."

He did look drained all right, but presently, when Jacoba heard the gurgle of liquid sloshing in a bottle, she knew it hadn't been the heat or the sun or working too hard that plagued Charlie. Hair of the dog, she believed they called the cure, in the belief a few shots of the very thing that worked against you, would also cure you.

Her anger grew. Useless anger, as it happened, because when she peeked in at him a few minutes later, she found her husband asleep and snoring like a rumbling volcano on one of the cots. So it was she who stood on an overturned bucket to reach high enough to thoroughly brush Pym and Tope. Their skin shivered with delight and, she was sure, gratitude. She'd found the salve to doctor Pym's gall in her satchel. Using the scented potion on a horse brought a smile to her lips. The tin showed Madame's trademark on the lid, a sight that made her feel nostalgic and, oddly enough, grateful. Madame did, after all, provide value in the effectiveness of her costly ingredients.

Setting to work cleaning Pym's collar, Jacoba fretted. What had gotten into Charlie? Or more appropriately, what had been taken out of him? The change from the sweet, considerate young man she'd married puzzled her. Hurt her. Frightened her.

His lovemaking— did she mean lust—that night did nothing to change those feelings.

Even during the winter they'd cuddled, before and after. Shared kisses. Caresses. Gentleness. Love. Most of the time. But not this night.

This night he reared above her, pounding, jerking, once even pinching a particularly tender spot. She'd cried out. Said, "Stop. You're hurting me," and he'd laughed and said, "You like it rough, don't you?" And she'd said, "No. Please, stop."

But he hadn't.

She'd cried when it was all done, but he'd just gone to sleep.

After a while, Jacoba disentangled herself from his heavy arm laid across her breasts, got up, and washed, careless of any noise she might make. It didn't matter anyway. Charlie slept on. To her relief really, because how could she face him now? She couldn't even bear to look at him.

Dressing quickly, she went outside into the chill darkness. Seeking out the horses for comfort, she found it in the warmth and the soft velvet touch of their noses as she pondered what to do now. Because if this wasn't a dire predicament she was in, she didn't know one when she saw it.

Finding a perch on a tree stump, first putting a piece of canvas over the cut part to prevent her skirt from contacting the sticky pitch ooze, she sat under the light of a half-moon. Although she would've preferred not to think at all, her memories drifted back to this time last year.

She remembered protesting Madame's plan to procure a rich husband for her. "I don't want to be married," she had said, flat out. Vehemently. "Especially to this . . . . this person."

Madame had watched Jacoba's horrified reaction to the proposal reflected in her dressing room mirror with a sly smile. Soft-skinned, perfumed, elegant in her dress and person, as a final touch, Madame tucked a sprig of tiny rose buds in her thick dark hair. She was hosting the best of St. Louis society tonight and had just now informed Jacoba of her dinner partner. And of his proposal.

"You object?" Madame had said.

"To Mr. Thorenson? Really, Mother? He practically dodders. Of course I object. His only conversation is of how rich he is and how he could've married into royalty if he'd wanted, but he thought the princess *too old*. Princess Elena is thirty-five!"

Madame's laughter pealed merrily as she fluttered a hand in a dismissive manner. "Haven't you learned anything from me? The best kind of rich man to marry when you're young is an old one. A very old one, by preference."

"As old as Mr. Thorenson?" Without stopping to think, because really, she knew the answer, Jacoba said, "Why?"

She'd had to withstand one of those looks her mother so proficiently administered when her daughter's apparent obtuseness thwarted her own ambitions. A Thorenson connection could be very profitable if they began selling Madame cosmetics in the Thor department stores.

"You know the answer to that." Madame touched up an errant eyebrow hair with a fine brown pencil. "Old men don't live forever, you know. When they're old you have much more freedom to pursue your own desires. And to control your own destiny when they're . . . gone."

Of course, Jacoba knew that. Madame had built her empire in just such a manner. But the idea repelled her. She was quite certain money, while important, didn't mean *everything*.

And then she'd met Charlie. A working man, young, good looking, kind, who spoke to her without condescending. Ambitious to make his own way, he said and she believed him, although he often spoke somewhat bitterly of being left out of his father and brother's plans for the future. She certainly couldn't understand why. And neither, apparently, could Charlie.

Although, she thought, coming back to the present and staring around the dreary camp in which she found herself, perhaps she understood now. Her eyes had been opened. She recognized that Charlie had most likely always been something of a slacker. He'd hidden it from her, but perhaps not from his father and his brother.

Anyway, she and Charlie had eloped and embarked on their great adventure. Became homesteaders. Here they were, on an Indian reservation in remote Idaho, with her sitting under the moon talking to horses and listening to crickets and a couple coyotes vocalizing in a song. The thought brought a wry smile to her face.

Could be Madame had been right. That rich old man might've been a better choice.

But that was before Ruel Gagne's visage drifted into her mind. Drifted in *again,* against every instinct telling her she shouldn't allow it.

* * *

Jacoba, stretching her body, sore from last night's . . . debacle . . . rose from the second cot shivering with cold in the early morning stillness. The sun, promising a warm day later on, found its way between trees to send a welcome shaft of light into the tent.

Charlie had yet to stir, although he no longer snored.

Already dressed, Jacoba pulled on her shoes and went outside to stir up the fire. Putting the coffee on to boil, she went around back to check Pym and Tope. To her satisfaction, the gall on Pym's shoulder already looked a little improved. She made certain they had grain, hay, and water before going back to start breakfast.

Preparing food would be tricky over an open fire. Especially for someone who really had very little cooking experience. Mrs. Griswold had given permission for her to observe the process, however, so she'd been learning. And, by copying every one of Mrs. G's moves, Betty had helped her successfully make a batch of feather-light biscuits. But that had been in a real oven. Not over a campfire.

Sighing, Jacoba set to work. Pancakes seemed a better option. And bacon. Anyone could cook bacon, the aroma of which soon drew Charlie from the tent, his nose twitching. A Charlie more like the one with whom she'd eloped.

But that, she heard a voice in her head say, remained to be seen.

"Jacoba," he said, warmth in his voice as he held his hands out to the fire. "What are you doing?"

"Fixing breakfast."

"You've learned to cook?" His astonishment struck a chord.

"Yes," she said. "After all, how hard can it be?"

But perhaps he didn't remember his own words the way she did. At any rate, they clearly passed over his head.

"I'll be damned," he said.

Not especially flattering. But then, as though struck by shame, he ducked his head and turned first red, then faded to pale. "Are you all right? I mean— last night. I . . . we . . . I . . ." He reached out to her.

Apparently his memory went back *that* far, Jacoba thought.

"Yes. *You*," she said coolly, moving away from his touch. "Am I all right? What do you think?"

His arms were still extended. "I think you're not." His arms dropped. "Jacoba, honey, I'm sorry. I didn't mean to hurt you. The whiskey. It was the whiskey. You've got to forgive me."

Squatting, she turned the bacon in the skillet. *Got to forgive him?* Forming an answer to the demand moved beyond her. The look on his face last night as he *raped* her. The satisfaction he took from using her body.

No. She didn't want to remember.

"Please." The entreaty came in his most soulful voice. "Say you forgive me. Jacoba, you're breaking my heart."

She looked up at him then, and stood to face him, trying to think if she owed any forgiveness. Owed an answer. Owed him for a broken heart.

At the edge of the timber, a large hirsute creature broke from the brush and dashed toward them.

Cursing, Charlie reached inside the tent for his rifle. A rifle she didn't even know he had. "Get out of the way," he yelled. "I'll shoot the sonofa—"

Jacoba put her hand on the gun barrel and pushed it down as the animal arrived and leapt against her. She staggered under the dog's eager onslaught.

"Hello, Quill," she said, laughing as his feathery tail whipped against her legs.

"Wait." Charlie's blue eyes snapped with instantaneous anger. "You know this dog? It's a damned pest." His gaze grew sharper. "You called it a name. You know its name?"

He snapped the gun barrel out of her hand and slammed it against her side.

Crying out, she winced away, knowing there'd be a bruise. "That hurt," she said, regaining her voice.

"Then take care. I won't stand for interference. I don't want that damn dog coming around here and I'll shoot any stray that shows up. Understood?"

She took the time to rescue bacon in danger of scorching and stood, a plate filled with crisp hot strips in her hand. Although certain her expression held an answering anger, she said, "You should make the acquaintance of your neighbors, Charlie. I'm pretty sure you'd do better with them than with this Jim Ledger I've heard about."

"Neighbors, indeed. A bunch of damn Indians, is what they are. Them or that dog, they'd better stay the hell off my land. I'd as soon shoot one as the other. And mind your own business. Jim is a friend of mine."

Jacoba stomach gave a lurch. Inwardly, rage gathered.

Outwardly, her voice sounded quite calm. Cool and restrained. Ladylike and measured. Like Madame, she thought, astonished at herself, only without Madame's sometimes charming accent.

"You haven't bothered to learn who they are. Your neighbors' names, I mean. Have you?"

"Why should I? I don't care."

"But you should. Does the name Ruel Gagne mean anything to you?"

"Yes. He's the man . . ."

Jacoba finished the sentence for him. "Yes. He's the man who saved your life. And this is his dog."

Chapter 15

Jacoba had the idea Charlie put in a full morning's work only because she was on site to urge him on. Taking frequent rests, he chopped limbs from the felled trees, and she, favoring her sore side where the gun had struck, gathered them into a pile to dry in preparation of burning. A slash pile, he called it, as if proud of a new word in his vocabulary.

The piney smell made up for the hard work. Almost. She wished she knew how to bottle the scent. When she came here to live, she resolved to discover if it was possible. Perhaps she could distill it and keep the fragrance true.

"I'll be such a mess on the train this evening. I hope people won't notice." She brushed in an ineffectual way at the dirt, dust, and, unfortunately, a blob of pitch stuck on her shirtwaist. Her dark hair, released from its usual neat twist at the nape of her neck, hung in tangles around her sweaty face.

Panting, Charlie looked up from his chopping, took off his hat and fanned himself with it. "It's no one else's business. This train, though, they're mostly local people. There'll be others who look worse." He studied her appearance. "Although you do look a bit . . . soiled. I wish you didn't have to go back to town, Jake. We're getting a lot done here today."

She pressed her hand against her side. "We are."

Jake. He'd called her by the old pet name, just as though last night and even this morning hadn't happened. As if he hadn't raged at her and struck her with his gun. Jacoba had mixed feelings about that. One part of her was relieved not to be quarreling with him. Another part fumed, to say the least, over the treatment he'd subjected her to. He hadn't apologized. Hadn't said a word. Had it been an accident?

It didn't seem like an accident.

Then there was the scene about the dog and Ruel Gagne. Another, a secret part of her, bristled over the way he'd dismissed Ruel. How she felt about her "savior" versus how she felt about Charlie. Although, thinking it over, sometimes she had trouble understanding anything when it came to Charlie. He was a bit of a Jekyll and Hyde character, a disturbing trait to discover at this date.

Take this property, for instance. Had winning an allotment on the reservation been a catastrophe rather than the boon she had first thought?

She couldn't help wondering if, once relieved of the responsibility of creating something fine out of sheer wilderness, Charlie would go back to being the man she'd married?

But then, there was the way he refused to answer her questions about Jim Ledger.

At mid-morning, when they stopped to reheat the coffee and eat a leftover pancake smeared with honey, she brought up what she'd heard about Ledger. People said he had put his hands on a young girl. A euphemism. They meant he'd done a lot more. A lot worse.

"Lies." Charlie's rebuttal came quickly. "Whoever told you that lied. Girls fall all over Jim. Those Indian girls, they want white men to . . ."

"To what? Force them? Who told you that? Him?" Jacoba didn't bother to hide her scorn.

"Everybody says so."

"Everybody!" She snorted. "Did the girls?"

He was silent.

"I don't believe it. Not for one second. Sounds like a man making excuses for his bad behavior to me." She closed her mouth on adding, 'And he's taking you down with him.' Push Charlie too far and he was likely to grow stubborn. Or maybe, given his behavior last night and this morning, worse than stubborn. Violent.

"You don't know anything about him," he said, eyeing her with a grim expression. "Jim is good man. A hard worker. These squaws? They're asking for it. Half of them are drunk, anyway."

He broke off, but Jacoba knew his denials for a lie. The quick excuses he made for Ledger showed that he'd known right away what she'd meant. Who she'd meant. And maybe even he correlated that story with the way he had treated her.

She did.

"Maybe he'd better be careful," she said in cautious warning. "Men have been shot for less. Decent men won't stand for their women—or children—being abused."

They didn't speak for another hour. Late afternoon found Pym and Tope plodding gently through the near dark, carrying her back to Rockford where she'd catch the evening train to Spokane. Jacoba found the silence between them a relief.

By then Charlie had made a list of necessaries for her to send to him. For one thing, the windowpane glass she'd already sent money for. Money which, as far as she could tell, had gone for gambling and drink.

"I want you to write to your mother, Jacoba." He stared ahead into dusk. "It wouldn't hurt to start making amends. I . . . we . . . have to get some money or we'll lose the homestead."

We? I? Jacoba had doubts about how much *she* figured into his plans. She didn't even have to think about his claim. She clamped her lips. "No."

"No? What do you mean, no?" His voice hardened, rising as if she sat yards away instead of just inches. "Listen to me. You need to do whatever is necessary to keep us afloat. It's not like Madame Ludke will miss a few hundred. Or even a few thousand, for that matter."

"It is not my mother's responsibility to give us money. We're young and strong. We can and will make our own way. I've managed so far. I guess I can a while longer."

"Dammit, woman, don't be so stubborn. It's not enough."

"It will have to do. I refuse to beg."

Hissing between his teeth, he snapped the rein's over the horses' backs, making them shake their massive heads.

Charlie's plea turned into a whine as he listed his demands. He needed a grinding wheel to keep his axe honed and the two-bottom plow sharp, he said. He needed buckets. He needed food, both for him and grain for the horses.

He needed, in Jacoba's opinion, someone to keep his head on straight and keep him working. Someone to make sure he stayed away from Jim Ledger.

Sighing over the length of the list, Jacoba resigned herself to at least one more month as a telephone girl.

At the train station, their goodbye, which consisted of a quick peck on the cheek, struck her as self-conscious and perfunctory, admittedly on her part as well as his. Charlie not only didn't help her off the wagon, but didn't wait to see her onto the train. He simply turned the team back toward the reservation as soon as she alit.

As if he can't wait to be rid of me. The thought rose and refused to leave.

* * *

"How is your new home coming along?" Mrs. Griswold greeted Jacoba as if they met by chance, although Jacoba thought *chance* didn't factor in. They were in the entrance hall, the landlady with the front door key in hand.

Mrs. Griswold's eyes widened as she took in her boarder's disheveled appearance. "My word, Mrs. DeGroot, is everything all right? Is your husband well? You weren't in another accident, were you? Attacked by wild Indians?"

Knowing she looked a fright, Jacoba cringed. *Not attacked by Indians. Just my husband.* Not that she could possibly say such a thing out loud.

Mrs. Griswold's pointed and probing questions did nothing to restore Jacoba's already low self-esteem. Nonetheless, she answered her landlady with every sign of assurance. Embarrassing to admit to a half-truth and lies.

"My husband is doing well," she said. *Or would be if he stayed off the liquor and away from bad influences.* "Everything is fine." *A flat-out lie.* "Our house is . . . coming along." *Only if one considered a dozen cut logs progress.*

"I'm very happy for you," Mrs. Griswold gushed. "I suppose I'd better start looking for a new tenant right away, then. You'll be moving to the homestead soon, I expect."

Jacoba, hoping Mrs Griswold wouldn't complain too much when she heated water for a bath, edged around the older woman and headed for the cellar stairs to light the boiler. "Not just yet, I'm afraid. But soon. My husband wants to spare me the hardship, right now." *And he needs the money from my wages.* But of course, she didn't say that part out loud, either. Tried not to say it even to herself. Was that her only value? It seemed so.

"That's very considerate of him." One of Mrs. Griswold's eyebrows crawled upward as she spoke. "I hadn't thought . . . Well, I'd better get the house locked up. I believe everyone is in for the evening."

Jacoba continued down into the chilly, and rather dank, dirt-floored cellar wondering what the landlady had meant to say. Mrs. G had grown rather impatient with Charlie over the winter. Impossible not to notice. And she wasn't the only one, as Jacoba discovered the next morning.

Worn out from a weekend of tension and physical labor, not to mention her bruised side, Jacoba slowly made her way down the stairs from the third floor, gripping the handrail as she forced stiff, aching muscles to respond. The bending, the lifting, the stretching. She wasn't used to such strenuous work.

Clamping her mouth shut on a groan, she paused on the second floor landing for a cramp to ease, which is how she came to overhear a private conversation. One she'd not only never been intended to hear, but one she'd rather *not* have heard. Still, when her name was mentioned, how could she not listen?

Cautiously, she peeked around the corner into the hall.

"I see you've set young Mrs. DeGroot a place at the table, Betty." The schoolteacher, Miss Madison, spoke in her precise, though rather nasal, tones.

"Yes, ma'am," Betty replied. "Mrs. Griswold says she got back from the reservation last night."

To Jacoba's ears, the hired girl sounded harried, probably because there'd be people demanding she be in two places at once—as happened most every morning. Right now, the two stood outside the bathroom door where Betty had just handed in a dry towel, which a hairy male arm had retrieved. The girl had kept her blushing face turned aside.

"I hope this doesn't mean that awful husband of hers is coming back here," Miss Madison said. "Have you heard whether he's gone for good?"

Awful? Jacoba cringed.

"No, ma'am." Betty's flat voice discouraged further questions, but the schoolteacher, probably accustomed to drawing answers from unwilling, or unprepared students, forged on.

"I was almost prepared to get up a petition asking Mrs. Griswold to evict him this spring, before he left. He'd gotten fresh with me, you know. Ask Mrs. Ellers. She saw him, and she told me he'd been very rude to her."

Mrs. Ellers was the old lady with the cane whom Charlie had wanted to utilize as a servant.

"Oh," Betty said, but not as if she were shocked.

Silent, Jacoba's brows drew down. What did the schoolteacher mean, *gotten fresh*? Surely not! It wasn't as if the woman was a raving beauty exuding sexual invitation, after all. More of a dry stick and a stickler for proper formality.

Unless . . . had he really been that bored? Harassed her for the sheer sport of it?

"I know you helped out when Mr. DeGroot was on crutches, dear girl," Miss Madison continued her probe. "Did you have any trouble with him?"

Silence. Then the teacher said in a crow's caw of what—delight? Vindication?— "There. I knew it. What did he do?"

Betty, almost inaudible, stammered, "I . . . I'm not supposed to say. Mrs. Griswold told me not to tell anyone. Especially not Mrs. DeGroot. And the missus talked to him. He stopped."

"Well," Miss Madison said, "I can understand that. His wife is a perfectly nice, hardworking and educated lady. But," her next words were loaded with drama, "the wife is always the last to know."

And Betty said, "Ya. But I say we should keep it at that."

Pain, embarrassment, horror, rage—every kind of worrisome emotion one could fall prey to landed on Jacoba in a merciless heap. How was she ever to hold her head up again? What Charlie did reflected on her. She knew that. Unfair, perhaps, but that was life. And while she might take Miss Madison's story with a grain of salt, she believed Betty. Had to. Especially after her visit to the reservation.

Swallowing hard, no longer noticing the aches and pains previously plaguing her, she continued down the stairs before either of the women could catch her listening.

She left the house without seeing the wave Mrs. Griswold gave her. Without stopping for breakfast, no great matter since any desire for food had been replaced by a wave of nausea, she followed the familiar route toward Spokane Telephone. A little café she'd often noticed marked the halfway point. Today, of all days, she felt justified in following the enticing aroma of coffee inside.

The morning had passed the normal breakfast hour, with Jacoba the only patron in the place. Prompt to a fault, the waitress snapped a large cup of coffee down in front of her. A small, gooey roll, pretty as an Easter ornament, adorned the saucer.

Jacoba, who'd sat with her elbows on the table and her head in her hands like some weary nightwalker, looked up. "Oh, dear. I'm sorry. I didn't order the roll, although I must say, it looks delicious."

The waitress, a middle-aged woman whose bibbed apron had passed from pristine to well-used during the course of the morning, laughed. "I know, but my dear, you are stick thin and, unless I miss my guess, hungry."

She waved away Jacoba's embarrassed protest.

"Please, don't fret. You see how small the roll is. It's a sample for a new recipe, one I'm thinking of adding to the breakfast menu. No charge. I'm using you as a test subject. Please, take a bite and see if you like it."

Relieved to have her worrisome thoughts interrupted even for a few moments, Jacoba complied. As she'd guessed it would, the roll melted in her mouth. "Delectable. Orange, pecans, vanilla bean pastry creme." If she'd been alone, she would've licked her fingers. Instead, she wiped them on a napkin. "Your rolls are bound to be a hit."

The woman, proprietor/baker/waitress, all wrapped into one, flushed pink with delight.

"Thank you. Ah . . ." she took another look at Jacoba, "might you be looking for a job? A small, temporary job? I'm only open six days a week from six in the morning until one o'clock. I need someone first thing in the morning to help serve the breakfasts. That's my busy time. It would only be for a month. My sister is coming from North Dakota to help, but until she gets here, I'm being run off my feet."

Surprised, Jacoba's mouth opened to say no. But something stopped her. "I've never waited tables before," she admitted. "And I do have a job already."

"Yes," the woman said. "I know. You're the telephone girl who saved that foreign man at the Holiday Hotel. I saw your picture in the paper. I also see you pass the café, most mornings. That's why I thought to ask. I hoped you could put in a couple hours before your other job. Just a little addition, you see."

Jacoba's mind raced. Whatever she made could be kept secret. Money just for her, put aside for her personal necessities. She needed to make up a batch of Madame's face lotion from her favorite recipe. And if she could get access to the utensils, some of the refined soaps she preferred.

Her own little secret and none of Charlie's concern.

"All right," she said, before she changed her mind. "When do I start?"

Chapter 16

The job at Delilah's Cafe combined with the hours at the telephone company kept Jacoba too busy to think of the conversation she'd overheard between Betty and Miss Madison. The situation suited her. She didn't want to dwell on what they'd said. What good would it do?

Hiding your head in the sand! That's what Madame would say, a fact Jacoba pushed from her mind as too awful to envision.

Since the cafe held only eight small tables and a counter no more than a dozen feet long, she sometimes had problems navigating between customers, whom she found were often as rude as the telephone patrons. Hands, especially male hands, were prone to reaching out just as she passed. Although, the cafe being a respectable place of business, they stopped short of touching. Mostly.

But, whether her presence was the cause or not, the cafe's cliental steadily grew.

Delilah, of course, reveled in the restaurant's popularity, a smile wreathing her mouth and creating a dimple on her left cheek. From the moment the proprietress unlocked the front door, every seat filled and refilled during the first two hours as a constantly changing barrage of city workers piled in for a breakfast of scrambled eggs and deliciously decadent sweet rolls.

As Jacoba whispered to Delilah during a short lull, "They may not know what the word decadent means, but they most certainly agree on what tastes good."

Delilah blushed with pleasure. "The customers like you," she told Jacoba on the third day. "You're pretty, polite, and quick on your feet. I must say you caught on to the work quickly for someone with no experience."

"Thank you," Jacoba replied with a blush of her own, "but it's not me. It's your delicious baked goods." A plan had formed in her mind that concerned Delilah. What would the lady say to stocking a small supply of Jacoba's soaps and lotions? Just to see how it would go. With so many shop girls coming in, it seemed a perfect outlet. Delilah could take a commission on sales, just as the big department stores did with Madame's line of cosmetics.

But then Jacoba scratched her head, metaphorically speaking. Orange pecan rolls side-by-side with lavender scented lotion? How would that work?

One thing about it, even when she moved to the reservation, she'd be able to carry on with her cosmetic goods if only she could find a reliable and honest source to market them. And Charlie need never know. She already knew he spent most of his time away from the homestead. She'd have time to take her product to Rockford and put it on the train. Perhaps she could make a deal with Mr. LeTevere to pick her up and take her home. Or—

But here she put the brakes on an alternate idea. She couldn't ask Ruel—Mr. Gagne, she meant—if he'd transport the products on his boat. It wouldn't be right. Something told her she'd meet with no objection from him. The objection came from within herself.

She went back to the first plan. She'd manage. If Delilah agreed. She might be putting the cart before the horse, another of Madame's surprisingly homey sayings. The older lady might even take offense at the mere hint. Jacoba planned to wait to broach the subject until just the right, most auspicious moment.

The very next morning she found herself in the unhappy position of once more listening to a conversation between Betty and Miss Madison. Before stepping onto the second floor landing, she heard the murmur of their voices and resolved to walk with a heavier tread. The women should have some warning.

And so should she.

"Where does she go, so early every morning?" Miss Madison's whisper carried easily up the stairwell to where Jacoba froze in place, one foot still raised to take the next step.

"I do not know. Is not for me to put questions to Mrs. De Groot." Betty, sounding unhappy at the question, made a prim reply, but Jacoba noticed her German accent had become more prominent.

"Don't you? But I thought you and she talked often in a friendly manner. Didn't you help her find the job at the telephone company?"

Since she heard no verbal reply, Jacoba visualized Betty shrugging or nodding. But yes. Betty most certainly had helped.

Without warning, her eyes filled. They had been friends, she and Betty. Almost friends, anyway. Until Charlie intervened. And yes, she blamed the schoolteacher too.

Miss Madison's whisper evolved into a stronger tone. "Do you think she's sneaking out and seeing someone? A man other than her husband, I mean? Not that we should blame her. Quite unsurprising, actually."

Betty sounded shocked. "Mrs. DeGroot? No. She does not sneak. And she would not do that. Betray her husband. He is not a good man, but she would not."

"Don't be so sure. A certain type of woman . . . well, I'm sure you know what I mean. And my dear, she is foreign. From some European country. Remember? She actually spoke to those . . . what were they? Russian—no, Hungarian? . . . people in their own heathen language. It just goes to show you."

"Show me?"

"But remember," Miss Madison's voice dropped and Jacoba strained to hear.

Remember what? She got her answer.

"Where there's smoke, there's fire. Mr. DeGroot hasn't been back since he left, you know. And I, for one, am grateful to see the last of him. But we have only her word that he's on that terrible Indian reservation. What if he's abandoned her? What if he's abandoned her for another woman? Or because she is the one seeing someone else?"

Betty made no answer for the longest time, then said, "I must go. Mr. Howard is waiting for his towels." She spoke carefully, any accent almost indiscernible.

Her pulse racing, Jacoba took note of Betty's frozen tone. Miss Madison might have overplayed her hand in showing her disdain of foreigners. Betty was already sensitive about her accent.

First feeling hot, then cold, Jacoba became aware of the hem of her skirt tickling against her legs. She looked down and found her hands balled into fists, her shaking legs causing her skirt fabric to ripple like running water.

And hoping—yes, hoping—Miss Madison would stumble on the way downstairs and break her scrawny neck.

Appalled at herself, she forced unsteady legs to continue down the stairs. Walked right past Miss Madison who took one look at her and flinched against the wall. Even caught up with Betty and went past her as Betty, too, shrank from Jacoba's path.

She'd speak with Delilah that very morning, presenting the baker lady with tiny bottles of a couple of her favorite lotions. Since the lady washed her hands frequently, her skin dried quite badly. Also, a miniature bar of her favorite coconut oil soap, wrapped in pretty blue paper.

She'd intended to wait another week for their relationship to build, but after this morning, even another minute seemed untenable. At the end of this month, willy-nilly, she was moving to the homestead.

This city, this house, this whole life sickened her.

* * *

Delilah, when broached, at first appeared a bit doubtful of Jacoba's business proposition, saying she'd have to think it over.

"I don't know where I could fit in a display, for one thing," she said, brow puckering as she examined the short counter with the cash drawer hidden underneath, "and really, cosmetics in a bake shop? Is that a good fit?"

Jacoba's spirits drooped even further as she handed Delilah the samples she'd brought along. "I think so. A good many women come by on their way to work, you know."

"Yes, to have their coffee and a roll, not apply lotion."

Delilah drew the stopper from the lotion and held it under her nose as Jacoba did her best to keep disappointment at bay.

"It wouldn't take much room, really, just to see," she urged. "We could place a basket, perhaps, here beside the cash drawer. In any case, try the lotion. I think you'll like it."

"Well, I will do that." Gingerly, Delilah kneaded a dollop of rose scented lotion into her hands where lye soap and hot water had taken their toll. Her face cleared.

"Oh!" Surprise colored her voice. "How very nice. It feels wonderful and smells even better. Better," she added in a whisper, "than those ever so expensive products at the Palace department store."

The concerned crinkle between Jacoba's eyes cleared. "You like it?"

Delilah stuck her hand beneath her nose for another big whiff. "I most certainly do. And the soap?" She sniffed this, too. "Lovely. Most every night my friend Randall tells me I smell good enough to eat, but I'd rather smell of flowers than of yeast rolls." Then she blushed, a wave of color that told a smiling Jacoba more than the lady perhaps intended.

"Then you'll do it?"

"Oh, all right. We'll give it a try." Delilah scooted a tray of oatmeal raisin cookies to the other side of the counter and checked the space. "Bring a basket that will fit here tomorrow and we'll see what happens for a day or two. I don't suppose it will hurt anything."

A premise that held true. On Jacoba's next day off, considering the products had flown from the basket, she spent most of her time combining ingredients for her favorite body lotion, then cooking up the best beauty soap recipe she knew to replace the items sold. By the time the small supply she had on hand had sold out, these flower-shaped bars would be cured and ready to tie into pretty packages.

And Delilah's bakery business continued to thrive. It turned out most ladies who purchased the lotions or soaps couldn't resist the temptation of a cookie or two as well.

By mid-month, as the heat permeating the roof gathered in Jacoba's third floor room—plaguing her with hot and sleepless nights—she began packing. She thought longingly of the tall trees shading the clearing where Charlie had set up camp. It was sure to be cool there, so close to the lake. Had he cleared any land and plowed space for a garden yet? She'd sent seeds. They needed to be planted immediately if there was to be any kind of a crop. And had he begun on the house? She would've thought he'd be champing at the bit to get started. He was a master builder, after all, or so he said. Although she admitted to doubts, these days.

The disloyal thought took up a place in her head and lodged there, right beside the memory of him striking her with the rifle barrel.

Because, if he'd done any of these things, he sent no word of it or of anything except another plea for more money. Worry became her constant companion.

And then, one evening as she dragged home from her shift at Spokane Telephone after a particularly trying day, she found a letter addressed to her written in typewriter print. It lay on the console table in the entry hall where Mrs. Griswold had an open-fronted cabinet with pigeon holes labeled with room numbers. Expecting it to be an overdue letter from Charlie, the return address gave her pause. Everything about the envelope really, because the address was not the only thing. Typewritten? And why hadn't the letter been placed in her room's mail slot? Why had it been left here where everyone who passed could see.

Something, a sort of premonition, told her to ignore the letter. Pretend she never got it. At that moment, Mrs. Griswold swept into the hall from the kitchen, holding the front door key in her hand.

"There you are. I was beginning to wonder if you'd be home tonight." The landlady's tone signaled annoyance. "I've been waiting for some time to lock up."

Jacoba glanced at the watch pinned to her shirtwaist. "I'm right on time, Mrs. Griswold," she said, making certain to keep her voice even. "Not late at all."

The other woman shifted her feet like a restless horse. "Everyone else is in for the evening and I'm tired. I have to wait for you every night, Mrs. DeGroot."

Lock-up time was at 11: p.m. and it was 8:30. Lips tightened to hold back a retort, Jacoba turned to start up the two long flights of stairs. She carried the letter in her hand.

"Oh," Mrs. Griswold added, "Make certain your room is tidy when you leave in the morning. I'm showing the room to a prospective boarder tomorrow."

Whirling, Jacoba stared down at the woman. "You do not have my permission to enter the room. Your prospective boarder will have to wait until I vacate. Which will be when my rent is up."

The landlady's face turned an alarming shade of violet. "This is my house. I can turn you out any time I like."

"Not," Jacoba shot back, "according to the terms of the lease we both signed. And I have done nothing to default on those terms."

"Your husband . . ."

"I am not my husband. Who, I may point out, is not currently in residence, nor has he been for three months, while I am still paying double occupancy charges. If you continue to press this, I'm certain my attorney can address the issue." Jacoba heard it then, an echo from her old life. It could've been Madame standing on those boarding house stairs—had Madame ever performed such a lowly act—

while saying those things in a harsh voice. And meaning every word.

Quaking inwardly, but showing none of those feelings to Mrs. Griswold, who'd fallen silent, Jacoba marched to her room, heels hammering on the stairs. If she awakened any of the other boarders with the stamp of her feet, at this moment she didn't care. Later, she might apologize. Might. It depended.

Her room, hot from heat gathered during the day, started a body-wide wave of perspiration the moment she entered. Tossing the letter onto the bedside table, she went to the single small window and reefed it upward. It stuck at a mere eight inches, but even so, a waft of cooler air entered.

She might have to move her bed to lie beneath the window, Jacoba thought, smiling wickedly to herself at the scooting noises the bed legs would make. If she wasn't mistaken, Miss Madison's room lay right beneath this one. But then she decided vindictiveness didn't suit her. Acting like Madame had served her well just now, or so she hoped, but truly, she had no wish to be cruel.

Stripping away her clothing, she poured cool water from the pitcher Betty had been kind enough to sit on the commode, and washed before donning a dimity nightdress.

Better.

But there was still the letter. Or more than a letter, given the thickness of the envelope. And the return address, with the authoritative title of Perkins, Howard, and Chesburn, Attorneys at Law.

What had these lawyers to do with her? Aside, she thought suddenly, from possibly convincing Mrs. Griswold the threat she'd made held true.

Taking up a letter opener, she slit the top of the envelope. Peeped inside and spotted a name.

So no. The proper question was, what had these lawyers to do with Charlie?

Only later did Jacoba realize she was wrong regarding one aspect. She had no attorney.

But evidently Charlie did.

Chapter 17

Dear Mrs. DeGroot, the letter began.

I am enclosing paperwork in regards to a name change on the homestead papers for the Coeur d'Alene Indian Reservation land, which is currently assigned to you. Mr. DeGroot requests the change from Jacoba De-Groot to Charles L. DeGroot. It is a simple matter that needs only your signature.

Mr. DeGroot has requested the transfer of ownership to be processed as quickly as possible, as he is in need of funds to further develop the land and this will allow him to process a loan.

If you will kindly make an appointment with me at your earliest convenience, I will have the conveyance paperwork drawn up and ready for your signature. There will be a fee for these services in the amount of $25.00. Please have these funds with you at the appointment.

> *Respectfully yours,*
> *Andrew Chesburn*

Perkins, Howard, and Chesburn
Attorneys at Law
Coeur d'Alene, Idaho

Jacoba imagined everyone in the house heard her indrawn breath—if they hadn't been asleep. And most surely the way her legs trembled shook not only her skirt, but her whole body and perhaps the entire building.

And her rage . . . why didn't its heat set the place afire?

How dare he? And how dare a slimy lawyer's office even take on such a . . . a soulless assignment?

Oh, Charlie.

In that moment she was certain she felt her heart break. Is this why Charlie had urged her to elope with him? Why he'd said he loved her? Because he believed Madame could be tapped for money and now, since Jacoba adamantly refused to ask for any, he planned to take what he could? If she signed those papers, would she ever hear from him again?

Legs no longer able to support her, Jacoba collapsed onto the bed, the mattress sagging beneath even her slight weight.

Or was she misjudging him? Heart beating hard, she read the letter again. No, she hadn't misread. The part where it said Charlie needed funds to develop the land. She knew people who put up assets—or even a property itself—as collateral to raise the money necessary to expand. Business deals were often conducted that way. Even Madame had been known to do it.

God knows she and Charlie had spoken often enough of how they'd have to tighten their purse strings until the homestead was self-supporting. Maybe—

But then, thinking of Pym and Tope and the gall on poor Pym's withers when he'd been neglected, the lack of progress on clearing land, and Charlie's constant demands for more money, what else was she to think?

Only later did Jacoba let herself admit that all the pondering, the second-guessing, the excusing, refuted the evidence not only in those things, but of the way he'd treated her. Taking her body as though she had no choice, no say. Hurting her, then acting as if it were his due.

And finally, he'd subjected her to the condemnation of her fellow boarders. Mortified her, so they reviled her as if it were her sin and not his alone.

Jacoba didn't sleep that night. Nor the next, although exhaustion made her fingers clumsy on the switchboard while at her job, and her speed lag in rushing about the breakfast tables at Delilah's restaurant.

But she made no appointments. Not with a certain Andrew Chesburn and not with anyone else.

She had a decision to make.

Time marched inexorably on, until she worked her last day at both Delilah's restaurant and the telephone switchboard.

Entering the restaurant as Delilah opened the door for her at 6 a.m., Jacoba found a stranger already inside. The woman, who bore a distinct resemblance to Delilah, stood by the cash drawer counter holding a bar of lavender soap to her nose. The sister, Sarah, had arrived, right on time to take Jacoba's place as the morning waitress.

Sarah pocketed the soap and tossed a coin into the basket. "I hear you're someone I'll have a hard time living up to. Delilah has told me, repeatedly, what a good worker you are. Then there's all this lovely stuff you make."

Jacoba didn't know whether she was hearing a compliment or a complaint. Deciding to consider the words a compliment, she smiled and shook Sarah's hand before adding some bottles of lotion she'd brought along to the basket. Stock had run low during the week. "Delilah has been a good teacher and a good boss. I'll miss this place—and your sister's wonderful baking."

"I'll miss you, too. A lot." Smiling, Delilah joined them.

Sarah's smile seemed forced. She sniffed and said, "I hope no one expects me to match your prowess. After all, you're considerably younger than I am. Not so heavy on your feet."

Not so heavy on your feet? Jacoba hid a smile. She guessed that was one way to admit to those extra inches around the waist.

"Now, Sarah. You just have to make up your mind to . . ." Delilah broke off, looked doubtful for a moment, then said, "Well, ladies, don your aprons. I see our first customer is at the door."

The two-hour rush flew by, so much so that Jacoba's leave-taking consisted merely of an assurance she'd be bringing—or sending by train—more of her potions within a couple weeks, and the women wishing each other well.

The final hours at Spokane Telephone & Telegraph were less friendly than those spent at the restaurant. Telephone girls, as a general rule, were kept constantly busy and they changed so frequently that Jacoba hadn't really made many friends. Eileen, the girl she'd assisted by answering the call for help from the Hungarians, was still employed and had gotten more assured in her job. Mr. Lehman, the supervisor, remained and enjoyed his long cigarette breaks while generally eyeing her with distrust.

This being Jacoba's last payday, she found herself standing in line just behind Eileen at quitting time. She hadn't told anyone she was leaving, and it came as a surprise when Eileen turned around and said, "Oh, Jacoba, did that Hungarian man ever send you a bonus or a tip or something for what you did to save his life?"

"Save his gunshot victim's life, you mean." Jacoba moved forward a step as a girl ahead of them received her pay envelope and walked away. "But no. I never heard from him again. Which is fine."

"Oh?" Eileen frowned. "But he called a couple days later and asked for you. I think you were at lunch. Or maybe it was your day off. Anyway, he asked me your name and if I knew where you lived and some other questions. I sent the call to Mr. Lehman. I hope that was all right."

What could she say? No? Too late.

Forcing herself to relax, she shrugged. "Yes. Of course. Really, it doesn't matter."

But Eileen cocked an eyebrow at Lehman who stood behind the paymaster as he dealt out the envelopes. "Do you suppose he took whatever the Barany fellow meant for you?"

Jacoba broke into a surprised laugh. "Do you doubt it?"

"It sounds just like him." But the girl looked relieved at Jacoba's peal of laughter.

And that, as they say, was that.

The next morning Jacoba, already exhausted, loaded herself and a variety of boxes and baggage aboard the train headed for Rockford. An hour later she found Mr. LeTevere and his wife, Mary, waiting for her with their wagon and small son.

* * *

"Mrs. DeGroot, hello. We are here." Mary waved to her from the LeTevere farm wagon as the little boy clambered over the side and followed his father—matching his father's steps and stance exactly—to Jacoba's stack of goods piled on the depot platform. His siblings had evidently been left at home this morning.

"Good morning, Mrs. LeTevere," Jacoba called in return. "Good morning to you, Mr. LeTevere. And to you, young sir." The boy had his arms held outstretched, the better to assist in carrying something over to the wagon.

Aha, so he was here to work. Then work he would.

Jacoba complied, laying a lightweight hatbox in his outstretched arms. "Thank you, Victor," she told him, remembering his name at the last moment. She received a flashing smile in return.

By the time the train pulled out of the station, Jacoba's possessions were loaded in the farm wagon. LeTevere jiggled the reins over his mismatched team and away they went, passing through the town of Rockford at a sedate walk.

"So." LeTevere looked over at her, his dark face serious. "You have come to stay."

Jacoba guessed it must be obvious given the many bags and boxes they'd loaded. "Yes. I thought . . . well . . . I thought I must give it a try. Something told me it was time."

Mary touched her arm with fingers as light as butterflies. "Something?"

When what her fellow boarders had said was added to the letter she'd received, well, it became hard to choose which stabbed deepest into her heart. Not that she was about to tell these people of either circumstance. One because of mortification, and the other because of hurt. Or maybe the two were so mixed together there was no separating them.

Forcing a smile, Jacoba let the question slide. "Yes."

Once they were out of town, she motioned to a flat box that had been the last thing entrusted to the little boy and which she'd taken on her lap when settled on the wagon seat. He stood braced against the back of the seat, his head on his mother's shoulder, swaying to the motion as if to the fluid movement of the sea.

"Would you like to see what's in this box?" she turned to ask him.

His eyes flashed from her, to his mother, to his father, who gave an almost imperceptible nod. "Yes."

"Do you think you could untie this string?"

"Sure." He reached over the seat's back and yanked the end of the bow. The string fell away.

Jacoba held the box. "And now remove the lid."

He was grinning when the lid came off, and then he squealed.

"Victor!" his mother said sharply, but then she squealed just a little too.

The box contained a baker's dozen mix of Delilah's best pastries, doughnuts filled with creams and frosted, twisted fruity fritters with a spicy glaze, elegant eclairs, rolls spiraled with fillings both orange flavored and cinnamon.

"What's your fancy?" Jacoba asked, and passed the box around. Their delight brought her own appetite to the fore, and she downed a cinnamon roll with as much zest as Victor devoured an apple fritter.

A blessing she'd thought to bring the treats, Jacoba thought, as they served as a fine distraction. The topic of her move became lost in the background and she was glad of it.

Having dreaded what she'd find, she was almost surprised to discover some small progress had been made to the homestead when the wagon came to a stop in the clearing.

Her clearing. Her property. She had papers to prove it—if she could hang on and pay for it. And keep Charlie from taking it from her somehow. She pushed the thought aside.

Alongside the tent, sagging even more pitifully than it had a month ago, a small house had been framed. Although, looking at the structure critically, it seemed less a house and more of a one room log cabin. At least it would provide shelter from the elements. As soon as it got a roof, anyway.

To her inexperienced eye at least, the work seemed well done. Square—Charlie had told her the most critical part of construction was starting it all off square. Twelve inch peeled logs lay on heavy sill plates, well-sited on a small rise for run-off in case of heavy rain or snow.

On their way west, Charlie had preached at length regarding these attributes. "Nobody wants a flooded house," he'd said with a grin, "and you'll never find a DeGroot built house with anything but even floors."

She guessed this would prove if he was as good of a builder as he claimed.

Louis LeTevere grunted as he stepped down from the wagon and eyed the structure. It had a long way to go to actually be livable. "Guess you'll have to sleep in the tent for now, Missus."

"By yourself?" Mary added as she gazed around.

Jacoba sighed. "Apparently so." *Where is Charlie?*

The place was as deserted as it had been the first time she visited, the woods surrounding it quiet but for birdsong, the buzzing of insects and the susurrant whisper of the tall tree tops. No sound of

axes chopping or horses clomping, no smell of woodsmoke pointing to recent activity. No one to welcome her to her new home.

If she could even expect a welcome. The way they'd parted, and
the notification from the attorney made it doubtful.

My property, she reminded herself. She didn't need a welcome.

Moving at last, she jumped from the wagon as Mary followed
more sedately. "You stay there," Mary told her son. "Pass things
down to us, yes?"

"Yes, mamá," he said, the French accent sounding strange issu-
ing from a small Indian boy's mouth.

Louis already had Jacoba's heavy iron soap-making pot lifted
to the ground. "Where do you want these things?"

She hesitated. Her heart quailed at entering the tent. The Lord
only knows what they might find in there. She made up her mind.
"Please, just stack everything under that tree and I'll make up my
mind later. I have a sturdy tarp so at least we can get it under cover." She indicated a lone cedar whose drooping branches formed
a cave. Luckily Charlie hadn't chopped it down. For once she was
glad of his sloth.

Later, finding herself and Louis out of earshot as Mary spoke
with Victor, Jacoba posed a question, one she hesitated to ask. "Do
you know where he might be?"

She named no names. Louis would know who she meant.

And he did, although he seemed disinclined to speak. Shrugging uncomfortably, he put a box of foodstuffs in a separate pile.
"Over by Plummer, there's a place, a saloon. Lots of men—white
men—go there nights. They gamble. They drink. They . . ." He
closed his mouth.

Jacoba swallowed. "A bordello?"

Louis frowned, finally nodding. "Not exactly, but there are
women who make themselves . . . available."

"Yes. Are they . . ." Her mouth compressed. "Are they Indian
women? Girls? Or are they white women?" Although perhaps, it
didn't really matter.

"Both." He smiled a little. "Or people tell me. I don't go there. Got a wife. Got a family."

Jacoba felt like breaking into applause. Got integrity, she thought.

The silence when the LeTevere family had gone, a delighted Victor clutching a quarter, his father with two silver dollars, failed to bring peace to Jacoba. A sort of nervous energy filled her. Energy all mixed together with dread and an unexpected dose of anticipation. The latter surprised her. Anticipation of what?

But she knew when the faint hoot of a steam whistle from out on the lake reached her. And then, from far away, she heard a dog bark.

Quill.

Chapter 18

Jacoba spent the rest of the morning and into the afternoon sorting through her pile of goods, but when suppertime rolled around she knew she'd have to enter the tent. Charlie's tent. Memories of the last time she'd been here flooded in, filling her with dread. What she might find there today? But, of all things, she couldn't find the matches to start a fire. They were somewhere within her pile of goods; she just didn't know where.

She rubbed her temples, aware of a headache coming on. A bonehead, forgetful as a lost cow. How could she possibly have forgotten the location of something as necessary as matches?

Willing herself to courage, she ducked under the tent flap and went inside.

Looking around, she held her breath. The hot, close air, funky with the odor of a man who neglected his hygiene, spread under the canvas like a disease.

Added to that, she smelled sex. And the cot where Charlie slept a mess of tussled blankets, one hanging onto the tarp-covered floor. A pair of women's drawers, ripped at the front seam, had been flung on top a box containing—well, she didn't know what.

Jacoba choked, bile rising in her throat.

She touched nothing, but found the tin where she knew Charlie kept his matches and took a few. His supply too, she noticed, had dwindled to only a handful. So careless he'd become, even of his own welfare.

How much did she care?

Although she searched both her mind and her heart, she couldn't find an answer. All she seemed to feel was . . . distaste. For the man she'd tied herself to, for herself, for a situation, no, a problem she didn't know how to solve.

Except for Madame's guidance. She knew what her mother would say to do, lessons learned from Madame's seven marriages.

Emerging quickly, Jacoba sneezed, the sound explosive in the silent surroundings. A symbol, she thought, her lips curling, telling her to let go of all she'd found inside the tent. It didn't help.

Only made her head ache all the more.

Having stowed the items she'd brought as securely as possible, she took the packet of papers the attorney had sent, as well as the official paperwork pertaining to her homestead, and paced slowly around the property. Heart heavy, like a weight in her chest, she knew she had to hide the packet. It was as if she heard Madame's voice giving advice, telling her she must keep the papers safe, out of . . . dare she say it? Out of untrustworthy hands. Her husband's hands.

But where to put them?

The route eventually took her to the edge of the lake where a flat stone protruded out into the water. Someone, at some time, had driven a spike into the stone, then hammered the top part into a loop. Jacoba imagined boats tied up there.

She'd like a boat. A small one, suitable to sit out on the water while gentle waves rocked her like a baby in a cradle.

Although she hadn't intended for it to happen, her gaze drifted toward the Gagne house in the distance. His boat—Ruel's big steamboat—was gone, but a small rowboat, an exact replica of the one she'd been thinking about floated up against the dock. A dog,

Quill, no doubt, although at this distance she couldn't be sure, was dashing along the shoreline chasing birds.

Jacoba smiled to see him.

But still she hadn't found a secure place to store the papers. It had to be dry, out of sight, yet readily accessible. Most of all, it had to be somewhere Charlie would never think to look.

In the end, she took the packet back to camp with her. Once there, she found a shovel, the handle dry from sitting out in the sun and needing some linseed oil. She searched out and began digging at the side of a rock layered with distinctive red streaks and embedded in the soil, one she thought too large for Charlie to move by himself. She dug under it, until she had a hole just the right size in which to insert a tin box that had held crackers. Now it held the oiled packet, her pearls, and a hundred dollars she'd scrimped to save. Carefully tamping the dirt in around it, she brushed out her own footprints and, in the end, tossed a few smaller stones artistically over all.

Then, taking a wide berth around Charlie's tent, she got to work. First job? Make a list of things to do. Number the items in order of importance, starting with, first all, hire some help.

Or was that number two? Shouldn't she speak with Charlie first? Try to come to an understanding? See if they could find their way back to the friendship—had it been friendship?— they'd enjoyed in those first happy days last year? Was that even possible?

She had doubts.

* * *

It was late when Jacoba heard a wagon rattling down the trail toward the campsite where she sat on a log pulled close to a small fire. At least, she thought, Charlie had bestirred himself enough to build a guard around the area. It would have been tragic had he allowed the fire free rein and started the woods aflame.

Now, at the sound of the wagon and the clomp of horse hooves, she tensed and prepared herself for battle—metaphorically speaking. Or was she wrong? Would he greet her with a smile or with a scowl? Did she care?

Those ripped female drawers in his tent reappeared in her mind's eye.

As it turned out, he greeted her with both. And a gun.

"Bessie? Is that you?" Charlie called as he broke into the clearing and apparently making out the shape of a woman in the firelight.

But not the woman's identity.

Jacoba saw the flash of teeth as he grinned. *Bessie?*

"No," she called back. "It is I, Jacoba. Your wife."

His grin not only faded as Tope and Pym plodded closer, but changed into a frown. "Jacoba?" he repeated as though she was someone he'd forgotten.

Firelight glinted off the barrel of the rifle he carried across his lap.

What is he afraid of? Who is he afraid of? When had he begun carrying the rifle with him?

All good questions she intended to ask later—provided he didn't intend to shoot her before she got the chance.

"Whoa." Charlie pulled the horses to a halt beside the fire and stared at her.

The horses, she saw, had lost weight, hides not so shiny, hooves in need of a trim and a shoeing. They looked tired, overworked and poorly fed. Anger trilled through her in a hot wave.

"What are you doing here?" he demanded. "You didn't need to come yourself. You could've taken care of that business in Coeur d'Alene. There or by mail."

"Business? What business are you referring to?" She wanted him to say it. Hear what words he'd use. Then she'd know.

Know what?

The question echoed in her mind as she waited for him to speak.

"You know what business," he finally said. Wrapping the reins around the wagon brake lever, he swung to the ground, the rifle still in hand.

Jacoba rose as well. "So, no, 'Jacoba, my love, how good to

have you here at last? No, I've missed you? No, let's build this home together?'" Her little speech mocked.

Charlie stared at her, coming closer until he loomed above her. "What are you talking about? Why are you here? You've brought the papers, haven't you? The signed papers? Or did you take them directly to the attorney?" He didn't wait for her reply. "I hope your work is going well, Jacoba, because we're going to need every cent you can bring in to hold on to this place if my plan doesn't go through. Debts are piling up."

"Debts?" she repeated, her voice soft. "Debts for what?" Glancing about the site, her narrowed gaze showed scorn, disgust, and finally, anger. "What have you done, Charlie? Or more importantly, what haven't you done?"

"I . . ." His chest puffed out. "You don't understand anything, so don't meddle. It's none of your concern. Do as I tell you and all will be well."

"Meddle? None of my concern?" She set her hands on hips, hoping the pressure would hide their trembling. "Anything that concerns this property is my concern."

He sneered. "Not anymore, Mrs. DeGroot. What's yours is mine, remember? That goes the opposite, as well. My debts are your debts."

Was he proud of it? His debts? Had he gone insane? Jacoba's eyes widened with astonishment. Anger flamed, building like the core of a gas lamp.

"Also, there's another little problem coming due," he drawled when she didn't say anything. "I decided it was time you talked to your mother. Since you refused, I wrote to her. I told her you. . . we . . . need $1000.00 right away. Lord knows she can afford that and much, much more."

Jacoba choked on a scream. A long, drawn out scream that would've reached through the woods and across the lake if she let it. Maybe even all the way to St. Louis and her mother, who'd been right about Charlie from the very beginning. As had Charlie's own father and brother when they refused to include him in the family business.

But she wouldn't scream. She didn't want to scare the horses. After a moment, she managed to say, "Has she answered?"

"Not yet. I expect a letter any day."

"Do you?" Jacoba was honestly curious. How unwise her husband had proved to be. He knew Madame's reputation. Did he really think she would whip out her pen and write a check at his demand? What kind of sob story had he presented to her, anyway, aside from something intended to arouse her sympathy? Not that it mattered. Any story he invented was more likely to make her laugh than to cry. Jacoba had a strong feeling Charlie would be waiting a very long time for that reply.

Charlie, to her unacknowledged relief, set the rifle aside. "So, what about the paperwork? You paid the attorney and filing fees, didn't you? The instructions should've been in the letter. When did Chesburn say everything would be completed?" His impatience showed in the spots of color on his cheeks. He hadn't shaved for a while, appearing unkempt, slovenly. Unwashed.

Jacoba's nose wrinkled. Where had he been? she wondered. What had he been doing? Her stomach lurched.

"I paid nothing." She set herself for his anger. "I ripped the papers into tiny pieces and burned them in Mrs. Griswold's fireplace."

"Burned them?" His face turned white, then red. "I told you . . ."

She stiffened her spine. "You told me to squander the single asset that is supposed to be a new start for both of us. You're telling me I have to pay *your* gambling debts, while you've done nothing but fritter away your time, using money I've worked hard for. And now you've tried to coerce my mother. Well, I won't do it, Charlie. And neither, you'll see, will Madame."

His slap came out of nowhere. A slap across her face hard enough to send her reeling backward, out of his reach. Blood welled from the cut on her lip.

"You'll do as I say. You're my wife." He followed her as she dodged back. Not fast enough. Another blow caught her in the stomach. Her diaphragm spasmed, her lungs refused to draw in air.

Suddenly without strength, she fell to her knees.

Dear God. Did he intend to beat her to death?

She held a hand out in front of her, as though to ward him off with those slender fingers, but he grabbed hold of them and twisted.

He must have seen the agony on her face, because he smirked. "You see what happens when a wife disobeys her husband? Be warned, Jacoba. I am the master here." He looked down at the pile of goods she'd brought. "Where's the money? I'm sure you have some squirreled away. A woman always does. Even my mother hid some from my father. For all the good it did her as it always disappeared into *my* pocket. And she was always afraid to complain."

He laughed and bent to the pile, cursing as he kicked aside her iron soap-making pot and rummaging through the stack until he found a small personal case where she'd been known to keep a few dollars. Jacoba managed a small breath. Her finger joints ached from the brutal twist. Blind, flaming fury surged through her. Fury, and shame, and . . . and she didn't know what to call those tumbling emotions. Hate. Maybe hate. And yes. The desire to see him . . .

With tremendous effort, she quelled the last thought. Best not to go there. Best not to let this fire grow.

But even as she told herself to wait, to let his transgression go this once, she struggled to her feet and thrust her hand, her good hand, into her pocket and brought out the pistol she'd placed there when she heard the wagon coming.

"Thank you, dear Mr. Finley," she whispered.

She was Madame's daughter. Nothing had happened here she hadn't seen before. With Madame, no less, which in part had made her the woman she was today. The result had sent a message Jacoba had never forgotten. And never would.

"Charles."

Ignoring her, he broke open the latch on her case, and found the envelope containing her last pay from the telephone company secured there.

"Charles," she repeated

He turned at her soft call. From his expression, he expected a conciliatory apology. From the way his jaw dropped, he most certainly didn't expect the bore of a pistol aimed at him.

"You will not touch me again," Jacoba said.

"What?" He took a step toward her.

The gun didn't waver. "No more. There will be no papers signed. There will be no more whoring, drinking, gambling. Nothing charged to my account. If you have debts, work to pay them yourself. I won't do it. Do you understand?"

Maybe he did, maybe he did not, his rage perhaps keeping him from comprehending anything but his desire to hit her. A desire he barely kept in check. She saw it written on his face.

It was a surprise therefore, when the next words from his mouth were neither curses nor shouts, but questions any bystander might have asked.

"Where did you get the gun, Jacoba? What do you intend to do with it?"

"I stole it," she said, and she had, from the trunk in Finley's room when she'd retrieved the money he'd stolen from her. As to what she intended to do with it, well, she hadn't quite thought that through. Not completely. But— "I intend to protect myself with it, Charlie. From you or anyone who attacks me."

He watched her, waiting for her to waver, she knew. If so, he was disappointed. But not quelled nearly enough. His core was still filled with bluster. "You have to sleep sometime, Jacoba. Do you realize that?" His smirk came back.

"And so do you, Charles." She smiled. "So do you. As I recall, you've always been a heavy sleeper. Oh, and you'd best put my pay envelope back where you found it. It doesn't belong to you."

He shook with rage, his eyes glaring, his face red, his hands clenched.

But he put the envelope back in the case. Another thing for her to hide tomorrow.

And for now, checkmate.

Chapter 19

Jacoba didn't sleep that night. Nor the next. Distrust and worry, all mixed with apprehension that threatened to overwhelm her, combined to keep her awake, eyes wide at the slightest sound. Charlie's barely veiled threat, after all, had not been hard to interpret. What did he plan to do?

What should she do? What steps should she take to protect herself?

Meanwhile, Charlie, whose raucous snores seemed strong enough to billow out the sides of the tent, suffered no such problem. He, unlike her, apparently had no expectation of being murdered in his sleep.

She saw the desire to strike out at her in his face. The quickly shifting hot emotion whenever he looked at her. He sneered, he frowned, he gritted his teeth as though barely able to contain the urge to violence. The impulse to subdue her, break her, hurt her. *Why?* She asked herself that question a dozen times a day, and even more often through the next endless nights. Never, *never*, had she thought of him as a violent man until last month when he'd ravaged her unwilling body—and now this.

By the third day, she'd taken to catching naps while he was occupied elsewhere. If she could hear his axe, it seemed safe for her to sleep. But lightly, so when the rhythm of his strokes stopped, she awakened. His smirk never once slipped out of place.

Why, indeed? What had happened to him on the day of the train wreck? Had the spear in his chest killed some essential part of him? Maybe, except he'd told her he'd been stealing money from his own mother for years and she, poor lady, was too frightened to complain. What kind of man did that?

He'd been so thoughtful of her until then. Had it all been an act? Looking back, she thought so. What a fool she'd been, her own desperation to get away from St. Louis and Madame pushing her toward marriage with an old man the driving force allowing her to believe Charlie's avowal of love.

How stupid the whole thing seemed now. How useless. She'd traded Madame's kind of tyranny for Charlie's, neither of them having her best interests at heart. Or, she thought wryly, any kind of interest, let alone best. To Charlie, her only valuable was as a means to an end. She had no idea what value Madame put on her. If any. Still, she'd grown wiser over this last year. Wiser and harder. She wouldn't be used again.

It struck Jacoba as odd, now she'd come to stay, how Charlie set to work clearing the land. From early in the morning until late in the afternoon the sound of his ax and the subsequent fall of trees would come to her. Smoke so thick it obscured the sky drifted over the site from the burning slash piles. Not only from their site, but from the other homesteaders busy clearing the land.

While he occupied himself in the woods, she bustled about digging a garden spot and planting a crop, although the season was already growing late. After supper, he hauled logs from those felled earlier into camp and began adding to the house walls.

"This is only temporary," he said, excusing the small, carelessly constructed structure. "Next year I'll build a real house, one more suitable for Madame's daughter who is so proud she refuses to ask for money. This will get us through the winter and later can be used for storage."

She heard sarcasm in that message. If she hadn't known better, she might've thought the words conciliatory. His expression said something different.

Otherwise, they seldom spoke.

A week passed. The cabin grew. Even she could see it would never be more than a makeshift shelter to keep out the elements. Or, so she hoped, most of them. Jacoba had real doubts about that. For someone who bragged of being a master builder, the gaps between logs warned of leaks and the need for a great deal of mortar to chink them.

Then, when the walls grew too high for Charlie and her and the horses to manage, Jim Ledger came to the homestead.

Late morning found Jacoba in the clearing, working on the garden and planting not only beans for food, but herbs and flowers for her potions. Her head lifted when she heard a halloo rising from the trail in from the road. Standing erect, she stretched to ease her back. Then, removing her gloves and brushing dirt from the old riding skirt she wore, she went to see who had arrived.

A stranger's voice carried clearly to her. A hearty voice. Deep. Resounding. Authoritative. She stopped, still hidden among the trees, and listened.

"Hey, DeGroot," the man called to Charlie. "How the hell ya doing? I ain't seen you around for a week. Thought for sure you was going to join us at Tom's shindig last night."

Charlie, who'd taken a break to sharpen his axe at the wheel set in the shade of Jacoba's favorite cedar, sounded sulky as he answered. "I planned on it. Something came up."

"Came up? What?" A pause indicated the man might be looking around. "Don't tell me you decided to get some work done around here. What's the matter, Charlie? A guilty conscience?"

Perfect words, Jacoba thought, to goad Charlie into anger. And

she was right. But his anger, obvious to her right away, aimed not
at the man who uttered them, but at her.

"I've had a visitor," he said.

A visitor?

The man chuckled. "Yeah? Did Bessie come to stay? I heard
you got tired of your own cooking and wanted her to stay, but she
declined. Or did she come after all and give you the clap? I've
warned you before. You gotta watch out for those girls. You'd be
better off to get you a young one that ain't been with too many
men. Get a real young one and have you a virgin. It's always fun
to break'em in the way you want."

Sickness rolled over Jacoba, and for a moment her vision blurred.

"Ah, hell, Jim. Quiet down, will you? No, it's not Bessie."
Charlie spoke in lowered tones, but even so, the sound carried.
"She said she didn't want stuck out here. She likes the parties."

More than sickness. Fury. Enough to erase the faintness and
make the blood thunder through her veins. Jacoba patted her
pocket where these days the pistol always resided. So this visitor
was the acclaimed Jim Ledger, who Charlie often mentioned as
his guiding light here in the wilderness. The man the LeTeveres
had accused of criminal activities.

Ledger had evidently been taking a sharper look around. "You
got a woman here, though. I see clean washed clothes drying on
a line. I see a second tent and the yard tidied up, not to mention
the horse line farther away. Most of all, I see where you've got the
walls up on the cabin. About time. You can hold the next shindig."

"I could use some help to finish the walls," Charlie said. "And
the roof. That was our deal when I helped you."

"Don't want to talk about her?" Ledger laughed again, coarse
and rough. "I guess that means your wife is here. Where is she?
You ain't killed her, have you? Not yet, anyhow. Or have you beat
her up and made her so ugly you don't want me to see her."

She heard him snap his fingers and say, "Or maybe you just
don't want to share her."

"Share her?" Even Charlie seemed astonished. "My wife is not one of your whores, Jim."

"Women," Ledger said as if preaching a lesson, "is women. They all got the same parts. Some are just better put together than others. How's your woman, DeGroot?"

Jacoba couldn't bear anymore. Slowly, quietly, she backed away, into the silence of the woods. She intended on circling around the garden and taking the trail down to the lake. There she'd stay, until this horrible, crude man left. Even if it took all night.

Where is your wife? Ledger had wanted to know. *Or have you killed her yet?*

Is that what Charlie had planned? Had they spoken about it?

But even he had balked at sharing her with Ledger. Or did his reaction only mean the idea hadn't yet occurred to him. But now his "friend" had put it in his mind, what could she expect in the days to come?

If she thought she'd been afraid before, it seemed insignificant to what she felt now.

Leave here, Jacoba. Run.

The thought blazoned across her brain like a bolt of light from the sky.

Once out of sight and hearing of the campsite, Jacoba walked quickly through the woods until she reached the lake trail. Lost in her thoughts, the animal rushing toward her out of the smoke made her stifle a shriek. Until she saw it was only Quill, tail wagging and overjoyed to see her. She bent down to hug the dog who reciprocated by licking her chin.

Ruel Gagne stepped from behind the trunk of a giant grandpa ponderosa pine with a movement so graceful and silent she gasped in surprise.

"Quill," he said, at which the dog returned to his side and sat.

Ruel's face may have been set, but his dark eyes flashed. "Are you running away? It seems the wisest thing to do."

"How did you know I . . ." she lost the question, unable to go on. "You heard them talking, didn't you?" Embarrassment made it difficult for her to speak. "Did they see you?"

He shook his head. "No. Earlier, I met Ledger on the trail and supposed he was headed here. So I came back. Quietly. They didn't need to know." Hesitating, he added. "I knew you were here. I saw you at the lake one day."

Surprised, she said, "Oh. I haven't seen your boat tied up at the dock."

"No, I came by land." Then, "Did you look for my boat?"

Slowly, almost as if guilty of wrongdoing, she nodded. "Why did you come back? When you met Ledger on the trail, I mean."

"I don't trust him. I don't trust either of them. I am afraid for you, Mrs. DeGroot. You should leave here and not return."

His stare questioned her sense of reason. "Their voices carry and neither seems concerned. Their talk is dangerous to you. Why do you stay, missus? Have you no place to go where you'll be safe?"

"This is supposed to be my home. I won't be driven out." Determined words, but her voice trembled.

"I am sorry," Ruel spoke softly, "but you should go."

Jacoba opened her mouth, intending to say . . . she didn't know what, but then, from nearby, Charlie called her name. Loudly, so that brilliant, orange-winged butterflies fluttered into the air and birds fell silent.

"Jacoba." His voice echoed with menace. "Jake. Where are you? Come here. There's someone I want you to meet."

"Don't do it," Ruel said. He grabbed Quill, who'd started off to find the owner of the voice, holding him by the ruff.

"Don't let Quill go," Jacoba whispered. "I'm afraid—" She couldn't finish. What could she say, except that she feared Charlie, or this Ledger, might shoot the friendly dog. But she could see Ruel knew this, probably better than she did, when he pulled a bit of twine from his pocket and used it as a collar and leash.

"Jacoba." Her name rang out again, louder now. Charlie was coming to find her. Pride stiffened her spine.

"Go," she said to Ruel. "I'll be all right. Take care Quill doesn't get loose."

She saw Ruel was unsure. Afraid for her, afraid for his dog, leery of meeting Charlie again, especially since he and Jacoba were together. Their meeting could be misconstrued and it was like Charlie to do so. Although why he would care struck her as a mystery.

"Jacoba—Dammit, woman."

Charlie had gotten very near.

"Go," she said again, and turned to take the path back to camp. Once she looked back. Ruel and Quill were gone, silent in their passage with only a rustling of leaves to mark where they disappeared.

"Jacoba!

Charlie's anger came through clearly.

Putting her hand in her pocket, she straightened and said, not very loudly, "What on earth is the matter? I'm right here."

Charlie burst through some brush to where she stood. "Where the hell have you been?"

She eyed him coolly, her face, she hoped, expressionless.

Especially hoped, as another man stepped out behind her husband, smiling as if at a good joke. She hated him at first glance with his narrow face harboring close-set, almost yellow eyes, above a burly body. His appearance struck her as goat-like. All he needed was the horns. So this was Jim Ledger. Why not call him Lecher as it most certainly must suit him better? It was a thought that made her smile as wicked as his.

But her attention returned to Charlie. "You know very well I've been working in the garden. If it matters, I've been down at the lake to cool off."

"Of course it matters." Charlie may have been taken aback by her ready response. "What if you'd fallen in the lake and drowned? I wouldn't even have known."

Jacoba's heart lurched. Had he thought of this before, or was drowning a new idea only occurring upon Ledger's arrival? Something else for her to guard against? Now, more than ever, the pistol made a comforting weight in her pocket.

"But I didn't. I assure you, I'm careful."

"I want to know where you are at all times, do you understand?"

"No, Charles, I do not. This is the first I've heard of it." Her tone was caustic in its dryness. "Now," she turned to Ledger, acknowledging his presence no matter what kind of itch it formed under her skin, "have we all lost our manners? Are you going to introduce me to your friend?"

Sulky with her implied chastisement, Charlie merely nodded toward the man. "This is Jim Ledger. We've been working together."

"How do you do," she said. She didn't offer her hand. "I've been hearing about you." She didn't say from whom.

Charlie, who had steadfastly refused to speak of him beyond saying he was his friend, sent her a startled glance. A worried glance.

From the corner of her eye, Jacoba saw Ledger move his arm as though to reach out and shake her hand, but she'd already turned away and started toward camp, hurrying, as though she had unfinished business there.

It seemed odd, but she found herself trembling. Why? The two men fell behind her quicker footsteps, talking in low tones to each other.

In spite of, in her estimation, looking like a goat, Jim Ledger might've been considered a strong, hearty man. Or had been in the past if one could discount the lines of dissipation forming around his eyes. Those, and the telltale signs of overindulgence in liquor and food. Plenty of muscle covered his big bones, but he also had a paunch and a double chin. Fair skin, fair hair, and those oddly colored eyes completed the picture. Except a closer examination revealed small red veins had broken around his nose, and he seemed to have the remains of an acne outbreak forming pustules around his mouth. Unless those stemmed from some more virulent cause.

She shuddered. He struck her as unclean, and Charlie—Charlie probably was unclean as well.

Or did she mean diseased? The thought chilled her. For the third time in as many minutes, she felt for the reassuring weight of the pistol in her pocket.

Thank God the coolness between them had discouraged Charlie from attempting relations. More than a month had passed since her last visit. She was clean.

And would remain that way. The pistol made her confident of it.

Chapter 20

Ledger had brought a brown glass jug with him in expectation, or so Jacoba suspected, of carousing long into the night. Every time the two men— and here Jacoba had to give some reluctant credit as both men worked hard during the afternoon—placed another log on the cabin walls, they had a nip from the jug. Sometimes more than just a nip. It struck her as almost funny, the way they replaced the cork with more care than if the jug had contained French perfume.

She couldn't stop herself from worrying about their safety. The thud of falling trees as they struck the ground, the hacking of axes, the shouts and loud laughter, even the neighing of horses as Ledger's team, along with Pym and Tope, hauled their loads, had her shaking her head at the lack of common sense and precaution. And there was the smoke from the fires that burned the ever-growing slash pile.

More smoke than fire, truth be told, as the green wood smoldered rather than blazed. Soon they all, including Jacoba were peering through reddened eyes and coughing almost continuously as they brushed sparks from their clothing.

And the horses? The horses suffered. Jacoba got out her tin of salve.

No matter how much she longed for the cabin to be raised, or how much she resented two drunk men, still she feared one of them would be hurt. And if so, it would no doubt fall to her to provide aid. Something, she admitted, not her forte nor within her desired occupation. She'd found that out a year ago at the train wreck.

Then she remembered giving advice to the Hungarian, Barany. Perhaps, even if she was helpless herself, at least she could learn from others and pass the knowledge on.

But these two men? Touching them, tending their needs? Especially Jim Ledger — Even the thought made her skin quiver in revulsion.

The men knocked off work early, unhitched the horses and took them down to the lake to drink. Both men, she noticed, simply dropped the dirty, sweaty harness and left it on the ground. It fell to her to wipe the leather and hang it on tree limbs to dry.

So, this is where Charlie settled into his careless ways. Ledger, again. Jacoba's lip curled in disgust. Would it occur to either of them to allow the horses to swim and wash the soil of their work from their hides? Would the men even bother to wash themselves? The shouts she heard rising from the lake were hard to decipher.

But in this she maligned them. When they came back, both men and horses had been cleansed. And of course, it all called for a drink.

After a bit, as Jacoba stirred up biscuit dough to place atop a pot of stewing grouse, the rattle of wheels coming down the trail from the main road reached her ears. She stood up, looking toward the sound.

At first, she thought — hoped — it might be the LeTeveres and she could invite them to supper. But then, looking toward Charlie and his friend, she knew she was wrong. Not the LeTeveres. The wary glances the men exchanged warned her.

But they'd been expecting someone. Someone they'd bathed for in anticipation of meeting. Who?

A quick motion from Charlie got Ledger onto his feet, a nod urged him toward the trees where the sounds originated. A small vehicle had just broken into sight when he stopped it.

Not soon enough. The two females perched on the seat of a buggy drawn by a single scrawny horse provided plenty of insight.

Her breath hissed as she sucked in air. "How could you, Charles? You and that . . . that . . . man." She couldn't think of an epithet bad enough to describe her opinion of Ledger. "How could you bring those whores to my home?"

If there was an emphasis when she said *my home* she didn't hear it—but he must have, or imagined so.

"It's my home, as well. I will invite whoever I like to visit here." Charlie's face reddened under her stare.

"Will you? And I will un-invite them." Her hand went to her pocket where the pistol made her skirt sag. "Whatever it takes to do so."

"You wouldn't dare."

"Try me."

"I sent Jim to tell them to leave," Charlie said after a moment. "There's no party tonight."

A concession. Jacoba saw how he struggled to make it. Afraid, she suspected, of what Ledger would think.

"Or ever," she said. "Not as long as I'm here to stop it." It was only when she saw the look on his face, the quick shift of his eyes, that she realized her last sentence should have remained unsaid. It sounded entirely too much like a dare.

Ingrained manners made her invite Ledger to supper. Mannerless, he outdid himself in the effort to be uncouth. Nothing would do except he wash down her good dumplings with whiskey while draining the jug dry and belching satisfaction. Afterward, he and Charlie exchanged whispers like schoolboys, laughing and watching her for a reaction she refused to give.

Ledger left after supper, his wagon rattling as he drove away. The din he made singing an off-key, ribald tune at the top of his lungs echoed through the woods. Most surely, Jacoba felt, with the intention of goading her.

Later in the evening, Charlie dug out yet another jug he had hidden away and drank himself into a stupor. He fell twice as he staggered off to his bedroll in the roofless cabin, scraping his hands and leaving smears of blood on the offending stump.

Jacoba didn't offer to bandage his cut. She simply didn't care.

Charlie dead drunk was easier to handle than Charlie with all his wits about him.

Drink, she reflected, never made anyone more intelligent, more wary, more reflexive. But it sometimes made him meaner.

On reflection, depending on the time of day, she rather thought she preferred Charlie drunk.

Charlie was sick the next morning. Exceedingly so, and he, perhaps disgusted with his own actions, set to work with an ambition—or a will—Jacoba had never seen before. Once he quit vomiting, that is. By noon, he deemed the number of logs the horses dragged to the cabin site adequate enough to build a barn in addition to finishing the cabin, and he set to work peeling them. Yesterday's still smoldering slash pile grew. Smoke again rose in trailing clouds, while the scent of freshly cut pine and fir spread all around.

And Charlie sweated, the odor of liquor rolling off him in a vaporous fog.

Jacoba, her hands covered in her strongest gloves and wearing her oldest skirt and waist, worked alongside him. Once, though dim in the distance, she thought she heard Quill barking. Her heart leapt with the realization Ruel was just over the hill.

She saw Charlie heard the dog, too, a strange expression crossing his face as his eyes swiveled toward her.

Why?

The question tripped across her mind like a fly landing on dung, settling as though for a long stay. *What is he thinking?*

* * *

Sometime during the night, she awakened. It was dark in the tent. It was always dark in the tent, but this —

She'd been nervous when she went to bed. Even so, worn out from her hard labor, she'd fallen immediately into sleep. Now she couldn't remember if she'd really closed the flap so tightly it felt as though she were encased in a tomb. She'd had to keep the bogeyman away though, hadn't she? All she really remembered was that she didn't like being closed in. It seemed to shut off her air. To blind her. To make her heart race and fear creep into her bones.

Lying motionless, she did her best to hold her breathing steady, shallow and light. To not give in to the foreboding. Her eyes were open, she knew, but unable to make out a thing. Then something, a living body, moved and enough light came in that she could see again. See too well, really, because the light grew and grew.

How odd, she thought. Is it morning already?

A voice called out. Charlie's voice. Panicked, she thought, and then horrified. "Jim," Charlie said. "What are you doing here? What have you done?"

"Taking care of a problem." Ledger sounded pleased with himself. "It's what you wanted, isn't it?"

"Yes. But not . . . not like this."

That's when she realized the light came not from the sun, but from fire as it ate at the canvas of her tent.

Mind-numbing fear paralyzed her for seconds—too many seconds— before regaining her wits, she scrambled to her feet. The gun she always slept with nowadays was in her hand. She started for the entry and yanked on the flap, only to find it had been laced shut on the outside. She knew better than to waste time trying to open it.

But Charlie, when he'd set up the tent, had been careless. Nothing unusual in that as she'd discovered of late, and in this instance his lack of care served her well. There was a spot where the floor tarp parted ways with the canvas of the tent. It flapped even in the slightest of breezes and over the last couple days, the slack had grown. Grown enough to allow a woman as slender as she to roll out the back as the flames leapt skyward.

Gasping for air fit to breathe, she crawled into the darkness and then lay still as a death. Flat on her back looking up with thankful eyes at a sky filled with sparks and ash. Until the remains of her tent and most of her clothing lay in ruins.

Hah. Death. That's what Charlie wanted.

Strangely, it wasn't fear Jacoba felt. The gun in her hand was a solid weight. Reassuring in the face of her fury. In her building need for retribution.

She was not Madame's daughter for nothing and he, Charlie and Ledger both, would find that out.

* * *

Jacoba pushed herself into the darkness, rolling beneath the sheltering branches of one of the bushes that had been so pretty only a week ago. The sweet scent of their white flowers overrode the smell of smoke and horse manure. Those flowers were showering down like flakes of dandruff as they dried. The fallen drift of white made perfect cover for the paleness of her nightgown.

Her teeth rattled in rhythmic time with her body until she clenched her jaw to hold it still. Inside her head, the click had seemed so loud she feared Charlie or Ledger might hear. Pressing the back of her hand against her mouth, she fought to suppress a coughing spell, afraid it would reveal her position.

She could see her husband from where she lay tucked into the least space possible and curled around her pistol. Outlined by the flaming tent, he stood still as a statue, arms at his sides as he watched the sparks soar into the midnight sky. He didn't cry out, nor did he make any move intended to rescue her.

On the other hand, he didn't cavort like a man overcome with joy, either.

A second man joined him.

Ledger, hanging around to watch his handiwork.

Charlie turned his head to look at his friend—or whatever he was. "I didn't think you'd actually do it." His voice carried clearly over the snap and crackle of the fire.

Ledger laughed. "I told you I would. Are you sorry?"

Charlie hesitated. "Yes. No. Part of me is. I wish she'd done what I told her. She always obeyed her mother. I figured she would obey me."

"Huh. She broke away and married you, didn't she."

"Yeah, her one fling at independence—or so I thought at first. But damn, she proved to be stubborn as . . . as I don't know what. She went to work at the telephone company. Refused to ask her mother for a dime. The richest woman in St. Louis and her daughter too proud and stubborn to ask for even a small share of it. Damn her!"

The last exploded from him in a fury of what Jacoba interpreted as anguish and disgust in a mis-mash of emotion.

"We could've been sitting pretty if only she'd done as I told her," he went on, his anger growing. "Now look. I'm left with is this piece of worthless land and a dead wife. Unless I can keep this—" a wave indicated the ruined tent and, he presumed, her body—"from getting out for a while. I've been thinking, Jim. I'm going to write to Madame Ludke tomorrow. Tell her Jacoba is sick and beg—yes, beg—for money. Talk her out of a few thousand and then her poor daughter can go ahead and die a peaceful death."

Ledger laughed. Loud, long, and uproariously. "A fine idea. That'll teach her. Teach them both."

"Yeah," Charlie said. "Well, guess we'd better get out of here in case that Injun across the bay saw the flames and comes to see what's happened. Best if we're not here."

Ledger looked around. "Gonna leave the horses?"

Pym and Tope, Jacoba finally noticed, were snorting and shifting about in their hobbles, disturbed by the fire and the excited voices.

"Yes." Charlie nodded. "Or no. I'll ride one and slip the other's hobbles. Make it look like he got loose, as if Jacoba couldn't even manage that. Like the horse wandered through camp and set the tent on fire."

Ledger slapped him on the back. "Good thinking, pal. You've got a head on your shoulders. Anyways, them squaws, they'll be so drunk they won't know when we got to them. I set them up with plenty of hootch. They'll say whatever I tell'em to say."

"That's if anybody ever even learns about this 'tragic' accident." Charlie eyed Ledger, an odd expression on his face. "I hope they never do."

"Yeah, well..." Ledger seemed to ponder a moment, then a crafty expression crossed his face. "We can come back tomorrow or the next day, and if nobody has been here, we can bury her in the woods where she can't be found—ever."

"Yes." Charlie thought a moment. "I'll say she ran off. That she didn't like it here. Thought herself too good to go digging in the dirt and be forced to live in a log cabin."

"Right." Ledger said, "She ain't been here long. Hell, hardly anybody even knows about her, and if they do, nobody will think twice about it. Didn't the Albers woman—remember her?—do exactly that? Run off from her husband?"

"So I've been told." Charlie, though he nodded, seemed hardly to be listening. He moved out of Jacoba's sight long enough to free Pym and haze the horse toward the fire before nervously looking over his shoulder. Finally, his nerves got the best of him. "Let's get out of here. Now. I think Gagne is coming."

They left, Charlie astraddle Tope, trotting out of the circle of firelight and disappearing down the road.

Pym, left free, avoided the dying fire and wandered about as though wondering why he'd been left behind. Soon, he dropped his head and sought better grass to graze.

Jacoba didn't waste time crying. She felt frozen, bewildered, resentful, scared, angry, hurt. . . So many adjectives she needed a thesaurus. Besides, thinking up the proper word kept her mind off of a husband who had planned to kill her. Mostly. Hadn't really protested, at best.

How could he? How could I ever have cared for him? Helplessly, she watched the fire die away to nothing.

After a while, Jacoba emerged from her hiding place and collected Pym before entering the big tent Charlie used and where most of her things were stored. She dug around inside a trunk that showed signs of already being searched, where she found clean clothing and shoes. She dressed quickly, uncomfortable being in Charlie's tent where the smell of him seemed to permeate the canvas and the clutter he left announced his sole proprietorship. To her overwrought nerves, he remained a presence.

Hungry now as she hadn't been at supper, she got food from the provision box. Leftover biscuits and jam helped restore strength, although she choked on crumbs.

Then she waited. And waited some more, a good long time in case Charlie came back. He didn't.

As it happened, he'd been wrong about one thing. Ruel didn't come either. Oddly enough, she was glad about that. She didn't want him to know the depravity of the man she'd married. Of what a fool she'd been.

Regrets blanketed Jacoba in a fog. She'd thought herself worldly and wise, but look at what she'd done. She had married a scoundrel, a would-be wife murderer. Simply traded the efforts of one person who wanted to control her for monetary purposes for another who intended to do the same. Considering her poor judgement, maybe she deserved no better.

But still. Murder?

Madame would've been shocked to see the wry smile that turned up the corners of Jacoba's lips. Charlie, too. Something Jacoba was aware of even as rage boiled in her heart and pain scoured her soul.

Murder. *Charlie wanted to murder her.* Thought he had, at

the instigation and help of his friend Jim Ledger. And then he'd simply gone off to consort with low women, as if nothing of consequence had happened.

It was a concept difficult for her mind to fathom.

But it made her smile, even as her nerves quaked and she shook so badly she finally set the revolver she'd been holding on a stump. Her fingers were cramping around the butt and she didn't want the gun going off by accident.

The revolver she'd taken—stolen, really—from a man who'd first stolen what was hers. Comeuppance. The thief had deserved the turnabout. She only wished he'd known who had taken those things.

Charlie had known, but he'd evidently forgotten she believed in retribution for one's sins.

He should have remembered.

And she would make certain he did.

Chapter 21

The look on Charlie's face was priceless. The surprise. The shock. The dismay.

The fear. Oh, yes. The fear.

The way he looked around, as though afraid he might be observed.

Well, and so he was, but not by anyone he might expect. For instance, the sheriff and a cohort of his deputies.

Jacoba, standing back among the trees where the horses usually grazed inside their makeshift enclosure, wished she had one of those little Brownie cameras. She would've saved the photo for posterity. Maybe have a copy made and send it to Madame. Or the newspaper. Anonymously, of course, with no mention of herself.

She estimated the time of day to be about ten o'clock of the second morning since the fire. Yesterday she'd been prepared for Charlie and Ledger to arrive at any second, so she'd kept near the edge of these woods where she'd be able to dart deeper into the timber and disappear. It hadn't been necessary. Evidently their debauchery had occupied them most of the day.

Or, it occurred to her, they'd gone around establishing a record of their whereabouts. Better, she supposed, in Charlie's mind, to be accused of two-timing his wife than murdering her.

A smile twitched her lips. So. Something else he'd failed at. He and Ledger both.

At any rate, by the afternoon, she'd come to the conclusion they wouldn't be coming back that day and begun, not cleaning up the remains of her burned tent—evidence of what had happened—but tending to the horse, her garden, and even hauling the rest of the logs for the barn from where they'd been cut. There were only half a dozen. Even harnessing Pym had been a challenge, but having watched the men at work, she knew how to do it. The only question had been whether she could do it. Not an easy job for a woman alone, setting the heavy choker chain, but manageable when one was determined enough. She'd even used Charlie's axe and limbed the logs, and added the slash to the burn pile. The hard work helped dispel the flames of her anger. Not the slow burn, though. That was etched forever on her soul.

And now Charlie, on his own without Ledger at his side, slid from Tope's broad back and stood staring at the camp. His mouth had rounded into an O amidst the stubble of the beard he'd taken to wearing.

Ah, yes. *Priceless.*

Jacoba wasn't entirely sure what he expected to see, but she didn't think it was this. Not the completed stack of logs, skidded into place under her own and Pym's efforts. Not Pym whickering a comfortable greeting to his mate. Not the smoke rising from her campfire in little puffs with a kettle containing a ham hock and beans bubbling over the coals. And certainly not the raked and cleaned yard—excepting only the blackened remains of her tent.

She stifled a giggle. Give him a minute more. Let her revel just one more minute in his reaction.

"Hello?" he finally called out. "Is anyone here?"

What did he expect, Jacoba wondered scornfully. That the pot had set itself over the fire?

Still she waited. What would he do when she appeared in front of him, very much alive? Did she really want to find out? And yet, what choice did she have? What choice had either of them?

She moved, a rustling in the tree branches that hid her from Charlie.

"Hello," he called again. "Who's there?"

Drawing her pistol from a contraption of leather straps holding it around her waist, Jacoba held the butt firmly in hand.

"Me." She stepped into sight. "Surprised?"

His face drained of color, a delicious sight. "Y...y...you. How—"

"How did I escape my intended murder?" She didn't plan on telling him. Not at this point anyway. She wanted him to wonder. To worry. To puzzle. Maybe to consider a miracle. "Suffice it to say I didn't trust you. I especially didn't . . . don't . . . trust Jim Ledger. I could tell the pair of you had skullduggery in mind. And that I was to be the victim."

"Not me. I didn't . . ."

"Oh, please. It was obvious."

This time blood rushed into his face, not out. "Obvious?"

"Conspirators should be more cautious. When plotting murder, only one person with his hand on the gun is the safest bet. A loose tongue can spoil the plan."

He couldn't seem to stop himself from repeating her words.

"Loose tongue?" he said quickly, as though that was the point. Then, "What are you talking about? I don't know what you mean."

Jacoba merely looked at him. "Or strike of the match," she clarified, as if he hadn't spoken. If possible, she would spread strife between the two men.

"I . . ." he started, then changed his mind and said, "Jacoba, honey . . . I . . ."

She raised her gun, noting with some amusement his sharp gasp for air. "I've a mind to shoot you, you know. Can you give me any reason why I shouldn't?"

He remained silent.

After a moment, she said, "No, there isn't one, is there? Except that I'm not a murderer...murderess. You're not worth the trouble I'd be in if anyone found out, not to mention the weight on my soul. Do you have a weight on your soul, Charlie? Do you suppose Ledger does?"

He had no answer.

She made a small gesture with the pistol. "Of course, that shooting idea depends on events. I could change my mind. But what has me thinking is something you said. You or Ledger, I can't remember now which one. Doesn't much matter, I suppose."

Charlie looked as though he might faint.

And wouldn't that be amusing? Charlie lying on the ground unconscious? Vulnerable. Jacoba smiled just thinking about it. "Don't you wonder what it was?"

"I was drunk, not thinking. So was Jim. When we woke up, we didn't think what happened was real." Sweat had broken out on his face. "An accident. That's all it was, Jacoba. Darling. A horrible accident. I love you."

"Come to think of it, I believe it was Ledger who said, 'We can come back tomorrow or the next day, and if nobody has been here, we can bury her in the woods where she can't be found—ever. You can say she ran off.'" Dreamlike, she spoke over him. "And you said, 'I'll say she didn't like it here, messing in the dirt and forced to live in a log cabin.' And Ledger said, "'Nobody will think twice about it.'"

Almost word for word. Her memory had always been good, a source of pride.

"Jim said that, not me."

"Oh yes." She strafed him with a mocking look. "And you argued against his every word, didn't you? His every intention. Did you say, 'No. Never. I'll protect my dear . . . my darling wife to my last breath?'" A wild kind of laughter roughened her throat. "Did you?"

Charlie swallowed. His hands hung at his sides, but an underlying tension seemed to be building in him. Jacoba saw it in the way his eyes shifted, as if testing for an escape route. His feet inched forward and he leaned in. Would he attack? Try to overpower her?

She raised the gun.

Yet when he spoke, he didn't bluster. "What are you going to do, Jacoba? Decide."

* * *

By the end of the week, she still hadn't decided on her next steps. With Charlie treading cautiously around her, Jacoba had relaxed her vigilance enough to go about her work. She'd begun keeping only one eye constantly peeled for her husband's whereabouts. Without Jim Ledger's influence, she believed she was safe enough. For now.

Besides, the night of her intended murder, Charlie had left his rifle behind when he and Ledger went to meet the women. She'd taken and hidden the gun in the woods and though she was aware of Charlie searching, he hadn't found it.

When Ledger reappeared, which he was bound to do sooner or later, she would need to rethink what she'd done.

She would never have allowed this had she not known Charlie was basically a coward. The kind that preferred always to take the path of least resistance, which included running from the trouble he caused and placing the blame on someone else. In this case, Jim Ledger.

Not that Ledger didn't deserve to be held liable. He did.

But she remembered how Charlie had also blamed his mother for turning a blind eye when he stole money from her. How he blamed his father and his brother for not trusting him to run the family business. How he managed to blame Jacoba for his slow recovery from the train accident.

How could she have been such a fool when she married him?

Allowed him to persuade her to run away from their troubles. The question ran through her mind like the eternal waves on an ocean. *Never again. Her blinders were off.*

She was not Madame's daughter for nothing. Madame would never run away. From anyone or anything.

Except Madame would've found a way to rid herself of him—permanently—before now.

But when push came to shove, Jacoba hadn't been able to do it. Divorce seemed out of the question and she wasn't about to shoot Charlie. Not in cold blood. Besides, she needed him. Needed someone more muscular than herself, at any rate. How was she to manage a rough homestead by herself? Sometimes she wondered why she even wanted to, except for being too stubborn to allow herself to be scared away.

And so she pretended to forgive him, and he pretended to be chastened and regretful. A detente that lasted from moment to moment.

On the day after Charlie returned to the homestead, Louis Tevere had come riding through the woods from the road. She'd been glad to see him although Charlie stood by scowling for long seconds before stalking off to where he was in the process of clear-cutting another patch of land.

Watching him, Louis' smile had faded, even as he handed her the letter he'd brought. "He don't like Indians," he said. Then added, "Indian men, leastwise. Me."

Jacoba shook her head. "I'm sorry," she said, helpless to deny the charge. "But then, he doesn't like me, either."

Louis, a puzzled frown gathering on his forehead, didn't say anything, but only studied her expression.

The letter was addressed to Jacoba. "It's from Delilah, at the bakery where I worked before coming here. You remember those delicious pastries the morning you brought me to the homestead?"

The concerned face he'd worn since he arrived faded a degree. "Yes. So does my son."

Jacoba smiled. "She says she's sold out of the lotions and soaps I left with her to sell. Customers are already asking for more." A trill of delight swept over her, a lightening of her heart. "That's good news. She needs me to replenish the stock."

Jacoba, having the advantage of hearing her mother speak of business for all of her life, had prepared for this in some small way. When she'd come here, she'd packed one of her trunks with the necessary supplies to make up several more batches. The soap would need curing for at least a few weeks, but preparing the lotions took only a couple of days.

Thank goodness the trunk had been stored in Charlie's larger tent and so survived the fire.

"Mary likes the lotion you gave her." Louis said. "Smells good and she says it feels good on her skin." His gaze sharpened as he eyed Jacoba's expression change to dismay. "What is wrong? You said good news."

"Yes, but . . ."

Louis' eyebrows rose.

"Logistics," Jacoba said ruefully. "How am I to get the product to her? I don't dare—" She broke off at the look Louis sent her. "I mean, I can't take the time to personally take it to Spokane. Or to shop for more supplies." Definitely not. Because if she left for even a few hours, she had no doubt Charlie would contact Jim Ledger. Who knows what kind of plotting they'd do then? What kind of reception she'd have when she returned. Her life wouldn't be worth a plugged nickel, as these westerners were wont to say.

You should leave. Leave and never come back. Her inner voice spoke again.

"I will do it." Louis, generous as always, cheerfully made the offer. "I'll collect the goods and take it to the train in Rockford. Have your lady pick up the box at the station. If you write a list, maybe she can buy and ship the supplies to you. I'll bring them here."

"Mr. Tevere, you are a lifesaver." Jacoba reached out to shake his hand. "Just tell me what I can do for you in return!"

Louis, his dusky skin turning red at her ebullience, turned away. "Nothing, Mrs. DeGroot. I am glad to help out. Be a neighbor." He climbed back on his horse, a long-legged sorrel, and reined it toward the road. He had gone several yards before he stopped again. "Gagne said I should keep an eye on you when he is away."

"He did?" *Ruel.* Jacoba's heart sped up.

"Yes. So there is one thing," he said, in a deprecating sort of way.

"Yes? What is it?" She moved forward.

"You remember them pups my female whelped?"

She did. Handsome and lively, black and white creatures with longish fur and curly tails. Like Quill. "Indeed I do. They're darling."

"Got one left. A female. I need to give her away, somewhere where the children won't be sad to see her go." He paused as if hoping she'd say something.

She didn't.

"Thought maybe you'd like a pup to keep you company," he said softly. "She'd be a good watch dog. Let you know about danger. Be company when you are alone."

Oh, dear. Was he saying what she thought he was saying? What if . . .

A puppy of her own. Maybe one that would turn out like Quill. "Yes," she said.

Chapter 22

True to his word, Louis Tevere brought his wagon around later that same afternoon and loaded a box filled with Jacoba's cosmetics to take to the railroad station in Rockford. Her soaps were wrapped in tissue paper and tied with thin, pale green ribbons. Small glass flasks—originally meant to contain illicit whiskey and for which she'd paid pennies a dozen to an out-of-business bootlegger—held lotions stoppered with a pretty cork. All bore hand-printed labels with an identifying logo she'd created, and a description of the various scents and ingredients. Making them had occupied many a long evening when living at the boarding house.

"I'll bring the pup when I bring the supplies." Louis concentrated on tying the box of glass-bottled lotions to the wagon bed so they didn't rattle around, even though Jacoba had filled in the spaces with pine needles and moss. "Maybe you can prepare him first. I heard he don't like dogs."

He had his back turned so that Charlie, the *him* in question and watching from the side with a sour look on his face, could neither hear nor even tell he was speaking.

Jacoba lifted the basket of soaps to rest alongside the box. "You must have spoken with Mr. Gagne about Quill. Charlie rather took against him. I don't know why. But I'll keep the puppy close by my side."

Tacit agreement to something that seemed like a warning.

It crossed her mind to think that Charlie wasn't good with any animal. Even the horses who worked so hard for him. It was always she who found little treats for them, sugar cubes or an apple or carrot to crunch. She cleaned their harness and oiled it, brushed the dirt from their coats, cleaned around their eyes and applied an ointment to keep the flies away.

Those early days, when Charlie had searched for a team, then spent time caring for them seemed a long-ago dream when compared with the way he acted now. She wondered what had changed him. Somewhere in her heart, Jacoba acknowledged it couldn't all be Ledger's fault. Charlie had a mean streak all his own that something had stirred into action. When he gained courage, as she was afraid he would, then he'd truly be dangerous.

More dangerous.

Wrapped up in this sudden dire thought, Jacoba turned to find Charlie standing close. Too close. But all he did was thrust a hand into his pocket and come up with a silver dollar.

He didn't hand it to Louis with a thank you, but instead flung the heavy coin down in the dust beneath the Indian's feet.

"That's good enough," he said. "Now get out of here. You're a delivery man, not a friend."

"Charlie!" Jacoba, after a horror-stricken glare at her husband, reached out to Louis. "I'm so sorry, Mr. Tevere. He didn't mean it. It's not true. I most definitely consider you and Mary my friends."

Louis' eyes flashed as he stared at Charlie. But then he glanced at Jacoba, his stare dropping to the pistol she wore at her hip and his mouth tightened. "I know who my friends are, missus," he said. "And what friends do for one another."

He left the dollar in the dirt as he trod around to step up to the wagon seat. "Don't worry, missus. I'll bring the supplies when they arrive."

He drove away without looking back.

Spinning around, Jacoba's hand touched the pistol. "That was stupid, Charlie. More stupid than you may know."

Charlie sneered. "Damn all Indians. And you. What kind of woman are you, anyway? You prefer them breeds to a white man? A damn Indian lover? Holds true for the one that lives over the hill, doesn't it? Want to go live in a teepee? Huh?"

She went ice cold and yet she managed a derisive half-smile. "Well, that's a change of attitude. After all, I believe you've consorted with plenty of native women. Just so you know, I'd prefer just about any man over you, Charles DeGroot. And for your information, the Tevere family has a home anyone would be proud of. Unlike most of the white people hereabouts I can name, and the ones who live on this homestead in particular." She couldn't help tossing those last words at him.

He reddened and flicked a glance at the half-finished cabin and the pile of logs. "You don't know any of the white people. You don't know anything."

"And whose fault is that? None of them will associate with you, or that scum, Jim Ledger and I don't blame them."

His fist lashed out but she'd expected retaliation. She stepped back, out of his reach and put her hand on the butt of her pistol. "That's enough, Charlie. Never try that again. I won't stand for it."

He stared at her for a long moment, his blue eyes narrowed and mean. "Stand for it?" His voice roughened. "But one of these days you'll lie down for it." He turned and walked away.

It wasn't safe, the quarrel they had. Jacoba knew it. She suspected Charlie knew too. Exacerbating the hard feelings went both ways, the anger growing in leaps and bounds.

They took separate paths, Charlie deeper into the woods where the breeze carried the sound of his axe as he hewed another tree. She to bring out her big iron pot where she mixed emollients and tinctures for her lotions, boiled down fat and mixed in lye for soap, stirring and stirring until the trace was perfect. She even experimented with a specialized balm for the lips, as she discovered her own chapped when outside so much. The formula of grated beeswax and coconut oil firmed up as it cooled, the mint tincture she'd mixed in adding a bit of taste and freshness. Next time she'd put in a dollop of honey for healing, and some wild rose petals to provide a hint of color.

With the work, her anger ebbed, and perhaps Charlie's did too although, come evening, the horses came back tired, with signs of the whip on their broad rumps.

Jacoba's anger flared anew, her heart beating hard, as she soothed the animals with treats and spread her good salve on broken skin, until they calmed and began to graze.

"Damn Charlie," she whispered into the horse's pricked ear. "Oh, damn him."

She very well knew he would rather have set the whip's lash on her.

* * *

Jacoba had fixed an area within the empty shell of the cabin to store her goods and the completed products she'd made for Delilah to sell in her café. During the day, Charlie finally got a roof on the cabin, so if rain came, at least it would be kept dry. Or most of it. She questioned the workmanship and imagined leaks in the future.

Oddly enough, she had no worries about her husband destroying the fruits of her labor out of sheer cussedness and the desire to thwart her. He might want to, but he knew their value. She supposed she should thank Madame for that, as the Ludke wealth stemmed from such small beginnings. So might the DeGroot, or so he may have believed. Jacoba said nothing to dissuade him. She thought her value might add to her safety, not that she gave up keeping her pistol at hand.

On this warm afternoon, Jacoba was inside the cabin out of a rather stiff breeze, sitting on a tarp and cutting some of her precious tissue paper into precisely-sized squares. The soaps, though not quite hardened to perfection, would soon need to be wrapped.

A shot and a shout followed by a small pained howl brought her head up with a jerk, her eyes wide. She jumped to her feet, unsure for a moment of what she'd heard. Another shout echoed. The sounds, she realized, were coming from the road.

Not Charlie then. Or at least, she didn't think so. But who? What?

A second later she knew. Louis Tevere was due to bring supplies today. And her puppy.

The shot.

Pausing only to check her pistol, she ran. Ran as fast and hard as she'd ever run in her life, grateful for the old full skirt she wore and not one of her fashionable hobble- skirted dresses.

Wagon ruts made running more difficult, but she skipped over them as sure-footed as a doe without noticing, right to where the path led into the homestead.

There, where the DeGroot's rough trail joined the road through the reservation, she spotted Louis' wagon stopped in the middle of the turn-off. Then Louis himself, pinned against the wagon's side where a large white man she'd never seen before stood holding a shotgun on him. A shaggy bay horse trotted loose as if it didn't know where to go.

And there. As she might have known, she spotted Jim Ledger astride his horse with a rope around a small dog's neck. He was dragging it up and down in front of Louis and laughing as the puppy screamed. When it had breath. Its cries were growing fainter.

She wasn't truly aware when she stopped, cocked her pistol and leveled it, until her shot took Jim Ledger in the arm. Blood spurted and he shouted his pain. Not that she was aiming for his arm. She'd tried for his heart and missed.

In a way, it was an unlucky shot, but at least the rope dropped from Ledger's grasp, releasing the puppy. It—she—lay as though dead in the road.

Another result was the man with the shotgun spinning around and blasting away with both barrels of what she knew to be an over/under sporting gun. The good part was that he was far enough away the birdshot never reached her, instead shattering the leaves on a bush a full ten feet short of where she stood and far to the left. Untouched, she was also aware that now the stranger was disarmed, Louis, released from danger of being decapitated or gut shot, grabbed the gun out of the man's hands and tossed it far off to the other side of the wagon. She heard the clatter as it fell among rocks.

Meanwhile, Ledger swayed in the saddle, his eyes bugged and his face gone white under a dirty stubble of graying whiskers. "You. You're supposed to be dead." His voice shook.

Jacoba laughed, a mocking delight at his shock that made Louis Tevere give her a startled look.

"Yes, me." She hissed out a breath of disgust. "And here you thought you'd disposed of me. Here I am, and not a bit sorry to disappoint you."

The big man made an awkward move toward her, but she turned the gun on him. "Not a good idea, mister. Stay where you are."

To Louis, who'd already reached the puppy and loosed the rope from around its neck, she said, "Is the little dog all right, Mr. Tevere? I ran as fast as I could when I heard the shot. Who fired it? And at what? Or who?"

Tevere stood up, the pup in his arms. He pointed at Ledger with his chin. "Him. He aimed at me but he is drunk and a bad shot." Running his hand over the puppy's neck and legs, he finally said, "I believe the pup will live. Is a tough breed."

His English lacked its usual fluid flow. He'd been plenty scared, she realized.

Ledger wrapped his good hand around the saddlehorn, holding on and cursing steadily as blood dripped to the ground from his wounded arm. The nervous horse, held on a tight rein, moved in circles around it, plowing the blood into the dirt.

"I'm dying," Ledger announced. "You stupid bitch, you've killed me."

Jacoba, thinking his voice sounded entirely too strong for imminent death, wrinkled her nose. "Harrumph. At least I didn't try to burn you to death."

Louis choked. "Missus!"

"A long, sad story, not for this moment, Mr. Tevere." She aimed her pistol at the big man. "You, what's your name?"

"Mac. Owen MacFarlane." His wild-eyed look shifted between her, Ledger, and once or twice, to Louis. "What's Jim talking about, you're supposed to be dead? And you. Burned?"

If he'd been drunk, and she rather thought he had, he'd gotten sober fast.

She shrugged. "He set fire to my tent with me in it. He didn't know I got out in time."

"Charlie —" It appeared MacFarland had the beginning of a question, but it didn't get asked. Charlie came running out of the woods just then.

"I heard shots. What the hell is going on here?" he demanded. He looked at Ledger and frowned. "Jim! What happened?"

Ledger shook his head, a sort of signal Jacoba figured she wasn't supposed to see. Or interpret, anyway. Had this been a plan between them? Had they intended for her to finally die and have Louis take the blame? But then she remembered Ledger's astonishment at seeing her alive. And where did MacFarlane figure in?

Maybe, this once, Charlie wasn't involved with his friend's shenanigans.

Jacoba clamped her mouth closed. What would Ledger say?

He didn't say anything right off, moaning theatrically instead.

MacFarlane turned out to be more vocal. "We was just gonna have us some fun. With the Injun, ya know, when we rode up on him and saw the dog running loose beside the wagon. Then . . ." He hesitated. "Then I don't rightly know. Things kind of blew up.

Jim said he wanted to play with dog. Hell, it's just a mutt. Ain't like it's a French poodle or something. But this here feller"—he meant Louis—"objected. He said the dog belongs to Missus DeGroot, so Jim laughs and says, 'Missus De Groot, eh? I don't think so. What the hell? Did you steal it?' and the Injun says 'No.' Says he's givin' it as a gift. So Jim says, 'I'll take it' and he grabs it by the scruff and starts haulin' it around at the end of his rope. 'Teachin' it to lead' he says, but he ain't."

The look he sent Ledger appeared disapproving and he continued. "The Injun, he jumped down off this here wagon and started for Jim, which is when Jim spooked, grabbed his pistol and took a shot at him. Blowed the hat right off his head. So I got out my shotgun and had the Injun penned up afore he got hurt while Jim dragged the dog back and forth. Then this here woman showed up and shot Jim." He stopped, then added, "That's about it—except, we shouldn't of been doing it."

The account, Jacoba decided, or at least her part, was long, but quite factual.

"I'm dying," Ledger said, and fell off his horse right at Jacoba's feet. The horse snorted and trotted off to join MacFarlane's mare, wandering loose and cropping grass.

She looked down at him and a spreading puddle of urine as his bladder gave way. "He fainted," she said and barked out a short laugh. "Looks like one of you ought to take care of him. Get him out of the road in case somebody drives by." An unlikely happenstance.

Turning away, she gestured to Louis' wagon. "If you're still of a mind, Mr. Tevere, we can get these supplies unloaded at the campsite. I hope the puppy won't be too upset, staying with me after what happened. Let me hold her while we drive on down to the cabin. I'm a good hand with the horses. Hopefully the puppy will make friends and trust me, too."

Charlie gawked at her. "Jim. Aren't you going to help Jim?"

"No."

"We need the injun's wagon for Jim."

Louis, shaking his head, cast a wary look at Charlie and Mac-Farlane who'd gathered on either side of Ledger, already coming out of his faint. Since neither man paid him any attention, he rummaged behind some rocks and found his hat, displaying the hole shot through the tall crown.

Jacoba, looking at it, swallowed. Close. Another inch and he'd be missing the top of his head.

As for her? She had the unsettling thought that she might have just signed her own death warrant. Ledger wouldn't stop until she was dead after this. Or until he was. One way or the other.

"My wagon is not for hire." Louis clamped the hat on his head. "I do not haul trash. Missus?" He gave her a hand onto the wagon and mounted himself. "Hyah,"

Charlie, running, passed them on the way to the homestead, shouting that he had to get the horses hitched to the wagon and get Ledger to the doctor quick, before he bled to death.

Louis looked over at Jacoba who sat primly on the wagon seat petting and crooning to the puppy. "Don't think Ledger is hurt bad, but what you going to do if the sheriff comes, Missus? Those men going to make trouble for you?"

She'd noticed a slight quaver in Louis' voice. "Something to discuss with Charlie before he leaves for town, I think."

"You're not worried?"

"No. And I don't think you need to be either."

"There's two of them, maybe three. Only one of me and I have dark skin. And you. A woman."

Oh, he knew Charlie and his associates very well. Jacoba dipped her head in shame. "I don't believe Ledger has a reliable reputation. And I'm sorry to say Charlie doesn't either. Why would anything they say be taken at face value? I don't know anything about this MacFarlane. I've never even heard his name mentioned. Perhaps the sheriff is an honest man. And if not—"

Louis shook his head in a grim sort of way, as if knowing better what to expect.

They pulled up in front of the unfinished cabin to find Charlie already hitching Tope and Pym to the wagon. He looked up at their arrival.

"I hope you're satisfied, Jacoba. You're going to be in trouble when Jim tells how you shot him," he said, smirking at Jacoba as he attached the strap to the singletree. "Could be you'll even go to jail."

Jacoba handed the puppy to Louis and clambered from the wagon. "And when I tell how the pair of you tried to burn me to death?"

"Nobody will believe you," he said, his smirk faltering only a little.

"Oh, I think they will."

"I'll swear it was an accident."

"There are penalties for perjury, Charlie. You should know that. Everybody is aware that Ledger, and you, are a pair of bounders. Men who try to cheat at whatever they do, who are known for dishonesty, for bullying and drinking and abusing the native women."

His mouth tightened. "Lies. Besides all men . . ."

She cut him off. "No, Charlie. All men don't. And you, you're on thin ice. The people at the boarding house know about you, if it comes to that, and wouldn't be averse to telling the world. In fact, I think they'd take great pleasure in doing so. As for me, well—" An ironic smile bloomed. "I'm known as the heroine of the telephone company. I saved a foreign man of minor royalty from dying. Or have you forgotten the newspaper coverage?" She met his eyes square on. "And how you thought it was improper to have my name in the newspaper? I think it was great good luck. Who do you suppose the general public will trust more? A hardworking lady heroine or her philandering husband and his disreputable friend?"

Charlie, silenced, climbed onto his wagon's seat and shouted to get the horses moving. It was clear he would've preferred to run her over, but she had plenty of time to step out of the way.

Louis stood watching Charlie leave, his hands clenched. "Did he? Him and Ledger, did they try to kill you?"

"Yes." She went to the end of the wagon and picked up a box containing several bottles of clean, fragrant oils, olive, coconut, and almond. "Why do you think I carry this pistol every moment of the day, and sleep with it at night?" Not, she reflected, that he would know right off that she did.

"Aren't you afraid?"

"Yes." The admission cost her.

"Good. You should be." He carried two more boxes inside, looking around the raw log walls with a disparaging expression he tried to hide. "Why do you stay?"

She tried to come up with a good answer.

Giving the puppy a final goodbye pat—and perhaps having second thoughts as to leaving her with Jacoba—he climbed onto the wagon seat. For a few seconds, he eyed her as she spoke to the dog. "Think if this property is worth the risk," he said after a moment. "Is it worth the danger? Worth your life? It would be better if you went away. Leave the homestead to DeGroot. Be safe."

Slowly, she shook her head. "I have thought of it, Mr. Tevere. But I have no place else to go." A single room in someone's boarding house for the rest of her life? She couldn't bear the thought.

"Then you are very brave," he said.

She thought he meant she was very stupid. Which she couldn't deny, but she'd told him nothing more than the truth. She had nowhere else to go. It was her name that had been on the winning lottery ticket. Which made this homestead *her* land. She wanted it to be her home.

"You should run," Louis said again. "Today. Missus, you should take this dog and run fast."

She gazed up at him. "If I were a man, Mr. Tevere—Louis— would you tell him to run away?"

His shoulders hunched. "No. I'd tell a man to fight. But missus, you are not a man."

Gently, he shook the reins over his mismatched team and drove away.

Chapter 23

Ruel came for a visit the next afternoon. Although Jacoba hadn't expected him, she wasn't completely surprised, either, and imagined she had Louis Tevere—perhaps at Mary's instigation—to thank.

Mixed feelings colored her greeting to him. She wasn't sure she liked the way her heart gave a glad little jump when she looked up and saw him striding across the clearing to where she worked with her tinctures and potions. She stirred the pot hanging over the slow-burning campfire embers more vigorously than it needed.

"Cooking up a witch's brew, Mrs. DeGroot?" Unsmiling, he gazed down at her and squatted to make a fuss over the puppy who promptly showed him her belly.

Jacoba, a little surprised by his apparent familiarity with a classical analogy, stood up and pushed a strand of hair from her eyes. "Perhaps, if one considers my potion a brew. I can't remember, do all witches come to a bad end?"

His dark eyes clouded. "I don't know. Depends, I think, whether they're good witches or bad."

"Who has the final word on that, anyway? But no. I'm not a witch at all, but plain Jacoba Ludke doing her best to help careworn ladies look and feel better." She didn't become aware of omitting her married name until later, when she thought back over their conversation.

Judging her potion to be heated and emulsified to perfection, Jacoba swung the kettle aside to cool before she began filling bottles already labeled. "Rose Scented Almond Milk" they read. "Puts the cream in your complexion." She mustn't forget to add a vial of Bulgarian Attar of Roses on her shopping list to give to Delilah. It was rather expensive, as ingredients went, but worth it. Madame swore its perfume made the mundane components more effective.

Ruel waited until she'd stepped back from the fire and gathered the puppy gamboling too close to it before he spoke again. "Louis Tevere came by my mother's house this morning," he said then, referring to the house by the lake. "He told me what happened yesterday. Showed me the hole in his hat and said he thought he was going to die."

"I thought he was too." She shuddered, able to admit it now.

"He's worried about you."

She didn't know what to say and settled for, "Is he? No need. I can take care of myself." Had Louis told him everything? About Charlie and Jim Ledger setting her tent on fire? She scratched behind the puppy's ear, thinking she was a different woman from that day on the train when Ruel Gagne saved her. She'd been an innocent girl then. A weak, innocent girl.

And in love. The very idea of love in connection with Charlie repulsed her.

His eyes flashed. "No need? DeGroot and his friend Ledger, they tried to kill you. Ledger admitted it. Louis says even the man with him was jolted by what he heard. And none too happy with the whole situation. I know MacFarlane. He is not an evil man and doesn't want dragged into any kind to mixup."

"I'm relieved to hear it. I'd hate to think every man—every

white man—on this reservation is a blood thirsty scoundrel." She
sounded unnaturally prim. "But here I am. Alive and well. I'm just
sorry Mr. Tevere got swept up in the trouble."

"Louis said he thinks you should leave here. So do I. You could
make your soaps and perfumes almost anywhere, Mrs. DeGroot,
and not have to use Louis for deliveries. Why don't you?"

Mute, she said nothing. What would he think of her, a woman
with no one to care what happened to her? But what did he think
of a woman who stayed? A more appropriate question, perhaps.

"When do you sleep?"

His abrupt question sounded harsh and she winced. "When I
can." Her smile was forced. "I manage."

"Don't you get tired, always worrying if he's going to creep
up on you whenever you turn your back or close your eyes? Your
husband or his friend?"

"I . . . I . . ." Jacoba hugged the puppy closer. "But now I have
a dog. She will help me keep watch." It wasn't a real answer
and she knew it.

So did he. "Are you sure of that?"

"Yes." Truthfully, no she wasn't, but still couldn't bring herself
to admit it. As for the dog, the small creature snuggling in her
arms was a baby, not some wolf-sized, fiercely protective creature
trained to attack.

Ruel was right. And Louis, too, when they encouraged her to
leave the reservation. Leave the homestead to Charlie and let him
fritter it away or abandon it when he got tired of the work. Why
should she care this much? She didn't understand it herself.

Yet something, the renowned Ludke determination and stub-
bornness, she supposed, kept her here. Qualities that—

She looked up to find Ruel's dark, dark eyes fixed on her.

"Where is he now?" He looked around the site, still more of
a camp than a homestead, and she felt certain he'd checked for
Charlie's presence before he approached.

She sighed. "I'm not sure. I think he went to town. He probably wants to see how Ledger is getting along. Maybe to see if he can discover what Ledger told the sheriff and the doctor. The sheriff hadn't showed up by dark last night, and Ledger was still rummy from the alcohol he drank."

"You shot him. Shot Ledger."

If there was disapproval in the statement, Jacoba couldn't hear it.

"I did indeed. He was torturing this innocent little being." She hugged the dog, causing it to blink at her sleepily, though only for a moment before it slept again in her arms. "I will not tolerate such things. Not while there's breath in my body."

It occurred to her he'd left Quill behind for the same reason. Perhaps because he'd been leery of meeting Charlie? Leery for the dog, though not for himself.

"Will they make trouble for you?" he asked. "Or trouble with the sheriff?"

She shrugged. "I believe my character references superior to theirs. My husband knows that. He'd be a fool to try anything like that again."

"Unless he is successful with no one to say different." Soberly, Ruel shook his head. "Maybe you can vouch for your husband's actions, although I wouldn't be too sure if I were you, but can he vouch for Ledger's?"

Her mouth tightened. "I don't know. Doubtful."

"I thought so." After a pause where they both were silent, he changed the subject. "Have you named the pup?"

Dare she tell him that she had not? And if he asked her why, could she tell him it was because she didn't want Charlie to know how much the puppy mattered to her? That she thought if the pup had no name, it would keep her safe? Silly reasoning, she knew.

Ruel was waiting for an answer.

"Not yet. A name will come to me, and when it does, it will be just right."

His mouth quirked. "Don't wait too long. My sister had a

puppy once. She waited, trying for a month or more to make up her mind before she named it Walks Along. But the dog never did come when she called and Annette could never figure out why. Until one day the grown dog had a bobcat treed."

Jacoba frowned. "What happened?"

"Walks Along was barking, jumping and bouncing around the tree while the cat sat on a branch spitting and hissing and preparing to leap. Annette, afraid the cat would attack the dog hollered "No" in the most commanding voice she could summon."

Eyes wide, Jacoba said, "Did the bobcat attack?"

Ruel laughed, his teeth flashing white. "Turns out the dog thought his name was No. When Annette yelled, he instantly obeyed and ran to her. The cat escaped."

Jacoba laughed too. It was as though the moment released something in both of them. Maybe only for long enough to catch a breath, but it felt good. Normal.

Long enough, in fact, for them to hear Charlie shouting at Pym from out at the road.

"He's back." Tonelessly, Jacoba made the unnecessary announcement.

"Yes."

They had a few moments yet and Ruel filled them. "If anything happens, Mrs. DeGroot, anything that frightens you, anything that seems wrong, shoot your pistol three times. I'll come."

"If you're here." Through her instant relief, Jacoba couldn't forget his boat took him away for days at a time.

He hesitated. "Yes. If I'm here."

* * *

In the following two weeks, Jacoba and Charlie fell into a routine reminiscent of what most couples would consider an everyday life. Everyday, if hard work and the uneasy way they walked circles around each other didn't count.

Charlie, without a laid-up Jim Ledger to lure him into slacking off, getting drunk, and carousing with fallen women, worked more diligently than he had at any time in the previous months. Since Jacoba had met him, in plain fact. Inside the cabin, he walled off a corner to serve as a bedroom, built a cupboard and some shelves near where the cookstove would go when they had enough money to order one, and even put down a partial plank floor. Partial because he ran out of lumber.

He started a log barn, which Jacoba privately thought more resembled a lean-to, for the horses. But better than nothing, she told herself. He even hollowed out a length of a cottonwood log to make a watering trough. Louis, on one of his deliveries of supplies and money from Delilah, had suggested the method. The most astonishing aspect to the endeavor was that Charlie listened to him.

Jacoba almost began to doubt what she knew. Had she accused Charlie unfairly? Or was he playing some kind of game with her? Lulling her into dropping her guard. Waiting, perhaps, for Ledger to regain his strength and function before they threatened her again.

A few days after the set-to, early one afternoon Charlie drove off to check, or so he stated, on his friend's progress. "Believe me, Jacoba," he said, the threat implicit, "you don't want Jim talking to the sheriff."

And in truth, Ledger must so far have kept his mouth shut as the sheriff had yet to show up with questions. Louis reported something about Ledger acknowledging he'd gotten hurt in an unfortunate accident. All innocent, no blame involved.

MacFarlane obviously remained silent as well because, Louis added when sure Charlie wouldn't overhear, while most of the Indians had heard the truth of what happened, rumors didn't seem to be flying between homesteads.

Then again, the silence might have been because everyone was so busy. Busy people had no time to listen to stories about a wastrel like Jim Ledger and his friends. In a wry twist, Jacoba surmised news of the shooting came as no surprise to the hardworking men

and women building homes. Had they known the truth of the matter they might even have thought he'd gotten no more than he
deserved. Or maybe they just weren't interested at all.

During the second week, Charlie hitched Tope and Pym to the
wagon and went into the settlement again. He stayed gone for the
better part of the day, leaving Jacoba to her peaceful work. She
spent the afternoon inventing a soap—no—a recipe for bars of
shampoo with, among other ingredients, egg yolks, lemon oil and
beeswax to make hair shine.

Near sunset, when he returned, the horses plodding home
without guidance, he stumbled into the cabin without speaking
and sprawled on his cot. In seconds he was asleep—or perhaps
unconscious.

Left to care for the horses, Jacoba took her time, glad of the new
watering trough so she didn't have to trek with the animals, in the
dark and one-by-one, down the hill to the lake.

Inside the cabin, she found Charlie snoring with raucous
power, the strong smell of liquor hanging over him for the first
time since the night he and Ledger made their attempt at murder.
She had grown wiser, living alone with him these last weeks on
the homestead.

The Charlie she knew had always been weak and easily led. He
had, as she remembered, stood back and let Ledger take the lead,
only agreeing with him after the fact.

She forced herself to believe he regretted what had happened
the night of the tent fire. Believed he was glad she'd saved herself
and that he would never repeat those actions. He hadn't tried to
slap her lately, nor even threatened. It was his eyes, just the glint
in his eyes, that held a warning.

And so, she kept careful watch.

Accordingly, she did nothing to awaken him, only drawing the
curtain that served as a barrier between his part of the cabin and
hers. The questions she had could wait.

Somewhere around midnight, the puppy startled her out of a

light, sporadic sleep. The pup, from a place on the floor beside her, was panting and making baby growls. Just then, a match flared beyond the curtain and she heard Charlie groan.

Opening her eyes, Jacoba reached under her pillow for the pistol. She didn't take chances nowadays. Caution stalked always at the back of her mind. She'd told Louis the truth about sleeping light. Besides, Charlie had always been of uncertain temper when awakened in the night. The liquor had only ever made him worse.

Stroking the puppy's soft fur in reassurance, she lay still, eyes wide.

From the bedroom corner, the match went out. A round of coughing followed by prolonged retching made her catch her breath. She thought she heard feet hit the floor.

Was he getting up? He wouldn't come looking for her, would he? Silently, Jacoba scooted her bedroll farther into the corner, a rough bench that substituted for real chairs providing a barricade of her own.

"Jacoba," Charlie hollered, just as if she weren't, to all purposes, in the same room with him. "Get me a cup of water." His groan made him sound pathetic. Tried, anyway.

Unmoved, she didn't answer.

"Please, Jacoba." The cot creaked. "Oh, Lord. I'm sick. I need some water."

Jacoba, tensing, raised up on her elbows as the puppy whined. Was this a trick of some corrupted sort?

But she remembered the way he'd slumped into the cabin and crawled onto his cot. Maybe he really was sick.

What could taking him a dipper of water hurt? Jacoba disliked suffering, no matter its form, even considering her husband's assaults on her. Except, she thought, she'd never lift a finger for Jim Ledger.

Setting the pistol aside, she arose. Charlie sounded too weak and woebegone to be a danger to her now. Just this once she would come to his aid.

"Please," Charlie said, his cot creaking again.

Please being a word not often in his vocabulary.

Always conscious of the danger of typhoid, Jacoba kept a bucket filled with boiled drinking water in the cabin. She washed the dipper every time she washed the dishes, just to be safe.

"I'm coming," she said against her better judgment and ignoring the sad inner voice that insisted it was a mistake. Starlight shining through the window openings provided enough light for her to fill the dipper and walk it over to him.

He slurped, his eyes watery in a pale, round face. But for all his begging not a word of thanks left his tongue. Not even when she reached for the empty dipper.

It was as she took dipper that he snatched her hand with hot, clumsy fingers. He jerked her toward him. Off balance, Jacoba lurched forward, her bare feet scraping on the rough plank floor.

She cried out as a splinter drove deep into her heel.

"What do you think you're doing? Stop it." She tugged at her captive hand, the bones crushed near to breaking. The dipper clattered to the floor.

Over by her bedroll, the puppy barked.

Powerful fingers dug into her wrist, broken and dirty fingernails like talons cut into her skin. He trapped her legs between his thighs, squeezing so tightly she couldn't twist loose no matter how she struggled. His free hand snagged onto a length of her hair.

"Here you are, the high and mighty Jacoba Ludke DeGroot. Madame Ludke's daughter. What're you going to do, Jacoba?" He gave her hair a sharp tug, the fiery pain enveloping her scalp. She barely held back a scream.

He sneered. "Maybe beg? I wouldn't mind a little begging. You're not so proud now, are you?"

All trace of weakness and suffering were gone. A worse situation for her because it meant he wasn't nearly as incapacitated as he'd sounded. He didn't seem drunk at all. Just mad and mean along with it. Oh, yes. And dangerous.

She stopped struggling, aware that fighting him would only hurt her more. "Stop this. Let me go, Charlie. Right now." Her demand came out in a whisper.

"Why? What are you going to do about it? Where's your gun, huh?" He laughed and let go her wrist in order to grope at her breasts with a painfully rough hand. "You know you can't make me. I can do what I want, and what I want is . . ."

But he was wrong.

Jacoba knew that in the ordinary way she couldn't fight him. But sure of himself and his superior size and strength, he'd left himself vulnerable. Still trapped between his legs, in his desire to manhandle her, he'd freed both her hands. Almost without thought, she lunged forward, aiming at his reddened, glaring eyes.

She missed with the left hand, merely scratching tracks across his forehead and cheek. But her right, fingers shaped into claws, found their mark. She dug into his eye as though to rip the orb from its socket.

Charlie screamed. His legs flew apart, his grip on her hair sliding away. Even then, she didn't retreat. Pressing her advantage, Jacoba scratched and clawed, her hands strong and fast until he finally managed to thrust her away.

Quickly, with him trying to steady himself, she ran across to her bed and snatched up the pistol. The puppy cowered under the bench as Charlie lumbered after her.

He halted, swaying as she pointed the gun at him and cocked it.

"Do not touch me. Come at me and I will shoot you." Her voice held firm and steady.

Long scratches ripped his face where she'd torn into it. The eye she'd attacked was full of blood and weeping, already swelling and closing to a slit. It would be days before he could properly see out of it. If ever. The thought gave her a thrill of satisfaction.

"Why don't you then? Go ahead." He gave a sob and touched around his eye. "You'd better. Because if you don't, I'm going kill you. Count on it. Be easy to blame those damned Indians you've been cozying up to afterward."

Threats and more threats! Jacoba was sick of them. Sick of being afraid and most of all, sick of Charles DeGroot.

Powerfully tempted to pull the trigger, she leaned forward. "You're disgusting, you know that? Why don't you just pack up and leave? There's nothing here for you. You and Jim Ledger together. Why don't you just move on?"

He stood up straighter. "Can't do that," he said. "See, Jim is dead. You managed to kill him after all."

Chapter 24

"What?" Blinking, Jacoba stepped away from the gust of Charlie's liquor-laden breath. "What did you say?"

He shouted his message. It remained the same as she heard before. "He's dead," he raged. "Jim is dead. You killed him."

"Well!" Struck dumb, she found no other words. Her hand trembled. "Well."

"That's all you've got to say?"

The question brought her gaze to his bloodied face, his ruined eye. Her pistol steadied. "What do you expect me to say, Charlie? Do you want me to cry?" She threw his own words back at him. "Don't count on it. Do you suppose he would've regretted it if he'd succeeded in burning me to blackened bones?"

His silence answered.

"I thought not." Jacoba gestured with the pistol. "Go back to your cot, Charlie, and nurse your ills. In the morning, you'd best pack up and go. We're done." Tomorrow, provided she lived through this night, she'd take the puppy and walk over to the Tevere place. Perhaps Louis would've heard the details of Ledger's death by now, if it was even true, and she wanted to know what people were saying. She wouldn't put it past her husband to lie just to see her reaction.

He lashed out suddenly, his arms flailing and falling short due to his upset depth perception. "If you've blinded me, Jacoba," he snarled, his lips drawn back over gritted teeth, "I will kill you. I swear it."

"Not if I kill you first." Jacoba barely recognized the voice as her own. Only the intention.

Unnoticed, the puppy had crawled from her spot under the bench. She barked at Charlie, her baby voice a warning to him even as she cowered from his loud voice.

"And that mutt," Charlie said. "You'd best watch out for it, too, because I'm going to wring its Siwash neck first chance I get. Or cut its throat. Maybe I'll drown it."

He acted as though he hadn't heard a thing she'd said. His threats spilled a cold intent that washed over Jacoba with chilling effect. She knew he meant it.

"You won't get the chance, first or otherwise. It's hard to kill what you can't see." She backed herself and the puppy farther away from him.

"Then it's a good thing I've got two eyes. And one of them is fine." His confidence showed she hadn't succeeded in damaging him beyond recovery. Hurt him, but not blinded him. Too bad.

"For now," she shot back, a threat of her own.

Somehow, and Jacoba hardly knew how it happened considering the wild words they both had spoken, they settled back down, each to a separate space. Vowing to keep her safe, Jacoba drew the puppy close, thinking of the story Ruel had told her about his sister naming a dog. It helped ease her fears in the dark, until her thoughts returned to Charlie's threat.

She had to take the puppy back to Louis before Charlie followed through, much as it added to her heartache. She already loved the little dog, but she'd never forgive herself if —

She pushed the vision of Charlie's avowed menace out of her mind, trying to take satisfaction from the sounds coming from beyond the curtain.

Did she hear him actually crying?

Oddly enough, the sound gave her no pleasure. She'd once loved him—or thought she did—even though she now saw the emotion for what it had been. Nothing but a desire to remove herself from the position Madame had intended for her. A desire to live her own life, not the one Madame chose. And so she'd let Charlie take charge.

A fool. She'd been a blind fool then and had remained one for far too long, allowing herself to be put in a cage of another's making.

No more.

She settled back on her blanket and lay shivering. The pain in her head from her sore scalp, as well as the swollen fingers on the hand he'd crushed, were a dire reminder of the danger her husband posed. But neither physical wound compared to the pain in her heart.

And the fear. A hard knot of terror that kept her from closing her eyes.

Charlie's intent was out in the open now.

What would she do if he refused to go? How could she make him? Would it all come down to one or the other of them dead? Did he really want to kill her?

She knew the answer to the last question. It was yes.

The same as the answer to the question she refused to repeat to herself.

* * *

In the morning, they got up, Jacoba first. She didn't look at Charlie. Charlie didn't look at her. Neither spoke. If it hadn't been for the visible wounds both bore, last night might've been a dream. Or if not a dream, then a nightmare.

Jacoba's scalp still burned and she found an actual wound as she gazed sadly into a small hand mirror. He had yanked out a dime-sized patch of hair from over her ear, leaving an oozing rent in the scalp. The area around it was red and swollen where his knuckles had pounded against her head. Arranging her hair to hide the damage proved a difficult and painful task.

She had bruises, too, mostly hidden under her clothes, and at least two fingernails broken down to the quick where she'd clawed Charlie's face while defending herself. Bruises circled her wrist like a bracelet. She would need to keep her long sleeves tightly buttoned

Once dressed, she wore the pistol prominently displayed on her hip. No bones about it, they were in an open war.

Charlie, when he looked up from hiding his face from her scrutiny, appeared to have tangled with a wildcat and she guessed he had. Scratched and bloodied, sick with a hangover, his damaged eye gave her pause. Not that she regretted the defense she'd chosen. She didn't. Only the necessity.

With a glare that would've peeled paint, if there'd been such a thing anywhere upon the cabin walls, he drank coffee and chewed some bacon before silently going outside. Jacoba heard him sharpen his axe then, hitching the horses, he headed off down the trail dragging the choker apparatus behind. Before long, all sounds of his passage faded.

Apparently, he intended to behave as though last night had never happened. Ignore her demand as though she'd never spoken.

Why didn't he just leave? Jacoba didn't understand what held him here. Did he still expect an influx of money from Madame? Was he really that much of a fool?

She could've told him—had told him, more than once—it would never happen.

What did he have planned? The revenge on his mind had been clearly stated. Any slight, real or imagined, had always made Charlie try for revenge. Even, it struck her, against his own family. And now against her.

Heart heavy, she made certain the campfire was out, dug her purse from where she routinely hid it, and attached a light piece of rope to the puppy's collar. She'd been teaching the little dog to lead, quite successfully as it happened, almost a miracle after the pup's experience with Ledger. But Jacoba had to get her away from Charlie. She knew the threat he'd made was one he'd follow through on first chance he got, even if it was thirty seconds before leaving—if he left.

If he didn't succeed in killing her first.

Her heart thudded as she, the puppy alternating between trailing behind and dashing ahead, set out walking. The Tevere homestead was only about three miles away. Three or maybe as much as four. When the puppy tired, Jacoba picked it up and carried it. Worry settling like a black pall over her, she was unaware of the rattle of a wagon coming up behind her until a woman called out. Taking it as a warning, she stepped to the side of the trail as the wagon came alongside.

"Halloo. Good morning." A woman bent toward her and peered down. "May we give you a ride?"

Jacoba turned to answer, her heart lifting as she recognized the Merrimonts. They hadn't aged a day in the months since she'd last seen them. Homesteading evidently agreed with the old couple.

Mr. Merrimont drew his team to a halt beside her. Mrs. Merrimont, leaning over the thin metal rail of the wagon seat, drew in an audible breath. "Why, it's Mrs. DeGroot, isn't it? Jacoba?"

"It is. I'm happy to see you again, Mrs. Merrimont. And Mr. Merrimont." Happy? More like embarrassed. Weary, bruised, a gun on her hip and carrying a dog? Whatever would they think?

"Where are you off to?" Opal Merrimont asked. "Surely you're not walking all the way to Rockford, are you?"

"Oh, no." Jacoba forced a smile that felt as though it cracked her lips. "Mr. Tevere gave me this puppy a few days ago and I'm afraid she isn't working out. I thought I'd best return her to him."

At his wife's blank look, Mr. Merrimont said, "That's the Indian fellow who has the homestead Oscar Hartson is after."

Enlightened, Opal patted the wagon seat. "Oh, well, climb on up and we'll drop you off. We're on our way to Rockford. We're going to take the morning train into Spokane and visit our son. Apparently we need to prove to him we're doing fine here on the reservation."

Nothing would do but that Jacoba pass the squirming puppy to Mrs. Merrimont, pull herself up and take a seat beside the lady. At least the side of her head where Charlie had pulled out her hair was hidden from the older lady's astute gaze. And come to think of it, she was relieved to get off her feet. Last night's splinter, though removed, had left a painful reminder.

Mr. Merrimont called "hyah," and the horses walked on. Jacoba reclaimed her dog.

Opal had been thinking. "Mr. Tevere, eh? You do mean that nice Indian man who is so good about transporting goods and passing messages to all of us, don't you? Why, I do believe he's got a profitable little business going for him."

"He'll need it, fighting Hartson off," Mr. Merrimont muttered.

Jacoba hadn't known Louis had actually gone into business, but it certainly made sense. He hadn't mentioned this Hartson business, but now she worried for him, for the family.

Opal reached over and patted the puppy. "Why is she not working out? She looks a dear little thing?"

"She is a dear," Jacoba said.

"What's gone wrong? Mr. Merrimont and I have had a good many dogs in our lifetime. Maybe we could give you some advice. Dogs are good company, you know, if they're trained right. She's not a chicken killer, is she?"

Jacoba ran her fingers through the pups fine and fluffy fur. "We don't have chickens," she said, "so that's not it. My husband doesn't want her."

"Oh, that's too bad." Opal looked as if she'd like to say something else, but at a look from her husband, refrained.

Half of her wished they'd just driven on. It was all too apparent

Mrs. Merrimont had questions dancing on the tip of her tongue.

But still, a ride as far as the Tevere gate sounded fine. She hadn't really slept last night, even before Charlie roused her. Or the many nights before that, if she were honest, and she was weary to the bone. If it hadn't been for Opal's constant talk, she thought she might've fallen asleep where she sat as she found the wagon's rattle and sway soporific.

In plain fact, her eyes closed for just a moment, only to open wide when Mr. Merrimont spoke. "Your man hear about Jim Ledger? I know they was . . . friendly."

At least he hesitated before saying anything more damning. Jacoba decided to lie.

"No. Or not that I know of. What about Jim Ledger?" She couldn't help the way her voice hardened.

Opal huffed out, "Nothing about him a decent woman should hear."

"Now, mother, it behooves all of us to be aware of what's going on with our neighbors. Folks need to know truth from lies," Mr. Merrimont said sternly. "Especially Mrs. DeGroot, seeing Ledger and Mr. DeGroot was birds of a . . ." He corrected himself. ". . . was friends."

Jacoba had always wondered why women were accused of being gossips when men were not. The old man was a perfect example of someone anxious to impart what he knew, whether true or false. But she doubted anything said about Ledger would ever be complimentary.

Stirring on the hard seat, Jacoba shifted the puppy to her other arm. "Please, what is going on?" It was easy to see Mr. Merrimont had disliked Ledger and that Charlie was painted with the same brush. The tone of his voice told her so, and of course, Opal had given her opinion outright.

"Jim Ledger is no friend of mine," she was inspired to add. "My husband and I . . . we've had . . . words. I told him Mr. Ledger was not welcome at my cam . . .cabin. My husband was very angry with me." She made the admission, calculating the old folks would approve.

They did. Oh, not of Charlie's anger, but that she'd stood up and asserted authority inside her home.

"Well," Merrimont flicked the reins over his horses's back. "Did you know Ledger had been shot?"

"Yes. I knew that." Jacoba kept her face expressionless. At least, she hoped she did. Even if her name avoided mention, didn't they know it had been Charlie who took him in to the doctor?

The old man emitted a short laugh. "First word he put around was that somebody ambushed him. Folks kind of figured he just wanted to make himself sound important. Then somebody said he figured one of the bucks got fed up with the man pestering the Indian women. That didn't settle well with Ledger. He went around saying no Injun could get the best of him, and to prove it, he went off to . . . ahem . . . that place where a certain element gathers to drink and carouse. He acted just like nothing had happened. Stayed drunk for three days, so I hear. A lot of folks got to thinking he accidentally shot himself on one of his benders. That or a woman done it. Talk is he weren't exactly a gentleman when it came to women."

"Especially Indian women." Opal's disapproval was clear.

Jacoba's breath sucked in as Mr. Merrimont continued his story.

"Anyways, a week or so later, he got to feeling poorly again. His arm swole up like a kiddie balloon and twenty-four hours later he was dead."

Opal's mouth pursed. "I hate to be uncharitable, but it served him right."

Soberly, Merrimont nodded. "He's lucky he didn't get lockjaw. Heard a man say Ledger had been rolling around in the bushes with some woman." His face turned red and he said, "If you'll pardon my bluntness. Anyway, Doc says the actual wound wasn't much. Bled a good bit, is all. Ledger just got careless and it turned septic. So blood poisoning is what done him in. Nobody's fault but his own."

"Well then," Jacoba said, "I can't feel so awfully sorry for him. He was not a good man."

"No," Opal agreed and Mr. Merrimont nodded. "He wasn't."

And they, Jacoba thought, didn't know the half of it. She hoped they never found out.

Shaken, Jacoba's anger at Charlie grew hotter. He'd known all this but still tried to blame her for Ledger's death. Yes, despite most everybody knowing the man had brought it on himself. She had no reason to fear a visit from the sheriff. And, apparently, MacFarlane was staying mum, too. Probably ashamed of his part of the whole mess.

As much as she enjoyed visiting with another woman and hearing other, better news regarding the families who'd taken up their homesteads, Jacoba was relieved when Merrimont drew his horses to a halt at the gate leading into the Tevere place.

"I still think we could help you manage the pup," Opal said, studying Jacoba's woebegone face.

Jacoba swallowed hard, fighting back tears. "I imagine you could. It's . . . it's . . . ." It took a moment for her to go on. "This is best," she finished. "I'm afraid my husband hasn't the patience to deal with her." She detested herself for making an excuse for Charlie.

The pup, fully awakened by the sound of other dogs frantically barking from the house a few hundred yards away, struggled to get down and promptly ran off when released.

"I'd better go after her," Jacoba said. "Thank you for the lift. I appreciate it."

"We'll see you again," Opal called, waving as they drove off.

Jacoba could only hope it would be under more open circumstances.

To her surprise, it was Ruel who came to meet her. He walked down the center of the drive carrying a shotgun in the crook of one arm. On the other, a red-splotched bandage wrapped around his forearm. "So," he said with a sideways glance at her. "He didn't kill you. Yet."

Chapter 25

Jacoba eyelids fluttered at Ruel's declaration, self-evident since she stood right in front of him with her heart beating and her lungs breathing in and out. Never mind the feeling that settled like concrete poured into her stomach.

"He?" Her mouth turned so dry she could barely speak.

"Your husband."

"What happened to you?" But did she have to ask? The way Charlie had gone off this morning gave a hint. The way he'd taken the trail toward the main road, not the path into the woods. He'd probably dumped the choker setup somewhere. And what about the horses?

Or did any of that even matter right now?

"Ruel, what happened to you?" She was unaware of repeating herself. Unaware she'd used his first name.

"Charles DeGroot happened. Him and his axe."

Jacoba's eyes rounded. Horrified, she whispered, "His axe? Did he . . .did he . . ." Her vision blurred into an ebony mat and she swayed in darkness. "Mr. Tevere? Mary? The children?" Near hysteria, her voice rose.

He went on as if he hadn't heard her. "And his fists. He's good with those, too."

She gave a soft moan. "But the Tevere's?"

"He came on Louis in the barn. Slammed into him with the axe."

Jacoba gasped. "Oh, no. No."

"Louis has good reflexes. Since he was cleaning stalls just then, he got the pitchfork up in time for the blade to get tangled in the tines. So DeGroot used his fists." Ruel's face settled into granite-like hardness. "He had Louis down on the ground when Mary showed up. She yelled for the children to run and attacked DeGroot herself. He flung her into the corner post of a stall and knocked her out before he went back to beating on Louis. That's when I showed up. Me and Quill."

She was panting as if she'd run a mile. Two miles. Three. "Dear God."

"Louis's dogs were going crazy, trying to get at DeGroot, but they were shut up in their pen. Louis's son Victor came out from behind the trees down at the corner and told me what was going on." Ruel was breathing hard himself at the recounting. "Your husband heard me shouting, which gave him time to retrieve his axe. He was waiting for me when I rode up. Nicked me once, but it was the only lick he got in."

Jacoba's hand covered her mouth. "Did you shoot him?"

"Shoot him? No. These are supposed to be peaceful times, Mrs. DeGroot. I don't usually carry a gun when I'm home. Unlike you, I see. Victor brought Louis' shotgun out to me." His corner of his mouth twitched. "But I'm not unacquainted with rough and tumble combat. I captain a boat, after all."

Though unsure of the meaning of his last comment, Jacoba took it to mean defending oneself and one's possessions at any cost.

"Where is he—Charlie—now?" she asked.

"Don't know. Quill tied into him and gave me time to grab the pitchfork and go after him too. He ran off, then. I didn't follow to see which way he went. I figured I'd best be looking after Mary and Louis."

Jacoba's mouth was so dry she could barely swallow. "Yes. Most certainly. How are they?"

At last, Ruel met her eyes. "Louis, he's bad. Almost unrecognizable. Mary was stunned, but says she will be fine. The children, they're terrorized."

Jacoba nodded, tears rising to fill her eyes. "I'm sorry. I'm so sorry." She paused to catch her breath, then burst out, "I wish I hadn't ever come here. Wish I hadn't won a spot in the lottery. Wish I hadn't brought this evil down on the Tevere's and now on you. Wish I hadn't ever met Charlie, let alone married him."

Soberly, Ruel glanced down her. "That's a lot of wishes," he said at last.

If she'd hoped to be excused, he obviously wasn't up to the task.

"What are you doing here?" he asked then, watching the trees, the road, the hills, as if searching for something. Probably a crazed man with a rifle. "Did you know he was going to do this?"

"No!" The denial burst from her. "I didn't know. He acted like he was going to work."

Ruel glared at her a moment before his gaze softened. "How did you get here? Did you walk?"

"I hitched a ride with the Merrimonts who were on their way to Rockford." She hesitated. "I had to bring the puppy back."

Ruel glanced toward the barn where the puppy was cavorting with Quill and the other dogs. "Why?"

"Charlie said he was going to kill her. And I believed him."

They were silent for a long moment before she spoke again. Her mind had been racing, and now a question rose up. "You said Charlie ran off. What does that mean? Didn't he have the horses here? The team? When he left this morning, he hitched them up and acted like he was going to work. But he didn't go toward the woods."

"I didn't see any horses." Ruel frowned. "And those sand-colored horses would be hard to miss."

Jacoba's heart thudded hard. And surely loud enough Ruel could hear it if he just listened. But if so, he made no mention of it. Just of his suspicions.

"Does he have a rifle?" he asked.

"Yes. I think so. Maybe." Her answer came haltingly. How was she to know? He hadn't when they came west, but now? There was the one she had hidden in the woods, which he could have found. She'd thought it probably belonged to Ledger. "Do you think he would've shot Pym and Tope?"

"That would make him a fool. A good team is worth a lot of money."

As if she didn't know.

"Is DeGroot a fool?" His question pushed at her.

"Yes." Her reply came without hesitation. "But maybe not to the point of killing the horses."

A stirring came from within the barn, at the same time a rattling wagon, the wheels of which squealed like a pig caught at the gates of hell, turned from the main road onto the Tevere's narrower one. Ruel shook his head.

"You'd better go, Mrs. DeGroot. The people are gathering to care for Louis and his family. They won't want you here." He turned away, then spun back to her. "I'll take care of the puppy. Perhaps the time will come you'll want her back." He left then, breaking into a jog as he went to meet the newcomers.

There was nothing she could do but follow his advice. *Better go.* Yes, even though she felt as if she'd dropped off a cliff. Did he mean she should be the one to abandon the homestead, leave it to Charlie and make her way alone? And really, that didn't sound like such a bad idea right now. Except for the horses. If he'd hurt them, she needed to do something. And her things at the unfinished cabin. She couldn't leave them for Charlie to destroy. They were all she had in the world. Those and the string of her grandmother's pearls, held onto through thick and thin were there, carefully hidden away in the box she'd buried in a secret spot. She couldn't—wouldn't—

leave those. But even with all of her possessions packed up, who could she hire to transport the boxes and trunks?

Guilt suffused her over the damage done to Louis and his family. They'd befriended her and paid a hideous price.

And the question looming over her like a smothering blanket of smoke?

Where could she go from here?

* * *

Sweat dampened the back and underarms of Jacoba's grubby shirtwaist by the time she got . . . well, home . . . for lack of a better word. It had gone afternoon by now, the hot weather turned muggy with no breeze to clear the air. Wind seemed in the offing, errant gusts already blowing her hair. Black clouds gathered on the northern horizon, portending a storm to come. She smelled rain, though as yet none had fallen.

The road, dry after days without rain, meant dust billowed from under her feet. She moved to the verge then, where grasshoppers sprang as high as her face and weeds crackled with an acrid smell. She walked as softly as she knew how, as if safety lay in silence. She watched for any movement amongst the woods, on the road ahead, sometimes the road behind, and once into the sky, as though those looming clouds might bring an enemy to ride amongst them.

But nothing stirred. She saw no one. Heard no one. All of which didn't stop her from being afraid.

Charlie, and his freshly sharpened axe, was out there somewhere. She had no doubt he lay in wait for her, and for perhaps the dozenth time, she touched her gun for reassurance. The question remained, could she bring herself to shoot if necessary?

I shot Jim Ledger. I clawed Charlie's eyes and protected myself last night.

Realizing she was trying to buoy herself up with encouraging phrases, the question remained. Could she shoot really Charlie?

She'd cared for him once, or thought she did.

No reliable answer came to her.

Starting down the trail to the unfinished cabin, a sharp whinny reached her from the still untouched part of the woods. She stopped. A few seconds later, she heard a snuffle. Pym and Tope had been missing from Charlie's attack on the Teveres, although Charlie had started in this direction with them. Had he tied them here, out of sight and mostly, out of sound, and left them to suffer from thirst.

Another thought struck a heavy blow. Had he counted on her coming to look for them when he didn't come home, and had set them up as a trap?

Jacoba touched her gun again.

If she looked for and found the horses, would she also find Charlie waiting to kill her as he'd promised?

The odd thing about the situation, she thought, is that he attacked the Teveres before coming after her.

Why hadn't he tried to kill her during the night? Why wait?

But then she knew. He wanted to make her fear him first. He wanted to punish her. He wanted to make her pay. And he wanted to find her pearls and to take the money she'd hoarded. Then he'd be free to take her life.

With an apology to the horses, she walked on, approaching the cabin in fits and starts. An anti-climax, as it happened. Charlie's tent alternately billowed and folded as the breeze beat against the canvas. She peeked in through the loose flap and saw nothing different from the clutter usual to him.

Although certain she'd closed the cabin door this morning, it now stood open. Easing around the tent edge, she edged to the cabin and flattened herself against the rough log wall. And stood, waiting for any movement, any noise, any sign of life.

Was this the anticipated trap?

But the cabin, too, was empty, although she saw where he'd dug holes in the dirt floor, torn apart her cot—and his—and rummaged through all her cosmetic supplies. Only the sale ready items remained intact. Potential profits he was unwilling to destroy.

Disgusted, arms akimbo, she gazed about at the damage.

Saw, too, that some of his things were gone. But only a few. His large whetstone. His canteen, with her supply of boiled drinking water depleted. One of her knives. A blanket from his cot. Also a loaf of bread, a couple cans of beans. Meaning, she thought, he didn't mean to remain away for long.

Recognizing the burning in her stomach as anger, she set salvageable things upright. Did Charlie really think her so stupid as to put her treasure where he could easily find it? If so, and the idea gave her great satisfaction, he greatly underestimated her.

* * *

Charlie made his approach just before dawn, after a heavy downpour of rain preceded the storm as it quickly passed on to the east. He trod almost on tip-toe to the cabin and flung open the door with such force one of the hinges, poorly nailed in the first place, rebounded and came loose.

His noisy approach is what woke her up.

She watched him plunge inside, stumbling over the uneven threshold and going down on one knee. It set off the warning signal Jacoba had rigged, a pile of emptied tin cans containing enough gravel to make a loud rattle when tipped about.

"Sonofa—." His curse echoed through the clearing, carried by one of those erratic gusts of wind. Sneaking about didn't seem to be one of his strengths.

She might've laughed aloud if her quaking insides hadn't made her feel sick. Jacoba couldn't help thinking she might be depending too much on Charlie's innate inadequacies. Even though she knew by this time that while he was prone to violence, he wasn't good at planning ahead or carrying through. A character flaw in this as well as in his daily life. She trusted it would serve her well in this case.

And if not, she relied on her pistol. Maybe, she thought moments later, too much.

What if that made her as guilty as he of underestimating an enemy?

Jacoba's warning signal had proved to be unnecessary. Earlier, she had been roused by the sound of Charlie's heavy and excited breathing as he emerged from the woods. Opening her eyes, she spotted him no more than thirty feet from where she had snuggled in behind a fallen log. Sheltered by her favorite cedar, she'd kept dry there through the rainstorm. Warm, too, due to a woolen blanket of a color that made her blend with the night.

Charlie had stood a moment outlined against the sky before making a final dash for the cabin. He was carrying something in his hand. She couldn't make out what, exactly, but thought she knew. The axe. The same axe she'd personally picked out, paid for, and sent to him only a few months ago.

And which he'd used to attack Louis and Ruel.

A shudder wracked her entire body, even shaking the thick leaves of an elderberry bush that helped hide her when she got to her feet and moved forward, following him. Charlie wasn't making a lot of effort to be silent. No doubt he thought it would be easy to overpower her.

And, she warned herself, it would probably be true. Prudence dictated she not let him get too close, to somehow keep him at arm's length. *Or did she mean axe handle length?*

She'd been wise to avoid being trapped in the cabin. And to ignore the horses' needs, as much as it made her heart ache. She had no doubt Charlie had planned an accident of some kind for her there. If, when this was all over, she'd have to be wary wherever she went.

If she lived to greet the sun.

At the cabin door, Charlie stopped and looked around.

She ducked behind a big pine.

Chapter 26

Jacoba had made a mistake yesterday. One she realized as she watched Charlie enter the cabin. She should never have righted the disorder he'd left as he rooted through her things. It would have been smarter, and safer, had he remained ignorant of her return to the homestead.

And yet, hadn't this confrontation been inevitable?

She came to that conclusion when Charlie reappeared in the doorway, ripped off the remaining hinge, and let the door fall where it may.

"Jacoba," he bellowed. "I know you're out there. Come here so we can talk."

He'd left the axe in the cabin, but Jacoba wagered she knew exactly where it was. Right on the other side of wall, where he could snatch it up at a moment's notice and whack away at her.

Would he go for her head using Marie Antoinette as an example? Or for her middle so to spill her guts, a phrase he often spouted. Although, she reflected, maybe not quite in this context. A fanciful mixture of visions, she decided, and not in a comforting way.

Needless to say, she didn't answer. Or not right off. She supposed the time would come.

"Jacoba."

Her name bounced off the hills, pattered in the branches of the trees. Somewhere a bird, she thought a quail, disturbed by his voice woke up and whistled a complaint at the noise.

Oddly, Charlie's tone changed.

"Jacoba. Honey, I'm sorry. I don't know what came over me. I've had time to think and I know I've treated you badly. Please, darling. I want to take care of you, my dearest girl. I need you to forgive me. I need you, Jake."

Charlie's use of her old pet name was softer. More conciliatory. As if he had taken hold of his temper and sincerely wanted to make amends.

She didn't believe him. Not for an instant. Should she tell him he'd be more convincing if every sentence didn't begin with "I?"

He didn't wait long before he started the spiel again. But then, due no doubt to her utter lack of response, the message grew more testy.

"C'mon, Jacoba. It isn't doing either of us any good to put this off. You know we have to . . . talk. Settle things between us. Yes, I got angry the other night, but so did you. I'd think you'd know better than to make me cross. You hurt my eye, Jacoba. You know that, don't you? That wasn't very nice or ladylike or very wifely of you."

He was working himself up into another temper. Deliberately? She thought so. In a strange sort of way it reminded her of a long ago night—she'd been what? Twelve, maybe?—when Madame had done the same. Worked herself into a real tantrum, that is. One worse than her regular hot temper and loose tongue.

Madame Ludke had been angry, in a rage, really, with her fourth husband. At least, Jacoba thought it was her fourth. Might've been the third or even fifth. She remembered him as the one who felt entitled to keep a mistress or two. He had also borne the old country title of count and been quite rich. When she thought of him now, Jacoba believed he might've had some connection to the man she'd saved at the hotel in the spring. At any rate, this one of Madame's husbands had been shot to death as he crept down the alley to the back garden gate. His killer was never discovered. Jacoba had always had her own suspicions about that. About why a murder taking place almost on their back doorstep had never been thoroughly investigated. To the contrary, hushed up.

In the here and now, the parallels between Madame's and Charlie's actions were striking. The pacing, the anger turned to cajoling, and soon, all too soon, the return to anger, hot and violent.

Charlie reached the hot and violent point in a hurry. Certainly faster than she expected. Enough so Jacoba, starting at the sudden insight into Madame's behavior at the time, made some small noise, some small movement.

And Charlie, by pure bad chance, happened to see or hear.

"Jacoba," he shouted. He reached into the cabin behind him then, grinning like a jungle ape, strode toward her hideout dragging the axe at his side. "I know where you are. Come out."

Whereupon she, determined to at least keep her dignity, did as he demanded. She emerged from concealment behind a tree and stood watching him.

In seconds, too few seconds, he stopped in front of her and reached out with his free hand. Only then did she step back. "Don't touch me."

"Why not? You're my wife. I can touch you when and where I want. However I want." He seemed very sure of himself.

"No." Her voice was steady. "You can't. You should go, Charlie." She could barely bring herself to call him by name. "Leave here before you're in even more trouble. People will not tolerate the attack on the Teveres. Or on me."

"People will mind their own business. You know they will." He moved closer and she took another step back. "They always do when they have no reason to care. Why would any of them care about an Indian? Or about a woman they've never met? You don't know anyone here."

He raged on, but he'd already lost her attention.

In her heart, she knew he was right. Or partly. The whites might not care about Indians or mixed bloods, but this was still the reservation. Charlie was wrong about no one caring about the Teveres. As for a strange white woman, he could be correct. She didn't know the people here and they didn't know her.

A sinking feeling made her legs go numb. The homesteaders, though mostly fine folk, or so she heard, wouldn't get between a man and his wife. Or maybe only if he succeeded in killing her.

But she didn't intend to give him the chance.

The resolve buried itself in her mind, bringing every other thought in her head to a halt. Right up until his hand lashed out, slamming against her cheekbone.

"Are you listening to me?" he shouted.

She hadn't been. Staggered, her feet went out from under her. If it hadn't been for catching herself on the log, she would've gone to the ground.

"You see," he said. "Last time you caught me by surprise and got in a few licks. This time, the licks are on you."

He struck again, almost paralyzing her with pain. She reached for her gun, but when she touched the makeshift holster on her hip, it was gone. Lost somewhere as she slept. A cry of despair broke from her, making Charlie's sneer grow. His cheeks flushed red with excitement. "You see?"

Leaning on his axe, he grinned and drew his arm back for another blow.

The only thing she could do was to run. Before he could strike, Jacoba ducked away, leapt over the log and ran into the woods beyond.

Of their own accord, her flying feet took her toward Ruel's mother's house by the lake. Where Ruel would be. Where he must be. She couldn't fire off three random shots to ask for help as he'd directed her to do. It seemed too much to expect for him to comply anyway, but if she showed up on his doorstep, she counted on him to hold Charlie at bay long enough for her to hide. Maybe to board the boat and get away.

But only if it didn't put Ruel's mother in danger. Or Ruel.

And only if he still wanted to help. If he weren't too angry over what happened to Louis and his family. If —

Charlie crashed through the trees behind her. Gaining ground. She didn't need to look back to know that even with her head start his longer stride would eventually let him catch her. If she couldn't reach the crest of the hill before he caught up, she had no chance at all to evade him.

Jacoba darted sideways between two trees and gained a step or two as Charlie, with his larger mass, was forced to slow and go around them. It gave her courage, and the momentum to try the trick again just as she broke through to the path where they led the horses to water. Clear going here. And panting, sweating, praying, she ran.

She'd never know at what point she stopped. Stopped running. Stopped praying.

The Gagne house lay below her, quiet and serene.

No Quill to bark a greeting.

No smoke from the house chimney to rise into the sky.

No boat rocking gently at the dock at the motion of the waves as they drifted in to shore.

No Ruel, his dark eyes full of concern as he strode to her rescue.

Death seemed her fate. Hacked to bits and buried like the entrails of a butchered cow.

She looked back. Charlie was only a dozen yards away now, the axe head glinting in the sun with the rise and fall of his arms. He saw what she saw and, his face flushed and sweating, he panted out a breathless laugh. Not amused though. Or not much. More angry.

"Your Injun lover not around? This is it, Jacoba. And . . ."

But she was off again, not waiting to hear the rest.

This is it? Maybe. She feared so, but she wouldn't make it easy. He'd have to work for it.

She dare not run directly for the main road bordering the homestead. Charlie could simply cross at an angle and cut her off. She'd be better served to take a more devious route. One longer, but less predictable. And one downhill from here, through the heavier woods, where Charlie proved to have trouble keeping his feet as he careened off trees and tripped over detritus on the forest floor that proved more of a barrier to him than to her grace. It was the only chance she had.

That's how she spotted Tope and Pym off to the side in a small clearing. The horses were hobbled and tethered so tightly they could barely move. And even now she hadn't time to help them, poor creatures. She whispered an apology, hearing Tope squeal a greeting—or maybe a plea—as she rushed past.

The Rockford road lay only a quarter-mile ahead. If she could make it that far, if anyone was traveling, if she found help, if . . . So many ifs.

Or perhaps Charlie would catch her there, and it would all be over.

Her lungs labored, breath coming in gulps that sounded like a fireplace bellows pumping air. Drawing on her last reserves, she jumped across a foot-deep ditch, dry up until now with the summer heat, where in the wet months water drained from the higher ground. But last night's storm had changed things. Water mixed with dust made mud.

And made stones as slippery as though covered in ice.

Stumbling as the softened soil crumbled at the ditch's edge and a stone rolled beneath her flying feet, she went to one knee on a burst of pain. Panic rode her. She pushed herself up, forging onward on hands and knees. The stone slid beneath her, setting her back yet again. She dug in with her toes and kept going.

Seconds later, she heard a clatter of metal on stone, and Charlie's yelp of glee. "Got you!"

He caught her foot, and with a yank, dragged her backward on her belly. Stones rolled beneath her as she dug desperately into the mud and kicked out with her good foot.

Charlie laughed, a demented sound like a jungle animal.

Twisting, she saw his face. Red, teeth bared, nostrils flaring. And above him, lifted above his head, his axe, poised to strike.

Jacoba screamed—or sobbed. Maybe both. And with every last bit of her strength, putting every last ounce of her weight in the effort, she kicked out at him.

With a jar felt down her whole length, her booted feet caught him on the knee making a peculiar mushy sound. And Charlie, crying out, toppled, even as Jacoba managed to roll away from him.

Over her own tortured breaths, she heard a weird grunt quickly followed by a thud. A single foul word, silence.

Then a scream.

She'd never heard a man scream like that before. Not the wounded at the train wreck, though there'd been plenty of moans and cries. Even Ledger hadn't screamed when she shot him, but only yelled a bit.

Nothing like this shriek, rising to a high falsetto and piercing the summer morning silence with despair.

Risking a look, she blinked at the sight of Charlie writhing on the ground. A blanket of red spread between his thrashing legs. His axe lay half beneath him, his hand where it gripped just behind the axe head stained the bright crimson of arterial blood.

"Help." He forced himself up on an elbow. "Help me."

Did he mean her? This was her chance to escape.

Even so, she stopped and looked again.

"Jacoba," he said. "Jake. Help me."

Jacoba stood frozen in place. Only a few yards separated them. Heart drumming, eyes widening, her gaze caught on the gaping wound that sliced across his left thigh. Blood. So much blood. The yellowish white of exposed bone. Horrified, and yet—

She moved toward him, knowing now that even if he somehow

rose from the ground, there'd be no more footraces.

"Help me," he cried again, then let out another of those terrified, and terrifying shrieks.

She edged closer, until she stood looking down at him. "Help you? Me? Why?" Something like a giggle rose up in her. "Charlie, you were trying to kill me."

A plain fact.

Tears ran down his cheeks, ashen now, replacing the high red from only moments before. His blue eyes begged her. "Please. I've cut myself. A tourniquet. Stop the bleeding. You can do it. You know how."

She looked down at him, wincing at the sight of the deep gash high on the inside of his thigh. He'd been so intent on catching her, he forgot the axe in his hand and fell on the blade. Hoist in his own petard, as Shakespeare put it.

"I'm afraid a tourniquet wouldn't help, Charlie. You've cut the femoral artery and there's nothing I can do." Eyebrows raised, she smiled down at him. "Nothing I want to do."

It was no more than the truth. She felt no sadness. Only a kind of coldness. Maybe a little regret for what might have been. "A terrible accident," she said, her voice without inflection. "Clearly lethal. You're dying, Charlie. Dying."

His elbow collapsed and he fell back. His eyes fixed on her. "Help me. You have to help me. You're my wife. I don't want to die."

Jacoba smiled again. A smile without mirth. "No. I don't suppose you do. I'll stay with you," she said, and sank onto the ground close to him. "You see, Charlie, I have a question I hope you can answer."

"Help me." It was barely louder than a whisper, and she went on as if he hadn't spoken.

"Why, Charlie? That's all I want to know. Why did you marry me in the first place? Why did things change between us? Or did they? Did you always plan to kill me?"

His eyes were unfocused as he looked up. "Damn rich girl. Money didn't even matter to you." His words slurred. "Mother richer than a queen, looking down on a man like me. Served her right when I took you away. And then you wouldn't even ask for a bit of money. If you'd cooperated, we could've lived the good life. But no. Not you. Too damn proud. This is all your fault."

He panted in short gasps. "I didn't want to be a farmer. Jim said I should . . ." The sentence faded.

She'd never know what Jim said. Didn't think she wanted to, truth be told. All this came down to envy? Envy and money? Jacoba stared at him. She couldn't help it. A laugh burst from her.

"You were so wrong, Charlie. Money meant . . . means . . . a great deal to me. It's why I worked at the telephone company. Why I've worked here, on the land. Why I've labored over making soaps and lotions to sell. I always wanted to make my own way, just like Madame did when she was young. Whatever made you think anything else?" But she knew why. The influence of Jim Ledger, egging him on. Making him think she owed him an easy life. That Madame owed him.

"Charlie, Charlie." She sighed. "If only you'd been the man I thought you were. If you'd become the man you pretended to be." She looked down at him. "We could have made it together, Charlie. I know we could have."

She drew away, careful to keep her skirt out of the blood pooled around him. She didn't touch him and she didn't touch the axe. Some part of her, warned by the example Madame had set those many years ago, reminded her to leave no trace of her presence. No one needed to know she'd sat there and watched him die.

But she'd see it through, until the bitter end.

A minute ticked by. Another. Blood, its metallic smell filling the air, no longer pumped from the wound. It slowed to a stop as his heartbeat faltered. His skin turned a ghastly greenish white. His eyes closed, he took labored shallow breaths, the spacing between them growing longer with each one.

After a while, he sighed once and those stopped, too. The breaths, the heart.

And still she sat, her breathing almost as slow as his had been. Minutes, hours. She didn't know how long. Finally, she reached over and touched his neck, feeling for a pulse.

Nothing.

If she'd been unsure he was dead, the stillness, the silence, proved the fact. Anyway, she felt it. A vacant spot in the universe. "Well," she whispered, "I guess that's that, Charles DeGroot."

She couldn't be sorry. Wouldn't be sorry. And to think she owed a simple loose stone for her life. If not for that, she'd be the one lying on the ground, hacked to pieces and drained of blood.

A commotion out on the road roused her from a daze. A dog bayed. A man hollered "Whoa" followed by, "What's got you in a tiz, Boomer?"

The dog, a hound from the sound of him, answered by baying again, then the deep voice said, "C'mon, dog. This ain't a hunting trip. Hyah." The rattle of wagon wheels indicated he was moving on, he and his dog.

Jacoba sighed with relief, grateful he'd been driving a team. Had he been afoot or on horseback, he might've investigated what had gotten his dog so stirred up. She had no doubt it was the scent of newly spilled blood.

The incident focused her attention.

She checked where she'd fallen and crawled out of the ditch. Here was sign of what had happened. The loose stone that tripped her, drag marks, mussed dirt. One of her own footprints clearly showing in the drying mud. She rubbed it out and checked for more. Found another and rubbed that one out too, along with every sign she'd ever been there.

She left the axe where it lay, the hickory handle darkened by the sweat and oils of Charlie's hand, the bloody head carefully honed to razor sharpness. Flies buzzed around Charlie's corpse, feasting on the fresh blood. Jacoba turned away, unable to linger more as her stomach churned.

In a surprisingly short time she found the horses again, led them back to where Charlie lay and walked them around before leading them home. Led them in the sense of a commander at the head of his troops. She allowed the reins to drag as the horses followed her like ducklings after their mama. The placid turn of their hooves effectively wiped out any further sign she might have left.

The rest of the day went by in a blur. She made certain the cabin appeared as if inhabited by a hardworking couple. She simmered a stew over the campfire, enough for a family meal, and retrieved her pistol from under the cedar. And lastly, she managed to fix the leather hinges and rehang the door, if not perfectly, at least passably.

Not a thing amiss at the DeGroot homestead. No indeed.

Jim Ledger was dead. Charlie was dead.

Jacoba was alive and free.

Chapter 27

The night, Jacoba found, lingered even longer than the ones gone before and turned out to be just as sleep depriving. Troubled, she couldn't get the vision of Charlie's last moments out of her mind. Not having lifted a finger to help him, did that make her a murderess? Truth to tell, she'd been fiercely glad to watch him die.

What should she do next?

Apparently, she wasn't free after all. Not until Charlie was in the ground, no questions asked.

Early the next morning, Hugh Bitner, the passerby from yesterday, aided by a little help from his dog Boomer, discovered Charlie's body.

Jacoba had been waiting, nerves drawn so tightly she believed if anyone touched her, her whole body would vibrate with a sound like an overly tight violin string. When she spotted a man on a horse riding up to the cabin with a black-and-tan hound running out in front of him, she felt only relief.

Even at a distance she was able to read that the man brought

news. What he thought was bad news, judging by the woebegone
and easily read expression crinkling his heavily bearded face.

At last.

She'd planned to wait another day, if necessary, then go to the
settlement and spread news that her husband was missing.

Jacoba touched her hair, assuring herself the sore bald patch
above her ear was hidden, and that her sleeves covered her bruised
wrists. Here came the test. The one that would show if her acting
ability was strong enough to convince this man of her innocence.

But then, she was innocent. She hadn't shot her husband, nor
poisoned him, knifed him, or used an axe on him. *I watched him
die and never lifted a finger.* The vision kept appearing in front of
her, worming its way into her brain like a disease.

Stooped from bending over the huge cast iron soap kettle she
had hanging over her campfire, she straightened, the long wooden
paddle used to stir the emulsion dangling from her hand.

Pasting a pleasant half-smile onto her face, she prepared to greet
the man as he drew his horse to a stop. A man in his forties, maybe,
or even fifties who had a face almost as lugubrious as his dog's. The
hound rushed over and sniffed the hem of her riding skirt.

"Good day," she told the man and presented her fist for the
dog to smell.

The man doffed his hat and held it over his chest. "Ma'am. Uh,
ma'am . . . Boomer, you get over here and leave the lady alone."
His deep voice resonated.

Jacoba already knew what he'd come to say. Had the moment
she saw the dog, and hearing his name proved it. And here was
the baying dog a man, this man, had yelled at yesterday. Sorry she
couldn't make what the man needed to say any easier on him, she
spoke up cheerfully. "Oh, the dog is all right. I had a puppy here a
couple days ago and he probably smells her on my boots. Is there
something I can do for you?"

Now came the acting part. She erased the half-smile and substituted a puckered worry crease on her forehead.

The man, twitchy enough to make his horse restless, stuttered as he said, "Ma'am, have you seen your husband around in the last while?"

Her head hung. "Not since yesterday, I'm afraid. He . . . my husband . . . was upset because he'd been to town and learned his friend Jim Ledger died. Blood poisoning, I believe." She was unable to keep a certain acerbity out of the statement.

The man's jaw tightened at the name.

"He'd been drinking," she continued as if she hadn't noticed. "Charlie, my husband, that is, and he's quite despondent. But he no more than got here than he went off into the woods to work. He hasn't come home yet and I'm getting a little worried. But he will be here soon, I'm sure. The horses—" She broke off. Her blink signed consternation, apprehension, a host of fretful emotions. "Can I help you?"

"You were saying . . .the horses?" Bitner reminded her after a moment.

"They came home without him. I thought . . . I thought Charlie must have let them loose, knowing they'd return on their own for their feed. He does that ever so often and he knows I'll take care of them."

"Not this time, ma'am," the fellow said gravely. "He won't . . . that is . . . I found DeGroot a while ago. Or Boomer here did." A jerked thumb indicated the hound. "There was an accident. Looks like it happened sometime yesterday."

"Accident?" she echoed.

"Yes, ma'am. Your man, DeGroot, he . . . uh . . . appears to have fallen on his axe and cut his leg open."

Jacoba widened her eyes and put on a stricken expression. "Cut his leg?" she repeated like a myna bird or some such thing. "Oh, my goodness. How badly is he hurt? Shall I get blankets? Some bandages? Does he need a doctor?"

He didn't answer, not at first. "Didn't you wonder where he was?"

She nodded. "Well, yes, of course. But he said something about keeping an eye on the slash pile while it burns. He's afraid of the woods catching on fire, you see. But sometimes he goes off and doesn't come home for a night or two. Did I say he likes his liquor and to . . . er . . . visit with friends? I . . . I've gotten used to his absences. I know better than to wait on him."

Bitner had no trouble reading between the lines. He probably knew where Charlie went better than she did.

"Well, Mrs. DeGroot, he don't need no doctors. He's layin' dead out there in the woods, this time. I'm sorry."

"What? Dead? Are you sure?" Jacoba raised her hands to cover her face. Her shoulders heaved. "No. Oh, no. But . . . but . . . what shall I do? Who. . .what . . ."

Bitner, she saw from the corner of her eye, eyed her helpless emotion with alarm. And though she'd believed acting a sorrowing widow might be a hard part to play, she found it wasn't. Not at all.

The excuses slipped out readily. Regrets and might-have-beens, along with her own foolishness, elbowed a way in. Her tears in this moment were real.

He got down from his horse and patted her on the shoulder. "Do you know anybody hereabouts, ma'am, what can help you out? I'm a widowed man myself, but I can fetch a woman for you, if you want. I can let other folks, like the town marshal, know what's happened. Even though you ain't in the village, him or doc can take care of seeing your husband's demise recorded at the county seat."

"His what?"

"The death. Me and some of the fellers'll get together and see your man planted."

She dashed at her eyes. "Planted, you say?"

"Buried." His face glowed red.

"Oh." Jacoba heard how small her voice came out. "Mrs. Merrimont. Do you know the Merrimonts? I think . . . I think she'll know what I should do."

Bitner's loud sigh of relief proved comforting. "Yes, ma'am. I know the Merrimonts. I'll ride over to their place right away and let the missus know you're asking for her. You just wait here. No need for you to . . ."

Leaving the sentence unfinished, he leapt aboard his horse, spurred the animal into a lope and headed back to the road. Boomer was hard put to keep up.

Jacoba had a notion Bitner was as glad to leave her behind as she was to see him go. She went back to stirring her soap. Delilah's last note had asked for a renewed supply and she meant to get a shipment off to her as quickly as possible. She planned to send the egg and lemon shampoo bars to Delilah, as well.

If Louis would still do business with her.

As it happened, the marshal beat the Merrimonts to the homestead, which actually pleased Jacoba. He and the mayor, a round-faced man who made use of a soiled red bandana to wipe away greasy sweat, rode out, looked around with what seemed like ghoulish interest, and announced themselves satisfied Charlie's had been a death by simple misadventure.

"Accidents," the mayor hastened to assure her, "happen more often than you might think with men working in the woods by themselves. A real pity for a man so young. Guess he didn't have a chance to learn axes and liquor don't work together real well."

Ah, yes. Charlie's reputation had gone before him.

And that was that.

* * *

What if you held a funeral and nobody came?

Almost nobody, anyway.

Charlie, as it turned out, had made no friends while he'd been here. Quite the opposite and the hardworking homesteaders didn't intend to spend valuable work time pretending to mourn a man most had never met. Worse, a man they'd heard about, who had no claim to respect.

Jacoba, dry-eyed and head lowered, counted the attendees on

her fingers as they walked through the woods to the secluded spot she deemed appropriate for Charlie's grave. There were the Merrimonts, who came on her behalf. The doctor, who for a small fee signed a death certificate stating accidental death. Mr. Bitner, the kind man who'd found the body and one of his friends whose name she'd heard and promptly forgotten. His role in the proceedings apparently consisted of helping dig a hole and bury the body.

She heard talk of creating an official cemetery, but for now, Charlie's body would rest on what the men referred to as "DeGroot's land." It was a nice spot. Jacoba hadn't cheated.

A wizened old fellow with a face like a springtime potato professed to have been a lay preacher in some little known religious sect. He spoke a few words over the body. Words that certainly proved he'd never met Charlie. Jacoba turned away to hide her wry smile.

Then there was Louis Tevere, who stood several yards from the others under Jacoba's favorite cedar. Jacoba wouldn't blame him if he were just making sure Charlie was truly dead and buried deeply enough never to rise again with his threats of harm.

And Ruel, his dark eyes watching her when nobody was looking. He'd tootled his boat's steam whistle as he tied up at the dock last night. This morning he walked up the hill from his mother's place, and left without speaking to her. Almost immediately she heard the boat whistle and knew he was leaving again. Her chest felt hollow.

Opal had words of comfort. And advice, speaking quietly as they dished up the funeral feast. "Your Charlie wasn't a good man, Jacoba. I didn't know about him before, but I've heard the men talking. Best to get your grieving over and done with, if grieve you must. But you're young. Don't waste your time on regrets."

Jacoba had stared at her, her surprise plain.

"I'm sorry, my dear. I saw your bruised wrists and, I'm not sure if you're even aware, but there's a bruise on your cheek as well. I see how thin you've gotten. How weary and how sad." She leaned nearer. "Sometimes, a man just isn't worth a woman's tears."

The food Jacoba and Mrs. Merrimont had prepared on that lady's advice disappeared down the mens' throats. Then, in a concerted rush, everyone mounted horses or stepped into wagons and within an hour, left Jacoba alone again. Except for the puppy she discovered tied up and sleeping in the shade.

Did she have a sense of loss? Yes.

Did she have a sense of relief? A thousand times yes.

That night she slept soundly, the puppy curled alongside her. The coyote that called from its den in the rocks above the lake failed to disturb either of them.

* * *

Two days after the funeral, Jacoba was heartened by the sight of Louis and his family piling out of the wagon in her dooryard.

Her first true visit from friends and her heart swelled.

Victor jumped to the ground without help and grabbed a box containing empty bottles. The box was heavy. His father retrieved it before it could fall from the small boy's hands.

"This one," he said, pointing to a knit bag where several bundles of tissue paper and a few spools of ribbon peeked out. Victor, wrinkling his snub nose, complied.

Mary got herself down from the wagon seat and helped the two smaller children. "See if the puppy has missed you," she told them, and when they'd gotten out of earshot, said to Jacoba, "I came to see if you were all right. You know. After."

Jacoba did know. She nodded. "And you? Ruel told me what my husband did to you and Louis. I'm so . . ."

A wave of Mary's hand stopped her. "We are well, although if it hadn't been for Ruel, I don't know." She glanced at the playing children and Vincent, swaggering as he helped his father. "We don't speak of it in front of the children."

"No need to frighten them now." But still, she felt the shame.

And a huge dose of guilt by association.

Mary's smile forgave her. Louis said nothing as he kept working just as he'd done before.

Her next visitors to arrive were the Merrimonts, and Jacoba's heart had another surge. Opal approved the puppy that frisked around her skirts, laughing and telling the little dog to "have a care." Mr. Merrimont poked around the homesite and told her about a young feller who was hiring himself out.

"A decent, God-fearing man," he said, "that a woman might give an eye to if she had a mind. He could fix this place up in a jiffy. Its bones ain't so bad."

"Hush, Papa," Opal said, even as she gave Jacoba a wink.

Jacoba pretended neither to see nor hear.

Mr. Bitner, along with his hound Boomer, showed up the following day with a beautifully put together wooden marker. He and Jacoba placed it on Charlie's grave in a sweet little ceremony, the man refusing Jacoba's offer of payment. He brought her a letter, too. A letter from her mother. When that kind man had gone, Jacoba, her fingers shaking, opened it.

Dear Daughter,

You should tell the man you married he'd best not try to fool me. I knew who wrote the letter. Did you know he asked for—no, he demanded—one thousand dollars immediately as you are failing, too ill to pick up a pen? I laughed when I read it. He is a born liar and a lazy thief. Even his own father says so. You probably knew nothing about the letter, but I expect you know all about Charles DeGroot by now. Whatever he has in mind, I know you can outwit him.

I know where you are. István Barany is a relative of the Princess, and of course, we are cousins, so I heard how you saved him from what could have been a serious charge. He said you worked for a telephone company there in the wild west. My daughter, I do not know what to think. You, working as a telephone girl? I hope you didn't tell anyone who you are. And yet, you sound brave and quick to action.

I am still angry that you threw away an advantageous marriage to What's His Name. He's dead now, by the way. Yes, he was disagreeable, but you'd never have had to worry about having money again. As it is, his estate goes to some hook-nosed, sauerkraut eating niece. Is your life with this DeGroot person working out like you thought it would?

You may write to me.

Madame

Jacoba laughed, folded the letter and put it away, surprised at her lightness of heart. Poor, deluded Charlie. Had he really thought Madame would relent and send money? He would've been so disappointed.

Days passed. They gathered into the next week when at last she heard the steam whistle sound from down on the bay. Dashing along the now well-worn path to the lake, Jacoba was in time to stand atop the hill and watch the boat tie up at the dock. Boxes, barrels and kegs were unloaded, placed in a wagon, and hauled off by a straining team of Belgian draft horses headed toward town.

That evening, she washed, brushed out her dark hair, and donned a clean dress. Not fancy, but not workaday plain, either. Then she sat by the fire and, holding the puppy on her lap, waited for Ruel.

He came as daylight faded from the sky. He and Quill.

Jacoba's breath caught as she watched him cross the meadow, his stride graceful and even.

She put down the pup, stood, and walked into his arms.

A Look at:
The Woman Who Built a Bridge by C.K. Crigger

Spur Award Winner for Western Romance

Shay Billings is pleasantly surprised at discovering a new bridge over the river, as it cuts several miles from his trip into town. Ambushed and left for dead, he has even more cause to be grateful when the bridge-builder saves his life. Shay's savior turns out to be a mysterious young woman with extraordinary skills. More importantly, she's a strong ally when he and a few other men are forced to defend themselves and their ranches against a power hungry rich man. Marvin Hammel seems determined to own everything in their small valley, his intention to gobble up not only their homes and their livelihoods, but the water that flows through the land.

January Schutt just wants to be left alone to hide her scars. She's rebuilt the bridge that crosses the river onto her property, and lives like a hermit in a rundown old barn. All that changes when she takes in a wounded Shay Billings. Now she's placed in the middle of a war over water rights. But has she picked the winning side?

About the Author

2019 Spur Award winner for The Woman Who Built a Bridge, and 2020 Spur Award winner for The Yeggman's Apprentice, C.K. Crigger lives in Spokane Valley, Washington, where she crafts stories set in the Inland Northwest. She is supervised by a feisty little dog with a Napoleon complex, and ignored—except when he wants to lay on the keyboard— by a reclusive cat. Not satisfied to write only of the historical west, she also writes contemporary mysteries and dabbles in the speculative genre. A member of Western Writers of America, she reviews books and writes occasional articles for Roundup magazine. Buried Under Books also features her book reviews.